HAVOC

HAVOC

A NOVEL

Christopher Bollen

HARPER

An Imprint of HarperCollins*Publishers*

Attributed to Caitlin Fitzsimmons: "Don't sacrifice the old, but we must repay our debt to the young," the *Sydney Morning Herald*, 22 April 2020.

HarperCollins books may be purchased for educational, business, or sales promotional use. For information, please email the Special Markets Department at SPsales@harpercollins.com.

FIRST EDITION

Title art courtesy of Shutterstock / Gorbash Varvara

Library of Congress Cataloging-in-Publication Data
Names: Bollen, Christopher, author.
Title: Havoc : a novel / Christopher Bollen.
Description: First edition. | New York, NY : Harper, 2025.
Identifiers: LCCN 2024008119 (print) | LCCN 2024008120 (ebook) | ISBN 9780063378896 (hardcover) | ISBN 9780063378919 (ebook)
Subjects: LCGFT: Thrillers (Fiction) | Novels.
Classification: LCC PS3602.O6545 M34 2025 (print) | LCC PS3602.O6545 (ebook) | DDC 813.6—dc23/eng/20240229
LC record available at https://lccn.loc.gov/2024008119
LC ebook record available at https://lccn.loc.gov/2024008120

24 25 26 27 28 LBC 7 6 5 4 3

FOR TCR

We should lift the coronavirus restrictions for the sake of the younger generation. Sacrifice the old for the young, rather than the young for the old.

—*Sydney Morning Herald*, APRIL 2020

———————

Only the very young and the very old may recount their dreams at breakfast.

—JOAN DIDION

The old believe everything, the middle-aged suspect everything, the young know everything.

—OSCAR WILDE

HAVOC

1.

Wise guests wake early at the Royal Karnak Palace Hotel.

That's not simply because of the heat—although by late morning, the desert sun torches all of Luxor, and even though it's only April, flowering springtime in the Sahara, heatstroke has already claimed a handful of guests. Just last week one of the honeymooners in room 207 collapsed on the terrace and grew so unresponsive she had to be airlifted to a hospital in Cairo. The rash of fainting spells has set a worrying precedent at the hotel. "It's always hot, but never this hot so early in the season," Ahmed, the Royal Karnak's manager, divulged to me. He decided it was best to draft up a sign at reception, and I helped with the English phrasing: *Honored Guest, it is _highly_ advisable to visit the Tombs early in the day, _before noon_, and please take a broad-brimmed hat and _plenty_ of extra water.* "Yes!" I said, knocking my shoulder against his as we reviewed our handiwork. "This is very good, Ahmed. Duly warned!" We placed the sign in front of the glass candy bowl on the reception desk so no one would miss it. Make no mistake, the temperatures in Luxor are lethal. You don't want to get caught outside with no shade in the grip of a scorching afternoon. But the real reason to wake early is that the hours around dawn provide the only peace in the day.

When I first arrived at the hotel three months ago, I made the novice mistake of taking a room with a Nile view. Who could resist such a temptation? To gaze out the window while flossing your teeth as the mythic river of pharaohs meanders by, and beyond its glittering brown surface, the cabbage-green edges of the desert and the dusty Theban Mountains jutting on the horizon like the blades of rusted knives. That view felt like the sweetest reward after two days of grueling pandemic travel—the swab tests and quarantine papers and the slithering lines at passport control and the sprint to catch a connecting flight only to sit for hours on the runway listening to the same Quran prayer drone over the intercom, terrified of the slightest sniffle or cough from contagious seatmates. And mind you I was only traveling to Egypt from a hotel in the Swiss Alps. The world has become a nightmare, more a box than a sphere, splintering at every edge. That first day, when I breezed into the lobby of the Royal Karnak, Ahmed surely mistook me for a wealthy American idiot. I am eighty-one years old, and try as I might, I can't knock the Wisconsin accent off my tongue. To Ahmed's credit, he had no reason to suspect that I would be anything more than a short-term stay—two or three days at most. He must regard our faces the way we guests treat our room numbers: essential information to keep at the front of mind for the duration of our stay, only to be forgotten instantly as soon as we walk out the door.

"It's a spec-*tac*-ular room," Ahmed exclaimed, his round, reddish-brown eyes trained on me over the pink-marble reception desk. Not a drop of perspiration rolled down his forehead to indicate that the hotel was desperate for bookings due to the pandemic's cataclysmic hit on tourism. "Of course, our 'premiere views' come with an additional surcharge. But it is worth it for the Nile, Mrs. Burkhardt. *The Nile!* Absolutely a once-in-a-lifetime experience!"

I discovered the hitch the following morning. Like clockwork at sunrise, the local touts line up along the corniche in front of the hotel, bright as songbirds in their blue and yellow gallabiyahs. When the first tourists trickle down the hotel's front steps, the touts begin their non-stop chorus—*A horse carriage to the market? A boat across the river to the Valley of the Kings? Want to see the body of the child-pharaoh, mister? Good price! Step into my uncle's shop, only for a minute, very cheap, no pressure, one scarab, just hold in your hand, a favor to me, to the people of Egypt. You don't have to buy, I give to you, no disrespect. How about some incense, the smell of the Nile! Where are you going? I take you. How dare you walk away! PLEEEEEEEASE!!*

These hsuckstering shouts continue without pause through the course of the day and don't fall silent until sunset. Naturally, the voices ring the loudest through those front rooms with "premiere views," a mad harmony of almost-accusatory falsettos set to the disco of horse hooves and tuberculotic car motors. That first morning I tried shutting the windows, then the curtains, then I ran all the taps in the bathroom, but the touts' cries still managed to penetrate the walls. On the third morning, riddled with a migraine, I marched down to the lobby and demanded to be moved to a non-premiere room at the back of the hotel. "I'll pay a surcharge *not* to hear those men!"

"Okay, Mrs. Burkhardt," Ahmed giggled, his face flushing only slightly. "I understand. From time to time, we do receive the occasional complaint from guests with more sensitive ears." *Occasional complaint?* I can never tell when Ahmed is being disingenuous. I tend to take him at his word, because, in the months since that quibble, he's become a dear and trustworthy friend. In a snap of his chubby managerial fingers, the bellhops relocated me and my three suitcases to the more modest room 309, where my windows now open onto the hotel's sprawling, orange-scented back garden. From this perch, I still hear the faint drone of the hawkers along the corniche, but for most of the day those shouts are drowned by the din of silverware on the lunch patio and the splashing in the swimming pool. Despite the unseasonable heat and the return of my uncontrollable compulsion, I have been extremely happy at the Royal Karnak ever since.

The compulsion: it scratches at my skull and wakes me up at night, drumming its long fingers on my forehead. *Are you just going to lie there and refuse to intervene when you see someone in pain?* I had hoped to leave my insatiable need to help others behind in the Alps. As it turns out the compulsion was only hibernating, lying dormant all these months to hatch back to life as soon as I found my footing. Believe it or not, I want people to be happy. Or if not happy, then free. I don't meddle, that's not how I think of it. No, I engineer a fork in the road, the miraculous moment when the prison door falls open, the rare and precious possibility of a second chance.

You might not agree with my tactics. Judge me all you want, but I think it's healthy to test others. Go or stay. Run free or remain trapped. I don't decide. That's for them to choose.

I wake at six, as I do every morning, in the blue hour before sunrise when the whole world seems wrapped in gauze. Even the birds in the garden haven't stirred yet. I perform my ten minutes of stretches—knee bends, leg lifts, "tornado arms," the muscle movements my physical therapist back in Klode Park taught me—as I grip the faux Louis XIV desk chair for balance. I'm surprisingly limber for my age, and taller than most women who have been relentlessly pressed on by the thumb of gravity for eight decades. Still, I tend to avoid the naked body that awaits me in the bathroom mirror—the tubular yellow sacs hanging on my ribcage, a necklace of maroon spots and ruched skin, upper arms that look as boneless as eels, a face chiseled by a lifetime of earnest expressions. I've discovered that it isn't so much the eyes of strangers you miss in old age as the pleasure in your own eyes at the sight of yourself. Mine now stare in dazed horror at my reflection, wide as if tricked—*how in the world did I get to be eighty-one?* I'm not talking about the wounded vanity of not being young anymore (I bore that tough verdict decades ago). I mean, how did I become this failing contraption on the tiptoe edge of extinction? Sometimes I honestly don't recognize myself in the mirror, and it's not simply because I dyed my hair black after my escape from the Alps. And it's not the new wardrobe of loose, long-sleeved kaftans covered in loud prints that I've adopted since starting afresh in Luxor. No, I genuinely don't recognize the dying, pitiful organism staring back at me in the glass.

I miss Peter. I *always* miss Peter, that's a given. But I miss him terribly right after I complete my morning exercises and I'm stepping into the tub to take my shower, alert to the danger zone of slippery porcelain (each morning we octogenarians take our lives in our hands simply to clean our bodies). I wish I could tell you that my grief for my husband is at its most intense at sunset, or as soon as I lift my head from the pillow in the morning. It's been six years since Peter's death, and the sadness of that loss tends to spring on me a half hour after waking, right as I rotate the shower handle and unwrap a fresh bar of hotel soap. Grief has no sense of theater; it nestles itself into the most ordinary corners of the day. Oh, yes, I do still break down in tears on occasion (music, don't listen to music, it shoots sorrow right into the veins). More often, though, I'm just left with the dull ache of the fact that Peter and I have been separated for more days than I can count. (For a while I did count; for the first thousand days I added a new digit every morning to the grief pile, in hopes it would eventually topple and crush me under its weight.) Peter and I had the fiercest love, inseparable from the day we met. For fifty-four years we didn't just finish each other's sentences; we could start them.

After I shower, I dry off and swallow down a fistful of medications, including my risperidone to calm my nerves. If the loss of Peter ever grows too overwhelming, I reach into my cosmetics bag and take out the single memento I've managed to save, a lock of his hair. Just brushing the soft white bristles back and forth against my lips reminds me of him. But I don't let myself linger for too long in my room. I slip on one of the Nubian-print kaftans that I buy at the local bazaar, and at 6:45 on the dot, I head downstairs to breakfast.

At this early hour, the hallways are as still as crypts. Housekeeping has yet to clear the discarded room-service trays left by the doors, each silver rectangle resembling a tornado-ransacked parcel of land strewn with food scraps, ticket stubs, wadded napkins, squeezed-to-death sunscreen tubes, and upturned wine glasses. No sound emanates from the rooms. A church-like quiet reigns for a little longer. Only the murmur of a vacuum can be heard running deep in the basement.

The Royal Karnak Palace. I once asked Ahmed the reason for the hotel's ostentatious name, and he tilted his head in bewilderment as if no one had ever posed that question. "The Karnak is Luxor's ancient temple complex located just down the river—"

I stopped him. "No, I get that part of the name. What about the rest of it?"

"Well . . ." Ahmed paused as he tried to concoct an answer gilded to impress. "Because it's a historic destination fit for royalty! Many dukes and princesses and dignitaries have stayed here during its storied existence!" A pretty dodge, I thought, to hide the deceitful nature of the name. Disregard "Royal." Ignore "Palace." The hotel was conceived purely as a capitalist venture bent on attracting rich Western vacationers. In 1907 an intrepid British tour company who'd invested up to their starch-collared necks in package Nile cruises was hampered by a dearth of five-star accommodations at one of its key ports. Thus the white marble Beaux-Arts "Royal Palace" was quickly erected in Luxor on the Nile's muddy eastern banks. From the outside, the hotel still looks much as it did in the commemorative photographs that hang in silver frames along the ground-floor hallway, the sepia prints foxed with brown freckles and bleached by that amazing airbrush artist, Time. (One shot, of a champagne picnic at the Valley of the Kings, shows a throng of long-skirted ladies with weak chins wielding donkey whips and fly whisks.) The hotel is constructed like an accordion, anchored in the center by an imposing square hall, with each side wing stretching out in a wide curve as if offering a conciliatory hug to the necropolis of ancient Thebes across the river. The Royal Karnak Palace's three floors of velvet-flocked corridors and scarlet Persian runners boast seventy guest rooms. It also holds bragging rights for maintaining the largest private garden in all of Upper Egypt. And Ahmed wasn't completely misleading with his mention of royalty. Early in its life, the hotel served as a watering hole for lesser nobles and ousted dictators who managed to spin a playboy lifestyle out of permanent exile. Famously, the hotel was also a refuge for wayward female mystery writers and gentleman grave robbers; in fact, almost exactly one century ago, the discovery of Tutankhamun's tomb was announced to the world from the Royal Karnak's grand staircase.

Back in the Alps, when I was frantically searching online for a viable escape route—limited to countries that were still accepting foreigners during the height of the lockdown—there were only a few decent hotels sprinkled along the Nile to choose from. Most of the finer establishments had shuttered during the pandemic. There's an equally illustrious hotel straddling the cataracts of Aswan farther up the Nile, but when I clicked on its website, I discovered it had undergone a massive renovation, transformed from a decadent nineteenth-century Ottoman retreat into something like a business-class airport lounge. Since the Luxor's Royal Karnak Palace had been acquired by the same Belgian hotel conglomerate that had soul-sucked its Aswan rival, I presumed it, too, had fallen victim to a "luxury upgrade." (The cultural vandalism of the Richesse Resorts corporation on grand hotels knows no limit.) Blessedly, perhaps due to the global pause button of Covid, the Luxor property had been spared. I don't want to sound like a snob. Everyone has their own vision of an ideal sanctuary. I happen to prefer the faded glamour of the grand hotels of yore. Yes, the Royal Karnak's interior is shredding, pilling, mildewing, and moldering before our very eyes, a fact evident in even the dimmest of lamp light. I like to think of it as *atticky*. A bit of advice: if you fear mice, don't peer too closely into the corners. I suggest walking around the hotel in a happy glaucomal squint. The satin curtains are tattered; the bald patches in the carpets have expanded to the size of continents; the velvet sofa upholstery feels like running your hand through the fur of a sickly Dalmatian; and yes, a covering of dust envelops most of the harder-to-reach windows to the point that I have to resist the urge to write my initials into it, the way Peter and I did on our car windows after snowstorms back in Milwaukee. Nevertheless, in the golden light of morning, all these minor housekeeping sins are forgiven. In the past five years of travel, I have been a guest at eighteen hotels, and the Royal Karnak is the only one I've ever considered my home. My plan is to stay forever.

My hip bones are clicking by the time I reach the staircase, and my ankles go wormy as I begin my descent, my hand clamped for safe measure on the banister, lotus flowers blooming in wrought iron. I could take the elevator, but I enjoy circling the grand staircase, following the links of the chandelier's chain as it plunges down the shaft and ends in a red scribble of Murano glass.

Even in the lobby, most of the world is still asleep. The hawkers won't start their chorus for another forty minutes. On the bony sofas nearest the front door sits a squad of listless tour guides, each waiting for their first bookings to appear, the guests eventually coming down by midmorning, yawning dramatically as if they deserve a standing ovation for waking so early. As usual Ahmed is at the reception desk, shuffling papers. I can see the shiny waves of his gelled black hair. He lifts his head as I cross the lobby and mimics checking his wristwatch. "You're late this morning, Maggie!" It's a joke, of course: I'm never late, I'm right on time, but this friendly sparring has become our morning ritual. I'm about to utter my scripted riposte, "I guess I haven't shaken off the jet lag," but to my surprise I notice a young woman standing across from Ahmed at reception. I try to blink her out of existence, but she isn't a hallucination. Her presence throws me off. It's too early for check-ins; the first commercial flight into Luxor doesn't land for another hour; the first incoming Nile cruise boats don't dock until ten. She's masked and backlit by the front windows, so I can't get a clear look at her. I'm so perplexed by this small glitch in the normal rhythm of the morning that I nearly overlook the little boy sitting alone on the sofa across from the tour guides. This skinny, quiet nothing of a boy. Later, I'll wish I had paid more attention to him, examined every part of his little body for clues, his moody face, his restless eyes, his jittery knees. He wears a pair of dirty round glasses, the lenses glowing in the lobby's gloom. The window light illuminates his giant ears, the skin covering the cartilage making an orange stained glass, brightened to the color of apricots. The boy—I couldn't guess his age, *seven, maybe?* It's too murky to see him clearly—is staring down at a device in his lap, his thumbs twiddling on the screen in the raptures of some video game. *Short-termers*, I decide, the primary breed of guests that checks in at the Royal Karnak for a night before embarking on a cruise or traveling south to the ancient temple of Edfu. They don't matter. Who can keep track of them? Their faces are like those of the dead strewn across battlefields in old war photos, already forgotten the moment you encounter them.

"I guess I haven't shaken off . . . ," I announce, but Ahmed has already turned to the young woman, handing her a waiver to sign, promising she won't sue Richesse Resorts if she contracts Covid during her stay. Then Ahmed points a gun at her forehead to take her temperature. I smile like a good sport, *No big deal, we can do our routine tomorrow,* and hurry past the trophy cases and bulbous Chinese vases sprouting ostrich feathers to hip bone-click down the hall.

I'm always the first guest to arrive at breakfast. Murals of yellow palm fronds and lime-green ivy dance along the cream walls. I take my usual table in the corner, which the sunlight never touches even as it expands through the room in the morning. The busboys are busy filling the samovar with pots of coffee, and Hamza, the hotel's chef, is behind schedule, only now lighting the torches underneath the silver terrines on the buffet table. Every morning I sit at my corner table until 10:00 a.m., when the busboys carry away the leftover eggs and gelatinous *koshary*, invested in the careful observation of my fellow guests. Today has already gotten off to a strange start, time out of whack so early, and I hope it doesn't bode ominously for my dangerous task ahead. I keep an eye out for the Bradleys. Once the compulsion becomes too strong inside me, there's no taming it—I wish for my own sake that I could.

Call it my sunset-years mission: I've decided, with what little time I have left on this planet, to put myself to good use. I know it's unfashionable to talk about soulmates, but when you've had the kind of love that Peter and I shared, you'll understand that going through the motions or settling for what's in front of you counts as a terrible loss. That's walking death to me, the years of brave-faced misery, permanently moored in the stormless coves of merely good enough.

What do I do? I liberate people who don't know they're stuck. I help them to press the eject switch. That's one definition.

Another? I sow chaos. I clean house.

I change people's lives for the better, whether they see it that way or not. Only once did my actions end for the worse. But I don't like to think about the murder.

2.

Egypt is a noisy country. The hawkers are particularly rowdy to-day, as if they suspect a dwindling supply of tourists and feel an urgency to compete for the remaining scraps of wide-eyed sightseers emerging like lambs into the sun. I can hear them shouting through the breakfast room's diamond-gridded windows. At nearby tables, a few newbie vacationers chewing on jammy croissants look genuinely frightened by the racket that awaits them. As I told you, most guests at the Royal Karnak stay only a few days; in Egypt, even during a pan-demic, there's simply too much to see. But for those of us long-haulers who have made a more permanent refuge of this hotel in Covid times, these temporary guests appear more as human place filler, background extras not worth engaging in for even the shallowest rounds of small talk. They're easy to spot, perpetually exhausted, trudging around with too many carry-on bags, fanny-packs girdling their waists; their hands are continually frisking their bodies to ensure they haven't lost their passport, vaccination card, or wallet. (*Debra? Debra! I think I've been pick-pocketed! Oh, false alarm, here it is.*) Due to the current hazards of travel, few of these vacationers are American, and an undesirable proportion are red-faced Russians, a population that doesn't seem one bit daunted by warnings of "the spread." Their lack of concern is likely bolstered by the Egyptian government, which has discovered a novel cure for Covid: it simply underreports its death toll. A few weeks ago, when I ducked out on an errand, my taxi driver boasted that Egypt had one of the lowest coronavirus contraction rates in the civilized world. "It's all thanks to our climate. The desert makes our lungs strong. The heat burns the germs away." I asked him if he knew anyone who'd died from the virus, and he reluctantly nodded. Yes, his sister, two cousins, his neighbor, and an aunt had all succumbed to the disease.

Despite the disinformation, tourism in Egypt has pretty much flat-lined. The country's most spectacular ruins have sat deserted (sand collecting dust, so to speak). In a desperate bid to fill vacancies, the Royal Karnak has agreed to play host to a slate of meagerly attended medical conventions frequented by doctors and their spouses, primarily from Germany, Serbia, and South Africa. I promised myself I would give up my calling once I arrived in Egypt. It isn't my obligation to solve the problems of strangers. But that vow proved easier said than done. Two weeks ago I noticed a shy thirty-three-year-old guest from Johannesburg whose pompous, bob-haired wife was delivering a keynote at one of the conventions on osteoporosis. He had soulful eyes and was especially polite to the staff, but he kept to himself, reading alone on the back terrace. Eventually, I coaxed him into opening up to me. His marriage toggled between listless and combative, but he was convinced it could be salvaged by an impending round of fertility treatments. I badly wanted to rescue him from the years of misery that lay ahead, but before I could act, the possibility was taken out of my hands. The man took violently sick one morning after drinking the Egyptian tap water, and the couple checked out without so much as a goodbye. Still, that little taste roused my longing to do good. Unfortunately, misery isn't hard to come by on vacation.

Here they are: the Bradleys, sitting at a table halfway across the breakfast room. They're a family of three from Manchester, consisting of a slim, middle-aged husband and wife and their ungainly teenage daughter, dressed as if she were headed to a barbecue in the Florida Panhandle rather than touring sacred sites in a modest Muslim country. All three are ladling bircher muesli into their mouths, each of them staring into space, lost in their own separate portal of oblivion, while a strip of sunlight blazes across their table, illuminating the miniature jars of orange and strawberry jam. A part of me had hoped that the Bradley family wouldn't materialize in the breakfast room this morning, saving me from my compulsion. It's not uncommon for guests to disappear as abruptly as they arrived. Families on vacation prefer to be on the move, their tolerance for each other liable to wither the longer they remain in a single location. The Bradleys, however, have defied all expectations, lingering on at the hotel for nearly a week.

The father is bearded, late forties, not unattractive, with tight blue eyes and a slender nose bent at the bridge. Geoff (that's his name) is the first to break from the group staring spell. He glances at his wife to ensure she's not paying attention before letting his eyes prowl the room, ogling any attractive women he sees. Those blue eyes rake over me without taking me in; I'm not what he wants, not worth even a nod of recognition. But I see Geoff clearly, have learned his habits and monitored his signs of discontentment. He wants out, but can't figure a way to the exit. He needs me more than he realizes. Really, though, it's his wife, Shelley, who most deserves a chance at freedom. She's the one whose pleading face is hounding me into the resumption of my services. Small-boned, with a miniature nose and mouth marooned between jowly, pale-pink cheeks, shoulders slumped as if she's mentally washing dishes even as she sits in a luxury hotel eating imported granola in the middle of an African desert.

Two days ago, I accompanied Shelley and her daughter, Stella, on an early-morning tour of Hatshepsut's Temple, after Geoff begged off to "catch up on work emails." It seemed as evident to Shelley as it was to me that her husband would be spending those hours admiring young bodies at the hotel pool. Hatshepsut's Temple is a massive stone shrine that juts from the base of limestone cliffs on Luxor's West Bank. It's devoted to its ruthless namesake pharaoh queen, and from a distance, its wide horizontal terraces look like the stacked keyboards of a church organ. The temple is a humbling sight, and only Stella, in her tight denim shorts and lace crop top, remained unmoved by it. Ahmed had insisted on pairing us with an eager young tour guide, fresh from university, and while I had already visited the temple complex, I feigned interest as our guide recounted rote anecdotes of back-stabbing and infighting among the soap-operatic Eighteenth Dynasty pharaohs. The guide, still so green, stumbled through his description of the ankhs and scorpions engraved on the walls. I could have corrected his occasional blunder, but I was attuned to a very different set of facts that morning. Chiefly I'd come to study Shelley Bradley. Did she need my help? Was she so hopelessly miserable that I'd be obligated to step in and save her?

"You and Geoff seem happy," I exclaimed as Shelley and I wandered into one of the tiny dark cells carved into the bedrock.

"Oh!" Shelley cried, as if spooked by the sudden turn of our conversation. Then frailly, she repeated, "Oh," and added faintly, "yes, of course . . . very happy." She studied a wall too drenched in shadow to discern any of its hieroglyphics.

"I don't mean to pry," I said gently, my voice sounding so harmless inside the cavern. "It's nice to see a successful marriage like yours. And your lovely daughter! How many years has it been?"

"How many years," Shelley echoed as she slowly circled a room that had been fashioned from rock in the fifteenth century BCE. She had the annoying habit of repeating questions back as answers. Finally, though, she submitted. "Well, let's see. Twenty-three years, I think it's been?"

"Oh, you must have married young! Twenty-three years of happiness!"

"Yes, of happiness . . ." Her voice trailed off. "Do you mind if we step outside? Stella has a habit of wandering off."

I was getting nothing out of this woman. We left the room, and I held my purple umbrella securely over my head against the sun. I have a skin condition that's aggravated by sunlight, and I was putting myself at great risk to be out here trooping after Shelley for clear answers.

When we emerged on the terrace, the guide gave us a pleading look. Shelley's daughter began reading aloud from her phone, and instantly I understood the cause of his agitation. "Were you guys aware that there was a terrorist attack at this temple back in the 1990s?" Stella turned accusatorily to the guide. "You knew about this massacre and didn't warn us?" The guide blushed and stuttered as he attempted a pacifying response. Stella didn't give him the opportunity. "It says that, like, sixty tourists were machine-gunned down right where we're standing.

Right on this spot!" She glanced around, as if assessing our current level of risk. "I mean, honestly, it was smart of the killers to choose this place, because there's nowhere to run. We're completely exposed, just left out in the open to be picked off one by one."

"Stella, I'm sure we're absolutely safe," I said, less to calm the teenager's nerves than for the sake of the guide. I knew he was forbidden to utter a single word on the subject of terrorism by order of the military government; he would be fired for spooking tourists if he even hinted at any dangers in Egypt's most lucrative industry. "I promise, dear, no one is interested in killing you."

But Stella wouldn't relent. "What was the name of the terrorist group?" she demanded. "Are they still active?" The guide glanced away. Her snotty voice, set in a British accent that elicited a kind of knee-jerk, old-empire respect, was obviously frazzling him. He attempted to tour-guide his way out of the subject, pointing out the repeating motif of cow horns holding the disc of the sun along a temple wall. "This is symbol of goddess, Hathor. She consecrate divine Ra to make the queen eternal . . ."

Stella shared an affronted expression with her mother and me, presuming we were on her side. "How can he be a guide and not know about a massacre that happened here twenty-five years ago? *Within his lifetime!*"

"Sweetheart," Shelley murmured, digging into her fanny pack to withdraw a wad of Egyptian pounds. "Why don't you get a soda from the vendor by the gate. Buy one for me, too, will you?" It was a bribe befitting a small child, but Stella grabbed the bills and flounced down the steps. As she crossed to the walkway leading to the front gates, two male workers began to trail behind her, taunting her with whistles and kissing sounds. Her mother and I watched the girl stride along the concrete path as if it were a fashion runway, this ungainly teenager in skimpy clothes mistaking a burst of horny male attention for the confirmation of her beauty—here, finally, in Egypt, Stella could be the pretty one. I know I should be more sympathetic. I had a daughter once, my dear Julia, the pride of my and Peter's lives, an intelligent, shy, beautiful girl who was taken from us too soon. That loss should have softened me to Stella, but I couldn't swallow my repugnance. The girl's only notable ambition revolved around the accumulation of social-media followers; on the van ride to the temple, she told me her Instagram handle three times, Stella$Forevr, as if I might be so infatuated with her that I craved even more access to her life and might want to savor each of her uploaded excretions in the privacy of my room.

"Go on, you were saying," I gently encouraged the guide, making it clear that he was now among friends, "about Hathor and the sun god?" I watched as Shelley struggled to fix her attention on another chapter of Hatshepsut's sordid court intrigues. As we continued through the complex, I began to feel that I wouldn't be able to unlock Shelley's confidence. Even if I did pry out a few unpleasant details about her marriage, perhaps this woman didn't need my help. Some people don't. Trying to save them is pointless. They're comfortable in their allotted parcel of quicksand, and so I let them be. Not every couple can have what Peter and I did—an eternal bond that nothing could break. There are those who don't want that kind of love, who prefer the hug of their own loneliness inside a dying relationship.

By the time we climbed to the top of the temple, my ankles throbbed, I worried about my skin, and I wanted to return to the hotel. As we entered a dark antechamber decorated in rows of human figures sprouting falcon heads, Shelley surprised me by grabbing my hand and confessing how relieved she was to escape chilly Manchester during the pandemic and that she didn't miss teaching physics at the local college. It wasn't much to go on, hardly a plea for help, but I could sense Shelley's despair bleeding through her words. In the end, it was an ordinary British expression that made me decide to help her.

"Things haven't been quite the same since we moved house last year," she said. *Moved house.* It rang like a bell in my ears. Yes, I thought, that British phrase is exactly right. In the United States, we would say "moved out of a house and into a new one." Houses don't move, houses stay fixed, increasing in value while the unvalued humans who inhabit them come and go like seasons. But right in that dark shrine to a dead queen, my heart sang with Shelley's notion that houses travel with us, that they aren't merely comprised of cladding, brick, and plumbing but are defined by the individuals inside them and the marrow of their years there, and that the soul of a house journeys with us when we move. It gave me pleasure to think that the fifty years Peter and I spent in our blue Tudor Revival in Klode Park had crossed the ocean and the mountains along with me to room 309 of the Royal Karnak and that I continued to live in our house even without its wide lawn and fat buckeyes raining their baseball seeds on the roof each autumn. I squeezed Shelley's hand in gratitude. I knew right then I would rescue her. Shelley doesn't feel she's brave enough to make a dramatic change, but I believe in her. Yes, right here in Luxor, Shelley Bradley will be reborn.

We were still holding hands while staring at the frieze of Set, the god of havoc. "Shelley, you deserve to be happy," I told her. "Take it from someone who has lived for as long as I have. You don't owe anyone your misery. Will you promise to remember that?"

She nodded uncertainly and withdrew her hand.

Now, sitting in the breakfast room, Shelley snaps out of her daze. She notices her husband staring at a table of giggling young women. He's so blatant about his appetites. Instead of calling him out, though, she redirects her attention to her daughter. Stella takes no notice of her mother's devotion, and when Shelley risks reaching over to fix a lock of her daughter's hair, the girl jerks her head away and gives her a vicious glare. Stella's sudden movement startles Geoff, and he squints at his wife and daughter as if they're a windstorm he's forced to withstand.

"I was only trying . . ." But Shelley's voice dies over the jam jars on the table. This poor woman, marooned with these people she calls her own. I don't have much time left to pull her from the drying concrete of her existence. I must act quickly. It's got to be done today.

Hamza carries his usual postprandial offerings to my table, three pistachio butter cookies on a blue tea plate. He bakes them first thing every morning and leaves them to cool on the kitchen rack so they can be served at the end of breakfast. No one except for me ever eats these treats that he lovingly prepares; the cookies must be a holdover from colonial days, a nod to the old tea rooms of bygone Royal Karnak Palace civility. Sweet, ogreous Hamza, rumored to have two wives and four sons, places the plate in front of me. "Eat up, Maggie!" he encourages with a familial wink. I thank him, patting his hairy forearm and laughing. "You'll kill me with all this butter! I know your plan, Hamza! I'm watching you!"

In the doorway to the breakfast room, I spot a woman trying to talk her way past the host who guards the door, writing down room numbers. She gesticulates at herself and then at the buffet. Eventually, he grants her entry. As she removes her mask, I realize it's the young woman who checked in early this morning at reception. The skin between her eyebrows is creased, giving her a permanently vexed expression, and yet she's also strikingly pretty, with wide, protruding eyes, high cheekbones, and stringy brown hair left stylishly unkempt. She must have been explaining to the host that she's a new guest whose room isn't yet ready. There's no sign of her little boy. Perhaps he's off exploring the hotel. As she wanders through the room, she knocks into a busboy carrying a tray of puddings. "I'm so sorry, excuse me," she says, and I can tell by her accent that she's American. She toys with the fringe of a blue *kafiya* wrapped around her neck, her small nails covered in clear varnish that glimmers in the window light. She scans the buffet table, but in the end she only nabs two rolls from the breadbasket and retreats into the hall. Her brief appearance, however, has not gone unnoticed by Geoff Bradley, who stares longingly after her as if the force of his lust alone might lure her back.

I wish this young woman had checked in two days ago. She would have been a much more convincing instrument with which to pick the lock on Shelley's cage. Instead, I've had to settle for Carissa, the Greek divorcée on the second floor who wears a different yellow silk scarf with each outfit. Well, I work with the circumstances given to me. I don't make fate. I only twist it.

3.

Zachary and Ben are my closest friends at the Royal Karnak. They're long-haulers like myself and had already been staying at the hotel for several months by the time I arrived, occupying the Sultan's Suite on the opposite end of the third floor. It's an exorbitantly expensive room that Ben's Ivy League university subsidizes, otherwise they couldn't afford Sultan status. Zachary (according to Zachary) was a successful corporate lawyer in Boston, pocketing nearly a million per year before the pandemic gutted his firm. He found himself in those first unthinkable weeks of chaos like so many other white-collar welfare recipients: living off a nest egg he never expected to touch. Unable to land a job interview during the apocalypse, Zachary decided to join his husband in Luxor. A breather from the stressors of unemployment. A chance to reconsider his values and ponder life's quick stopwatch. Zachary spends most of his waking hours idling around the pool.

Ben is half-Japanese, half–French Canadian, born and raised in Montreal. Although already waist-deep into his thirties, he's approximately fifteen years younger than his muscled, dolphin-smooth, unemployed husband, and he has a wispy teenager's starter mustache. Ben is (again, according to Zachary) something of an archaeology wunderkind. When Covid struck, he was midway through a sabbatical in Luxor, 3D scanning every artifact in the local antiquity museum (a minimalist cinnamon-brown building a seven-minute carriage ride up the corniche, its most popular attraction being its industrial-grade air-conditioning). Both men are vigilant about their diets, although it is Zachary who is neurotically addicted to vitamins and exercise. If the pair didn't skip Hamza's high-carb morning buffet, preferring to chug green smoothies up in their room, I probably wouldn't sit alone at breakfast. "The boys," as I call them, tend to congregate at the pool around noon—Ben prudently sitting under one of the peach-canvas umbrellas during a long lunch break from the museum, while Zachary lies supine, glittering like a human sacrifice under the pounding desert sun.

As a couple, they're unwreckable. I admit, when I first befriended them, the urge stirred in me to make them my next mission. You see, I liked them immediately, and yet I sensed an undertow of resentment in their cheerful, sarcastic banter—Zachary's resentment over Ben's insane work hours at the museum, and Ben's resentment over Zachary's utter lack of purpose beyond the confines of the hotel's pool and fitness center. In a further development, I clocked Ben rolling his eyes on several occasions when Zachary goofily entertained children at neighboring tables. It seemed to me there was a festering antagonism that, if needed, I could exploit for maximum effect. At the end of the second week, when I spotted Zachary leading a handsome young Egyptian up to the Sultan's Suite while Ben was at work, the truth elbowed me in the stomach. But that night at dinner, Zachary beat me to the shocking revelation, winking at Ben as he relayed the exciting afternoon he'd spent with a handsome university student he'd met at the market. I waited for the inevitable fallout, but Ben didn't erupt in a tear-soaked jealous rage. He merely told his husband that he needed to be careful about random hookups in Egypt. Then he let out a self-pitying moan. "Figures you'd be the one to get some action. I've been here for nearly a year, and not so much as a pat on the ass!"

I was stunned, confused, even a little distressed. As I sat between them at the table, I felt like a child struggling to understand the complicated behavior of adults, two sophisticated men who were in full control of their private lives. Eventually my shock turned to amusement, and finally I said over my entrée of honey-glazed salmon, which is *not* Hamza's specialty, "Wow, you two really have it figured out!" They loved that I was blushing, each throwing an arm around me. "Look, Zee," Ben said, "we've shocked Mags!" and ordered a bottle of red wine to celebrate Zachary's lucky find at the market. I learned later that the boys have one stipulation: never the same guy twice. I could have done wonders with that tiny loophole, but I no longer felt the urge to test their bond. Ben and Zachary belong together. They don't need to be saved.

I yank open the lead doors that lead into the back garden and begin my slow pilgrimage to the pool, keeping my purple umbrella pinned directly over me to block all sunlight. Lounging by the pool at lunch with Ben and Zachary is one of my principal daily activities, our boats briefly meeting on the vast ocean of the day. I've found that it's essential during these extraordinary times to establish a few dependable routines to prevent the whole world from spinning into madness. Even with the umbrella handle tight against my chest, I can feel the intense noon heat pawing at me from all sides. It's so hot, the moisture is sucked from my lips, and the air burns the insides of my nostrils. Even if I hadn't decided to drastically alter my appearance after fleeing Europe, the weather in Egypt would have forced a transformation. In the Alps I wore tweed, high-waisted skirts, starched round-collared blouses, and leather flats, and my then-gray hair was tied in a strict bun. Here in Luxor, I don't even bother to wear a bra under my kaftans, and I clap the sweat from my Velcro sandals out my window in the evenings. Thankfully there are plenty of shady spots along the garden's winding brick paths: the puddles of jet-black shadow that collect under the helicoptering fronds of the date palms; the dense pools of darkness amid the shaggy hibiscus and bee-laced lemon branches; the cool stone bench under the mango tree.

The Royal Karnak may have let its interior go to rot, but its garden is fastidiously tended by an army of workers. Nile rats can be a problem in Luxor, but not at the hotel, thanks in part to seven feral cats that patrol the grounds, mostly harmless except for the occasional unprovoked swipe at an ankle; gray, calico, and the meanest one, the tiger-orange female who sphinxes in the coral bushes. From my third-floor window I once watched this orange cat scale a palm tree to attack the bats who perch there at night. The most noteworthy element of the garden, though, is a large aviary, built, as its plaque states in semi-oblique English, "in the year 1921 after War." Inside this green-painted wood-frame structure, metal-netted on all sides, sit three yellow-mohawked lutino cockatiels on a network of artificial branches. They are the main suppliers of the hotel's whistling birdsong throughout the day. These birds are the unofficial mascots of the Royal Karnak, cared for by the grumpy head gardener, Seif, who has a calloused prayer knot in the center of his forehead and teeth as black as his fingernails. Seif barks at any guest who dares to rattle the mesh in hopes of attracting the cockatiels. He is the least likely man to work in hospitality, and even I, practically a family member of the Royal Karnak at this point, have yet to merit so much as a nod from him. As the winding garden path brings me in view of the aviary, I'm astonished to find Seif standing at it, pointing out his precious cockatiels to the bespeckled boy with the apricot ears who I saw playing a video game in the lobby this morning. No one wins Seif's favor, let alone on the first day of their arrival. But this little boy has somehow convinced Seif to reach into the cage to cajole the smallest bird onto his finger. The boy mimics a dove's gentle cooing. In the dappled sunlight, I take the opportunity to examine him. A puggy nose with a dash of freckles, a gapped front tooth, the scrunched muscles of his face laboring to keep the glasses high on the bridge of his nose—he bears only a trace resemblance to his pretty mother. Suddenly, as if sensing my eyes on him, he turns and stares directly at me over the bougainvillea hedge. There is something hard and defiant in his stare, as if *I'm* the intruder in *his* garden, and yet also curious, his eyes taking me in with a focus so rarely bestowed on an old person. His fierce attention nearly makes me blush. I quickly continue along the path, not slowing until I climb the putty-colored steps to the pool.

"Mags!" Ben calls from the other side of the turquoise water. He sits in the shade of a table umbrella next to his sunbathing husband. I wave back from across the water. The swimming pool was added to the garden in the 1950s, a giant rectangular crater of pastel blue with two wings jutting from its deep end and curving around to create two hidden "adult" alcoves. Pink and peach umbrellas shelter teak lounge chairs and tan mosaic tables. As I walk around the perimeter to reach the boys, I spot one of the pool's chief attractions. We call him the gigolo, although none of us knows whether he really is a prostitute. In truth, the boys and I can't make heads or tails of him. His mysterious identity is part of the fun. Sitting (never lying) on a teak lounger, with one leg hitched up and an alabaster ashtray between his thighs, the young Egyptian in his late teens (guestimates Ben) or early twenties (speculate Zachary and I) perches poolside, with sun-dark skin and black caverns of eyes. He is a thing of absolute beauty, a sight to behold whenever he struts to the deep end in his maroon Speedos and completes five laps before climbing back out, dripping wet, skin aglow, to return to his lounge chair. We don't know his name, and we've never spoken a word to him. But he orders his nonalcoholic drinks from the waiters in Arabic, and since he's been a mainstay at the pool for months but isn't checked into any of the hotel rooms, we deduce he must be a local. And yet local Egyptians aren't allowed to use the hotel facilities. Therefore, this gorgeous young man must have a special connection to the hotel. But what kind? This question has been the debate of many lunches among us. We'll seize on any trivial clue for analysis. "Have you noticed he always tips the waiter from a roll of bills he keeps in his bag?" Zachary once pointed out. "To me, carrying that much cash indicates an illicit, under-the-table money source." The gigolo exudes a cool, cosmopolitan menace that suggests he belongs to bigger cities, like Cairo or Alexandria. Zachary, naturally, was the first to propose that he's an escort, retained by the hotel to satisfy . . . well, the contingent of lonely old widows like me. That could well be the case. Perhaps I'm too old even for his client base, though, because he has never batted his long black eyelashes at me. But I've noticed that he doesn't deign to look at any of the other guests either, lost in his own world of ripe, delicious, muscular sloth. He absorbs our admiration like it's a life-sustaining nutrient, a second sun rich with vitamin D, as if we're insignificant scenery and he's the true heir to this oasis under the Saharan sky.

To counter Zachary's male-prostitute theory, Ben's offered two alternate possibilities. The first, judging by his stomach muscles, is that he works as a trainer at the fitness center (although Zachary swears he's never once seen him in the gym); the second is that he's a bartender who usually mans the front-terrace bars overlooking the Nile, but since they've been temporarily closed due to the dip in tourism, he's simply biding his days until the pandemic ends and the terrace bars reopen for business. "Bravo," I said to Ben, "that must be our answer!" But Zachary wondered out loud, would the hotel allow an out-of-work bartender to lounge by the pool among the paying guests all day? That brought me to suspect that the gigolo might be a relative of an executive at Richesse Resorts; perhaps a wealthy Luxorite family contributed money to the conglomerate's recent acquisition. (Both Zachary and Ben think this notion of needing a local investor a stretch for a billion-dollar European hotel chain.) "I'm going to settle the matter once and for all," I decided. One afternoon, I casually quizzed Ahmed about our resident beauty. To my disappointment, he refused to traffic in tawdry gossip. "Ahh, yes, that one." He tittered. "He is not important to you. Pay him no mind, Maggie. It's best you let him be." Unsatisfied, I went to a different source for intel: Yasmine, the portly, chatty head of housekeeping. To my surprise, she proved equally tight-lipped. When I brought up the curious young man, a look of trepidation passed over her. Holding a pile of fresh sheets to her chest, she said, "I keep my distance from that sort. I don't want to get mixed up with him." Added up, these warnings do hint at a criminal element. Maybe Zachary isn't too far off the mark. Who knows for certain? In the end, our handsome, muscled pool muse remains a riddle, sitting and glaring at no one in particular through his impenetrable cloud of cigarette smoke.

Smoking, smoking, smoking, sucking hard on his brown cigarette, biting the smoke, and swallowing it down before letting it flow back out from his lips. Then a swim. All eyes are on him as he struts around the pool. He has strong, hairy thighs, a smooth, defined chest permanently flexed, nipples the same maroon as his Speedos, a prominent but not egregious bulge filling the front of them, shaved armpits (his only flaw in Zachary's eyes), a military buzz cut, and he never smiles or looks farther than his feet. He zooms past me now en route to the deep end. When I turn to look at my two friends, Zachary is all teeth, a smile of appetite, his veneers blindingly white in the sun. I shake my head, doting-aunt style, and watch this gorgeous human swan-dive into the water without stirring a splash. Maybe, in the end, this is his job, to be an unattainable object of desire, something upon which all of us splotchy white westerners can cast our daydreams. We are all thankful for his dedication to the role.

I must tell you before I go any further that, last month, I stole a master keycard. I took it from one of the maid's carts, swept it right up and put it in my kaftan pocket as I asked for more towels and hobbled down the hall. The keycard provides access to all seventy guest rooms as well as the few common areas that are locked at night. I haven't used it, not once, even though I've been tempted. Time had to pass after the maid misplaced it in case anyone (rather laughable when you consider the hotel's skeleton staff) was monitoring rogue electronic swipes. To-day, though, I finally plan to put it to use.

I double-check that it's safely tucked in my pocket as I duck un-der the table umbrella where Ben sits in the island of shadow, a towel strung over his legs. He hates direct sunlight almost as much as I do. I close my purple umbrella and tap it against his knee to let me pass, before plopping into the empty chair next to him.

Zachary is a mere three feet from us, lying on his back in the sun. It almost hurts my eyes to look at him through his coating of suntan oil. He locks his hands behind his head and freezes mid-situp to showcase his impressive fifty-year-old abs (in case the deity in the pool happens to be watching). He studies his husband and me slumped together in the shade. "You poor, pathetic creatures. Why are you here if you hate the sun so much?"

Why am I here? It's been so long since I've asked myself that ques-tion. The answer: there was nowhere else for me to run.

Ben grabs the laminated menu off the table and flaps it at me. "Do you want to order something, Mags? We're getting the pizza with anchovies and capers." The boys wouldn't order pizza if there were a healthier option on the pool menu—usually they only peck at the toppings. Zachary would probably skip the meal altogether, sating himself on the various multivitamins that he doles out on the table with the fastidiousness of a bank teller separating coins. But it's the ordering of lunch that provides Ben the excuse to leave the museum for an hour and spend it with us.

"No lunch for me today," I reply. I'm about to ask how Ben's scanning session at the museum is going. There's always a new relic he's uncovered in the disorderly bowels of the museum's storage rooms. Even though he's technically prohibited from removing artifacts from the premises, once in a while he sneaks out a small, priceless trinket for us to marvel at during his lunch break—a gold-falcon brooch inlaid with lapis lazuli or a carved totem of a kneeling peasant, eyes shining with volcanic glass. As I glance over at him, I notice him staring at me with a horrified expression, as if he has finally seen it, *the wrongness*—has realized something terrible about me that I won't be able to explain away.

"What's the matter?" I stammer, my heart hammering in my chest.

"Your lips are fluorescent green."

I laugh in relief and try to scour off the food coloring with my fingertips. "It's Hamza's pistachio cookies. I've got to stop eating them for breakfast. They're packed with butter."

"Why stop?" Zachary wails from the teak lounger, flipping onto his stomach to spread the cancer evenly over his skin. His voice rises to a note of anguish. "Eat cookies all day if you want! Drink martinis with your eggs at breakfast! Enjoy as much of this life as you can while you're still kicking!" I don't think Zachary is alluding specifically to my advanced age. No, he's referring to the terrible mortality accelerant of Covid. The three of us have a rule not to mention the daily news reports on skyrocketing death tolls or the emergency rooms on the brink of collapse or the new viral strains chewing on America from both ends. Nevertheless, this heartbreaking information has a way of trickling into our brains no matter how many screens we mute or news alerts we deactivate. "If nothing else," Zachary declares, "this whole thing has taught us to run around full commando with our hearts, don't you think? Live for today! Do whatever the hell you want! Eat the cookies!"

Ben scowls, not a fan of manifestos for irresponsibility, having devoted his pandemic days to a marathon of fifteen-hour work shifts meticulously cataloging the world's oldest fragments. It's the very definition of failing to seize life with aging-party-boy abandon.

"I have a novel idea, Zee," Ben retorts. "How about, instead of deciding our only option is to embrace anarchy, we trust that rational science will find a cure and save us from this mess?" Ben turns to me with a grimace. "Even in pre-Covid times, Zachary could use a stubbed toe as an excuse to promote hedonism. An upcoming dental appointment! A missed train!"

"A caught train!" Zachary adds, delighting in this cartoon rendition of himself. "And wasn't I right all along, Ben? It didn't take a plague to clue me in to what's important." He squirms onto his side and presents his most wicked, leonine smile. "But I did come to a few new conclusions this past year. I'm never going back into an office. Or helping a bank draft a contract. Or drinking stale coffee in a conference room. Mags, here, is my new role model. A full-time hotel-hopper, leaving the past in her wake!"

I don't recall sharing that potentially incriminating detail about my previous hotel experiences with the boys. It must have slipped out on one of those nights at dinner when they goaded me into a glass of wine. As a rule, I try to avoid the subject of my whereabouts before I checked into the Royal Karnak, who I was, what happened at those places. To eclipse any further talk of my hotel-hopping, I feign a distraction, dipping my head to the side and staring up into the asphalt-colored sky. The sun is directly overhead, a white eye rolled back. It's well past noon by now, but the huge unblinking eye seems to hang in place directly over us for longer than it should, refusing to tilt west, cruelly applying an extra dose of intensity. As I stare at it, I see an amulet of a falcon with blue jeweled wings, its gold beak dipped in blood. I see beautiful, naked young men drowning in the Nile, their mouths going under, foreheads wreathed in gilded laurels.

"Mags? Earth to Mags?" I don't know how long I've been away. I'm leaning back in my chair, and Ben is on the verge of shaking me. A waiter stands in front us, tapping his pencil against his notepad. "*Yoo-hoo.* Do you want a glass of iced tea or not?"

"Not," I manage. Zachary and Ben share concerned glances, their indication that I'm having one of my senior moments. I worry it's a sign that my dosage of risperidone, prescribed to me after Peter's death by Dr. Reiselman to keep me grounded, might need to be upped a few milligrams. Anyone past the age of seventy is familiar with the forced vocation of playing amateur pharmacologist, regulating our medications when our doctors aren't available: a nibble more of one pill, a nibble less of another. But to ease everyone's fears, I smile serenely. *Nothing wrong with this old lady.* The waiter turns on his heels and heads back to the clubhouse.

"Have you met the new woman?" Zachary asks, inspecting a freckle on his arm. "We did, just a few minutes before you got here. Apparently, she and her son are staying awhile. I took her as British, but it turns out she's American."

"Why did you think she was British?" Ben asks.

"She has a British chin," Zachary says.

"What on earth is a British chi—"

But Ben's inquiry falls silent as the very woman in question appears by the pool, brimming her eyes with her hand. Standing stone still, she looks almost like she's saluting the hotel. She's changed from her earlier drab clothes into white pants and a short-sleeved linen shirt, which means she's finally been given a room. She scans the pool's perimeter with the same vexed expression she used to survey Hamza's buffet offerings. As her eyes reach our table, they narrow in a flicker of recognition, and she heads over with a hand raised in greeting.

"Hi again!" she says buoyantly to the boys, who respond with a hello in unison.

Zachary reaches for his sunglasses. "Tess, have you met Maggie? She's one of us, the human version of hotel furniture, permanent and unbudging."

Tess extends her hand, but I don't want to reach out to intercept it until her fingers cross the threshold of the umbrella's shadow. It's not worth the risk of aggravating my skin condition with any unnecessary exposure. Only her hand doesn't make it that far, and she retracts it, dropping it awkwardly to her side as if I've deliberately snubbed her. I try to make amends with an ecstatically welcoming voice.

"I saw you check in this morning!" I exclaim. "With your little boy! Is his father here too?" For a second my question hangs sourly in the air. I realize how old-fashioned I sound, making such an outmoded assumption about families, a loyalist to the nuclear that blew up a long time ago. Sure enough, Tess's pained, deerlike expression deepens and she turns to perform another perfunctory scan of the pool area.

An uncomfortable quiet descends, and I'm thankful when Ben changes the subject. "They better hurry with that pizza. I have to get back to the museum."

"Museum?" Tess asks, bringing her attention back to us.

"Didn't I tell you? Unlike my lazy husband here, I'm in Luxor in a professional capacity. I'm an Egyptologist." Zachary grunts from his lounger, mocking the overblown job title. Admittedly, "Egyptologist" seems a bit fanciful for a man who spends most of his day as a glorified scanning technician. But far from home, it's easier to simplify one's job into a generic cutout for the sake of strangers. No one wants to listen to the dreary micro-details of an actual profession.

"Fascinating!" Tess croons. "I'm sure Otto will have tons of questions for you."

"Otto?" I ask.

"My son," Tess says, eyes smiling at me, as if her love for him can even bridge the distance with an irritable stranger. "He just turned eight last week, so it's his namesake year. But please don't make that joke to him. He's already tired of it."

"Eight!" I repeat to commit the age to memory. "Eight years old. Otto."

"Speaking of, has anyone seen him?" Tess gazes around again, her brow furrowed. "I told him to stay by the pool."

I lift my eyes in the direction of the aviary. There, not fifteen feet beyond the bougainvillea hedge, her boy is standing right where I saw him last. Seif has placed one of the cockatiels on his shoulder and he's grinning behind his round glasses. He's the picture of innocence, just like my Julia was at that age. An eight-year-old child, he has not yet built hideaways or secret cubbyholes in his head for the concealment of strange desires and fixations. All of that comes later. For now he just *is*, a larval human, simply a boy with a cockatiel on his shoulder. Tess is calling out his name, staring in the wrong direction, the last *O* of *Otto* soprano-ing in concern. I'm about to point him out to her when I catch sight of the woman I've been waiting for. The Greek divorcée walks toward the pool, wearing a floral bikini. She has an impressive body, breasts too globular to be real. She has one of her yellow silk scarves tied around her neck, pulling it up over her mouth as a Covid mask whenever she encounters a new guest. Carissa is a long-hauler like we are, but she keeps to herself, lost in her own fog, and each week she makes plans to return to Athens but she never departs, fearful, no doubt, of the worldwide leper colony that exists just beyond the hotel gates. Today, as usual, she's right on time. The feral cats scatter as she clomps along the garden path in her espadrilles. I open my umbrella and struggle to my feet. "Time for my nap, dears. Enjoy your capers."

4.

———————————

Unraveling a life never takes as much work as you'd think. If enough suspicion exists, the seed is already in the soil. You simply need to encourage it to grow, nudge it along into sprouting. To help Shelley, I'm relying on a gambit I previously employed to great effect last year at a ski resort in Courchevel (that couple, now separated and sharing custody of their two children, should be writing me thank-you notes, although they never learned that I masterminded their freedom). Yesterday afternoon, I prowled the hotel for one of the communal courtesy phones located in a quiet corner—the calls had to be seen as coming from somewhere in the Royal Karnak but not traceable to a particular room. I found an unattended phone in the lobby of the fitness center and sat down in one of the pink club chairs, prepared to camp out for as long as it took for Shelley to answer. As luck would have it, on my very first attempt, her voice erupted on the line. "Hello?" she squeaked into the receiver, as meekly as if she were entering the dark house of a suspected serial killer. Anyone could hear a plea for rescue in that voice.

I didn't respond. Not verbally. I allowed a breathy silence to fill her ear and then sharply hung up. I waited exactly six minutes before dialing her room again. Shelley answered with the same unassuming "Hello?" This time I summoned a guttural whisper from deep in my chest, what I imagine a thick-accented Greek woman might sound like. "Geoff?" I uttered, steeped in lovesick doubt. "I, I . . ." I hung up. I waited three minutes and called again. "Hello!" Shelley demanded, her anger proving she had nibbled the bait and liked what she tasted. "Who is this? Geoff isn't in!" I inhaled deeply and let my breath blow over the receiver before returning the phone to its cradle. The seed had cracked open, a throb of green bursting from its shell toward the surface. A minor miracle, the beautiful raw matter of life.

The next part of the plan involves a greater degree of risk. Thankfully, in the early afternoon the Royal Karnak's upper floors shiver with emptiness. My cushioned sandals produce only a muffled patter on the hallway carpet. I take the master keycard from my kaftan pocket and perform one last check to ensure that no nosy maid has wandered into view. The Greek divorcée's room is directly across from the elevator on the second floor. Carissa usually spends an hour or two at the pool, which should give me plenty of time, although I'll only need a minute. Room 202. I swipe the card through the electronic reader, hear the permitting click, and quickly slip inside. The interior is dark, shadows tangling over the furniture, the window light caught in the inner curtain's translucent net. A heavy lilac perfume curdles the air, mixing with a note of stale wine. A glass of red, half drunk and crusted at the rim, sits on the credenza. Housekeeping hasn't been in to clean yet. Balled-up sheets tumble across the bed, white and fuzzy like Wisconsin clouds, and a smear of bronzer streaks the pillow. The hawkers along the corniche are chanting and whistling—*Ride? Miss, come with me? Please! Why you don't like my horse?*—and I'm grateful all over again that I switched to the back of the hotel. I hurry to Carissa's suitcase, which is splayed opened on the luggage stand. She's one of those travelers who doesn't unpack, not a homemaker by nature, failing to take advantage of the cedar hangers in the closet or the copious dresser drawers. Her bras and underwear stew with her blouses and shorts. There's an expensive silk negligee in her suitcase, the only item neatly folded as if she's still waiting for a reason to wear it (how sad, like a man returning from a vacation with all the condoms he brought still packed in his shaving kit).

Three years ago, when I was still learning my trade, I would have grabbed a pair of underwear. But with experience, I've learned the importance of subtlety. You can blow the entire operation with heavy-handedness, turn hints and clues into something that plunges headlong toward a practical joke. Unfortunately, Carissa's suitcase doesn't contain her signature yellow scarves. I scan the room until I notice a leather satchel on the floor below the flat-screen television, a hairbrush handle protruding from the top. Bingo, her collection of designer scarves, the kind marketed to upscale travelers held hostage by endless layovers in airport-terminal malls. I grab the brightest yellow—there's no way to mistake these scarves for any other guest's, the way Carissa makes a show of wearing them. But in case Geoff tries to pass the scarf off as a surprise gift, I pluck a few long strands of black hair from her brush.

Housekeeping will have finished its morning rounds on the first floor by now, and the Bradleys occupy the last suite at the end of that hall. It shouldn't be difficult to determine on which side of the bed Shelley sleeps, and thus under which pillow to slip the evidence of an affair. The rest is up to her—whether she chooses freedom and a riskier but brighter horizon or the safe prison cell the exact size of her husband and daughter in their new house in Manchester. I shove the scarf in my kaftan pocket and leave the room as quietly as I entered.

The boy. Just as Carissa's door clicks shut behind me, the boy comes careening into the hall from the staircase, his glasses gleaming, his cheeks rouged from sprinting up the steps from the garden. At the sight of me, he slows, chastened, as if I'm a volunteer hall monitor cracking down on the reckless walking speeds of guests. Or maybe it's simply that children prefer to keep their missions secret from adults (Julia, at Otto's age, was forever cloak-and-daggering around the house, pretending her chores were clandestine adventures, refusing to admit the truth when I asked what she was doing). I'm hopeful that the boy's inherent self-absorption, coupled with the natural confusion of being a new guest in a foreign hotel, means that he hasn't registered that the room I've just exited isn't mine.

He has a keycard in his hand and veers to a stop at the door across from Carissa's room. He and his mom are staying in 201, which tells me, in light of all the current room vacancies, that Tess must be experiencing money troubles. The 01 line is the cheapest, because these rooms share a wall with the elevator shaft; day and night the elevator groans like a dying water buffalo as it ascends and descends, rumbling those sad, cramped rooms with the force of a minor earthquake. Before Otto swipes his card, he turns to look at me curiously, just as he did earlier in the garden. I've shuffled a few steps away from Carissa's door to discourage any association. But what does it matter? He can't possibly have already worked out whose room sits across from his or which adult belongs where. He is nothing to be scared of. A little boy.

"Hello," he says in a testing tone, as if he's not certain I speak English.

"Hello," I respond affably. "You're Otto?"

He nods. "How did you know my name?" He has a careful, quiet voice, not as high-pitched as his scrawny body promises. I recognize the American accent, but there are unidentifiable weeds of European vowels growing among our flowery homegrown consonants. I wonder where he and Tess live.

"I'm psychic!" I tell him with a broad smile. But my eagerness to dazzle him might have been a mistake, for the boy is now taking a more considered interest in me, memorizing me, staring at my face. Why didn't I simply ignore him and shrink down the steps? As he studies me, I study him back, more than seventy years separating us in those five feet of carpeted hallway, the distance of an entire lifespan.

Underneath the thick glasses, Otto's eyes are two different colors, one brown, one green, making it unnerving to choose which orb to concentrate on. His pouty lips hide the gap between his teeth. His nose has already reddened from the sun. As we gaze at each other in silence, I sense an understanding growing on his face, the sparkle of a kindred soul, misunderstood, mischievous, a touch too lonely, but someone preternaturally wise to the difficulties of an imperfect world.

"You are not psychic," he balks, the watery line between reality and fantasy only starting to solidify at his age. There's still some belief in him that an old woman in an Egyptian hotel could possess special powers.

"You don't believe me?" I close my eyes, feigning concentration. "Let's see, you're seven . . . no, eight! You're eight years old! Ahh, but only just recently. Brand-new to the big, uncharted greatness of eight!"

He flinches, gullible, briefly taken in, before his homely freckled face tightens with intelligence. "Mom must have told you down at the pool." *Down at the pool* reminds him of his mission. "I need to get her phone. She wants to take a photo of me with the bird. The gardener said he'll let the big one sit on my head."

"Well, don't let me keep you, Otto," I say, laughing. "I'm Maggie, by the way."

He doesn't say "Nice to meet you," but merely purses his lips. This boy is not won over easily. He makes you work for his affection. "I can do tricks too," he announces.

"Really? I can't wait to see them. But you'll have to try very hard. I'm not easy to fool."

He doesn't respond. He only gives me a final survey with his eyes, considering me from knees to head, pausing an extra second at my waist. Then he offers the smallest, sweetest hint of a smile. Before I can return it, he unlocks the door, pushes it open, and barges into the room. I catch a glimpse of sunlight pouring over the bedspread, and two suitcases stacked by the foot of the bed, not yet unpacked. The door slams shut. Looking down, I notice a corner of Carissa's yellow scarf sticking out of my pocket like a lizard's tail. Hurrying, I take the steps to the first floor and knock softly on the Bradleys' door. I want to make sure that I'm not intruding.

5.

It wasn't until the second week of my stay that I discovered the sunsets. For the first week I kept to my room, resting on the bed as I watched night slowly erase the back garden. But one afternoon I returned from a visit to the market later than usual. Climbing the horseshoe staircase from the corniche, I noticed that the hotel's white marble facade had turned an exquisite salmon pink. Turning around, I gazed across the Nile and understood immediately the reason that the pharaohs had chosen those jagged peaks as their eternal resting place. The molten red sun was melting behind them, its last light scattering across the choppy river and falling like a blush over the hotel's pale Victorian face. Even the touts had gone silent during this miraculous rupture in the sky. I held on to my umbrella handle but let it tilt slightly so that the desert colors could wash over my face too. I didn't realize I was crying until Ahmed stepped outside to ask whether I was okay.

"It's just so beautiful," I said, wiping my eyes, feeling a bit foolish, and laughing at my tears. I wasn't the only guest enjoying the view. An elderly Malaysian couple held up their phones to live-stream the phenomenon.

"Yes, Miss Maggie," Ahmed said (in the second week, he hadn't entirely dropped the formality yet), "the Royal Karnak is the premiere spot in all of Luxor for sunsets. In old times, in normal times, just a year ago, we used to invite the guests out here to watch the sunset with cocktails." He gestured toward the terrace bars, now covered in plastic tarps and wrapped in chains.

"Why did you stop?"

"Too few guests these days, with the virus. We had to let the bar staff go." It was one of the few moments that Ahmed broke from his performance as the unfazed, jolly manager and hinted at the brutal hit the hotel had taken from Covid.

"We could still do it," I protested with ripening determination. "We don't need cocktails. Just gather everyone out here for five minutes to bathe in this divine miracle."

"Oh, I wish we could, but——"

"No buts, Ahmed! So help me, we're doing it!"

Starting the very next day, and every day since, it's become my self-ordained vocation to grab the silver bell off the reception desk fifteen minutes before sunset and ring it up and down the halls so that anyone who wants to—guests and staff alike—can gather on the front terrace. "Sunset time!" I cry, and occasionally I add a bit of obscure Americana that must puzzle the Europeans: "Get your fresh, hot sunsets!"

At first the maids and the junior staff were reluctant to mix with the guests (Seif and his team of gardeners still refuse outright). I had to grab Yasmine by her arm and drag her out the front door on that first evening while the rest of her housekeeping flock followed timidly. In the end, only the Russian guests spurned my overtures, resistant to group activities or at least those that involved mingling on equal footing with the help. Ahmed thought perhaps it was wiser to include the Russians by excluding the workers. But I was reminded of a maxim etched on the face of a clock in downtown Milwaukee that I always loved—The Sun, It Shines for All—and Ahmed couldn't argue against its logic when I quoted it to him. "For *all*, Ahmed. For Yasmine too! For everyone!" As the sunset's herding dog, I'm always the last one on the terrace, and I keep my back pressed flat against the wall, my umbrella at my side. All of us, whoever we happen to be, like a caravan of shipwreck survivors, stare west toward Thebes and watch the sky swirl sherbet and the palm trees stiffen into blackness as the Sahara turns red and then purple, and finally is lost in the night.

I no longer weep like I did that first day. Yet every evening, right as the last sliver of sun dips below the mountains, I think of Peter and wish he were beside me. We weren't big travelers. When we were first married, we dreamed of hopping on a plane to faraway places—the Great Wall, the Great Barrier Reef. But back then we didn't have the money, and the thrilling adventure of starting our life together superseded even the most exotic escape. By the time we did have the money to travel, our daughter had been born, and most trips out of town were relegated to our lake house. It was a three-hour drive from Milwaukee, accompanied by Julia in the back seat, who fell head-over-heels for cabin life and accrued a gaggle of friends along the shoreline. Whenever I suggested a family getaway in Europe, Julia stomped her feet— "It's *my* summer vacation and I want to see my friends!"—effectively smothering the plan in its crib. Peter was always too lenient with her. He always gave in on what she wanted. "*Your* summer?" he drawled lovingly. "Ahh, now I understand! I thought your mother and I had summers too, but I see, it's *your* summer! We apologize for our misunderstanding! Julia owns summer, and Julia alone!" His indulgence toward her put an end to the Burkhardts in Paris or Amsterdam or Rome—all those brochures I collected from the Klode Park branch of AAA that were never more than thumbed through, like fashion magazines at a hair salon.

Naturally, Peter and I assumed we'd have our retirement years to take our adventures. He served as the board chairman of a firm that located and extracted natural-gas deposits throughout the Upper and eastern Midwest. For most of his career, that business seemed about as lucrative as selling divining rods. But in the last two decades, business boomed, and we made a lot of unexpected money, which also unfortunately increased Peter's workload in what turned out to be his final years. One May afternoon, Peter went directly from his office to the hospital, complaining of abdominal pains. He never stepped foot in our house in Klode Park again. I spent seven months sleeping next to him in a chair in his hospital room. The ICU was pilot-testing a new service for the families of patients, where you could watch your loved one in their hospital bed on your phone while shopping or relaxing on your sofa, the way babies are monitored by an electronic eye above their cribs. But I couldn't take care of Peter long-distance, couldn't keep away from him for a single night. I needed to be next to him, holding his hand while there was still time left together. I became a hospital nomad, washing my face and body in the women's restroom, eating out of the vending machines. Peter never regained consciousness, but I held his hand for those seven months, and I believe for most of them he was holding mine. Guess how many times Julia visited her father in the ICU? Once. That was all. She said it was too painful for her. A grown adult. Too painful for her to visit her father, the man who'd spoiled her at every turn. Julia. *Her summers.* The only one who feels pain.

One reason I decided to spend my widowhood overseas was that it proved far more convivial than the homebound version. I'd worked for twenty-seven years as a "senior loan ambassador" at our neighborhood bank, but I retired shortly before Peter's illness. I floated the idea of returning to my job, even part time, but the new management wasn't accommodating (you can't exactly volunteer at a bank). Yes, I could have stayed in Milwaukee, haunting our Tudor Revival in a vigil to the past, turning the lights on and off by clockwork as if they were set on a security timer, bringing in the newspapers, taking out the garbage, checking the mailbox—a life whose movements seemed organized around the objective of preventing a burglary by keeping up the impression that someone was always at home. Someone always was. Klode Park is a tight-knit community, wealthy without much ostentation, the neighbors as sweetly invasive as butterflies, everyone called by their first name. The neighborhood worked hard to earn those flower-lined, leaf-blown sidewalks and the front doors left unlocked and the local green markets running on an honor system. But in the last years, crime had begun to seep in—car windows smashed, kitchen window break-ins, garages looted while families were out getting groceries or enjoying a stroll along Whitefish Bay. After Peter died, people would ask me, "Maggie, aren't you frightened in that big house all by yourself?" No, I assured them, not one bit. I never told them the fuller truth: that there were nights when I would have welcomed a burglar. I went for weeks at a time after Peter's death unseen by anyone. Friends, they were mostly sympathy cards and five-minute condolence phone calls. Daughter gone. An occasional cold lasagna left by a neighbor on the porch. A younger sister, Claire, with whom I never got along, calling or texting every other week to threaten me with an impending visit. Maybe I was too unresponsive, because Claire never turned up at my door.

I wasn't trying to escape my grief by booking a red-eye ticket out of Chicago five years ago. Not exactly. Nor was I lured solely by the glamorous nostalgia that the five-star European hotels promised on their websites. I left (or *came*, as I like to think of it) because of the plain fact that I missed being seen. I don't mean, looked at with deep affection, like the way Peter's blue eyes, as cloudy in those final years as freshly shucked oysters, held me in their sights with absolute devotion. No, I'm talking about being seen in the most basic terms: serving as the fleeting focus of another set of human eyeballs. That's what I missed: being recognized as a physical entity that takes up space. Most of the new "boutique" hotels built today discourage guest interaction; you can check into several of them without even being greeted by a live receptionist. That's the reason I was drawn to the castles, chalets, schlosses, and old-world creakers riddled with unavoidable common rooms where strangers can't help but congregate. I'm not always hotly desired in such rooms—most often I would be lingering in a library or ballroom (now doubling as a Pilates studio), when a young mother would mutter "Madam, could you," and gesture that I step out of the way so she could snap photos of her cereal-bowl children in front of a giant picture window. "Oh, of course, I'm so sorry," I'd reply. I was happy to oblige, apologizing for my presence, uglifying the room with my oldness. Very few people want a wrinkled, old witch lurking in the background of their vacation photos. Still, after Peter died, it was a luxury to be noticed at all, even as an obstacle, a woman who existed, who could ruin pictures by being so obtrusively there, *in the world*, even if she was in the way.

Peter. I didn't need to bring any souvenirs of our marriage to remember him by. As Shelley said so eloquently at the mortuary temple, *we move house*. But I did pack two small mementos of sentimental value when I left Milwaukee. One I've told you about, and the other I haven't because it's no longer in my possession. It was a silver-framed photo of Peter and me taken professionally twenty-five years ago. I remember when we got the selections back from the photographer, how horrified I was by the gray sheen of our faces and hair. "Oh Peter, we look like our parents!" What a wicked joke pictures play, the punchline taking so long to arrive. All through Europe I kept that photo of us propped by my bedside, and every night as I reached to turn out the light, I would look at it and think, god, those were the days, we were still filled with so much possibility, still young and healthy, Julia the light of our eyes, deep in the thresher of our happiest years together. I lost that framed photo—I won't forgive myself—when I fled Europe. I neglected to grab it when I frantically packed my bags to sneak out of the hotel in Sils Maria in the dead of night. It must still be there, in the snow-bonneted peaks of Upper Engadin, Switzerland. Perhaps that photo is now being used as a dart board, a shooting target, or the image on a Wanted poster.

That's why I've been so careful about the ribboned lock of Peter's white hair. I clipped it as he lay in his hospital bed. I never remove it from my cosmetics bag, where it's doubly protected in a Ziploc baggie. On the morning I landed in Germany from the States and passed through customs, the agent searching my belongings pulled out the rolled-up plastic baggie holding a strange, unidentifiable substance. "Is this marijuana, ma'am?" he asked me. "No, Officer, it's my husband." When I told Ahmed this anecdote a few weeks ago, he hooted in laughter.

I've considered carrying the lock of hair in my pocket, keeping it with me at all times. I'd like to rub my fingers over Peter's soft bristles during the terrace sunsets. But as safe as I feel at the Royal Karnak, I can't risk losing it. That desire isn't so creepy, is it? Holding onto a memento of the dead isn't such an oddity. In Europe, they build entire churches around a saint's relics—a jawbone or a rib or a kneecap. Here in Egypt, it's the whole body—a human god, wrapped and sheathed in gold to last for eternity.

During sunsets I stand with my back against the hotel's warm marble facade and wonder, right as the light vanishes: Could Peter have imagined that his wife would end up staring into the Sahara Desert as the sails of the felucca boats tilt in the Nile breeze? Six years ago, on his deathbed, could Peter have imagined a virus ripping apart the patchwork of nations that quilted the world? Would he have believed me had I been able to explain the future to him? *In a few years, sweetheart, a deadly plague will spin the earth faster than it was ever meant to turn and millions of people will go flying off the face of it—the rich and the poor, the ignorant and the blessed.* Peter would shake his head—*No, I don't believe you, stop saying that, you're crazy, the world can't get any madder than it already is*—and I'd squeeze his hand in sympathy. *Yes, dear, this happens, so many will die, and the biggest cities will turn into ghost towns, and hospitals will become as chaotic as Black Friday sales, and on top of that, your wife will be chased out of Europe, fleeing with three suitcases into Africa in the middle of the night, running for her life.* His eyes would clot with tears, and he'd ask me, *But where am I? Why aren't I with you, rescuing you, fixing the situation? And where's Julia? Where's our family and our house in Klode Park?* I'd squeeze his hand tighter because I won't be able to tell him that part of the future. It would kill him. *Oh, my darling, so much happens that you'll never learn. So many misfortunes, one after another, that you could never have predicted. So many lies and deaths. Our marriage was so strong, but even our Tudor Revival couldn't protect us. I had to handle it all alone.*

Tonight, as I do every evening, I apply a thick layer of sunscreen to my face, wet two fingertips with lavender oil to dab around my neck, and head down the grand staircase to ring the bell for sunset. As I descend to the second floor, I briefly glance down the hallway. At the end of it, on a chintz sofa so anemic that the cushions feel embalmed rather than stuffed, sits the boy's mother, Tess, all by herself, perched side-saddle and staring out the window behind her. That view looks out neither on the Nile nor on the back garden but on the Nubian rug store that closed last month, as well as the hotel's blue dumpsters, where the cats mate. The boy isn't in sight, and the door to their room next to the elevator is closed. I don't like being late in ringing the bell—the elderly guests need time to mobilize—but I can't resist this opportunity of catching Tess alone. I move down the hall, affecting a casual manner, using my purple umbrella as a walking stick.

Tess lifts her head, her small hands clasped together in her lap. It's clear that she's been crying. Unfortunately, she's recovered enough that it feels like prying to ask her what's wrong. How old is Tess? If Otto is eight, that means she's likely in her late twenties. Right now, though, this young woman on the sofa could pass as a college sophomore. Her smooth skin glows bluish white, like a blank canvas primed with gesso, the skin of a woman who must reap the benefits of scientifically advanced lotions and serums that weren't available to my generation (our pores clogged in the haze of mid-century secondhand smoke). Tess has the kind of plain beauty made more beautiful by a trace of sorrow. She's prettier than my Julia was at her age, although there is a similar quality in their expressions, a frazzled, lost look. She has the expression of someone who can't quite thread the needle in her grip. She stares up, helplessly, as she takes me in, her face practically begging me to take her troubles off her chest and make them my business. Her eyes are hazel green. I know nothing about the genetics of eye color, but I assume, since Otto's green eye matches his mother's, that his brown eye must belong to his absent father. For a second, I stand in front of her in silence, considering whether a question about eye color is a non-invasive icebreaker. I feel a sudden, uncontrollable need to learn the whereabouts of Otto's father.

"Maggie!" Tess says before I can launch a salvo of hellos. I'm flattered she remembers my name. No one ever remembers it. Sometimes I'm still introducing myself to guests on day eight of their stay. I'm momentarily tongue-tied, and I feel my cheeks reddening.

"Tess!" I reply, jump-starting my voice. "I saw you sitting here, and I wanted to invite you and your son down to the terrace. We do a sunset gathering out front every evening. It's absolutely gorg—" I make a show of studying her face, crumpling my own in increasing degrees of concern. "Are you okay? Is it allergies? If it's allergies, we all get them when we first arrive. It's from the native flowers in the garden. It takes a little—"

"No." She shakes her head and blows air from her lips. "Sorry. I don't know why I'm sitting here. I don't even know if you're supposed to sit on this antique furniture. I guess I was just resting a minute. It wasn't even a very long flight."

"You didn't come from America? I assumed by your accent—" I snail my shoulders to seem frailer, and Tess immediately scoots over in invitation to share the sofa. This ancient piece of furniture is ungodly low, and it's not all an act when I cling to the armrest to lower myself onto its sunken cushion. Tess's small hands help guide me.

"Yes, I'm American and so is Otto. He was born in San Francisco."

"Oh, Tess, I love California!" I exclaim. Do I? I've only been to California once, on a long layover from Hawaii after our honeymoon. Peter and I drove up the coast from Los Angeles to that seaside town where Clint Eastwood later became mayor. I was hardly bowled over by the state on that trip. But it sounds right when I say it out loud. *California*. It does sound amazing to my ears!

Tess sighs. "I love home too. My mother is still there, and, *ohh*, well that's a long story. I guess you could say we had different ideas about how to raise a child. Religion, you know. She found it, and I didn't. Anyway, for the past three years, we've been living in France with Otto's father. In Paris."

"You know, I thought I picked up a foreign accent in Otto's English."

Tess nods demurely, as if it's a compliment to hear a French accent sprinkled into the Americanese of an eight-year-old. "Yeah," she says. "He was raised in the tenth. Attended school there. We were happier in Paris than in the States, really happy, for so long." Her eyes begin to shine, on the brink of tears. "It was going so smoothly for a while." Tess pinches her eyes. "Well, we're here now. And I'm glad we are. A break will be good for us. Or . . ."

I lower my hand gently onto her back, like a plane brought down to land by an expert pilot. The nodes of Tess's spine are pronounced. I can feel them bulging through her linen shirt. My palm moves with the rise and fall of her breaths, like the hotel elevator, up and down, which is sure to keep her awake tonight.

"Otto's father?" I risk. She stops breathing. Her back stiffens, but she doesn't squirm from my touch. "Is he still in Paris?"

"Yeah," she whimpers. "Alain. He's a cinematographer. He works on limited-series shows, and he's booked on a period piece there. They just keep making more episodes. You see, the crew is in lockdown together, to keep the virus away from the set, so he can't just, he can't . . ." It's such a sensible excuse for his absence that it comes off as rehearsed, as if she's prepared it to fend off any suspicions of unhappiness from inquiring strangers. How can you blame this man for being locked on a set working overtime to pay for his family during a global disaster? And yet I intuitively sense all of Alain's betrayals and broken promises—to Tess, to Otto—swimming underneath the excuse's calm surface. Repeating this cover story out loud crushes her. She sinks her face into her palms, and her back jitters with a series of sobs. It's clear that Alain has a history of dodging his responsibilities, preferring the excitement of a film set to his pretty wife and homely son. I've been wasting my talents on the bland Bradley clan. Here, Tess, whose last name I don't even know, is all but begging me to lift her out of her pain.

She drags her fingers down her cheeks, leaving white contrails on her skin. "Alain says he might fly down tomorrow and spend a few days with us. If he can get permission from the production team. So maybe he'll come. We'll see." She wipes her eyes, and I let go of her back. It's important not to smother her.

"I didn't know there were flights so early from Paris to Luxor," I remark to shift the subject. She looks over at me quizzically. "I go down to breakfast early. I saw you checking in at dawn."

"Oh, that's right." She laughs. "We actually arrived in Luxor last night and were booked into one of those new modern hotels on the other side of the temple complex. But Otto hated it. For one, it didn't have a pool, and it was sterile and unfriendly, and well . . . he threw a tantrum. So I promised him that we'd find somewhere like—" She waves her arm at the baronial hallway with its chinoiserie vases clashing with the red damask. Clever boy, I think. I like Otto for his refusal to be stowed in a soulless cabinet of steel and reclaimed wood. His tantrum has brought us all together, washing up on this same safe shore. "It's better for him here," Tess decides, "because I don't know how long we'll be staying. I really hope Alain decides to come. For Otto's sake."

I nod. I've heard it all before. "The good news is," I exclaim, "there's so much in Luxor to captivate an eight-year-old, especially an intelligent one like your boy."

"Yes," Tess agrees. "Can you tell he's intelligent?"

"I absolutely can," I assure her. "And there are so many phenomenal ancient sites here to keep his interest piqued."

"The tombs. He definitely wants to visit them. Maybe if Alain doesn't show up tomorrow, we'll try to make it out to the Valley of the Kings in the afternoon."

"You really should go in the morning."

Tess bites her lip. "I would rather wait for Alain. In case he manages to clear a flight down with his shooting schedule. I want him to see Otto right away, so going in the morning won't work."

"Well, the afternoon can be fine too!" I reply. "In fact, it's less crowded if you don't mind the heat. I'm happy to go along with you tomorrow. If Alain doesn't show up, I mean. I can steer you and Otto toward the tombs that are worth visiting. There are dozens, but only a few that have the goods that your son will love!"

I worry I've shown my need too nakedly. Tess's face is an unreadable instrument as she angles it into the shaft of dying light that's streaming through the window. Her hazel-green eyes are almost yellow in the sun. There's a small dimple on her chin filled with shadow. It's the only feature that lends her face any toughness.

"Maggie, we'd love for you to show us," she finally says. "If it isn't too much of—"

"It's no trouble! I haven't been to the Valley of the Kings in weeks. I'd be delighted to see it again. It's better than any video game. Please tell Otto that!"

Tess laughs and wipes her palms on her thighs. "Yes, how did you know? He's passionate about video games. About all games really. And quite good at them. Sometimes I worry he's becoming too competitive, the sort of boy who can't lose graciously. I really don't know how I raised such a fighter. I was so bad at games when I was little."

"I never trust children who lose graciously," I reply. I don't tell Tess that Julia was such a child, a pushover at board games, no blood or strategy in her playing, too quick to concede defeat, yawny at the threshold of victory. "Why don't I have Ahmed arrange a van to transport us tomorrow!"

I grasp the sofa's arm to hoist myself up. I want to escape before Tess can rescind the offer. I feel an unbearable need to spend the afternoon with her and Otto. It feels like a second chance to be part of a family, or at least to exist in close proximity to one. I live in fear of Tess suddenly blurting out, *Actually, I forgot, tomooooorrow doesn't really work . . .* Before I can stand up, Tess places her hand on my leg to stop me.

"What about you, Maggie?" she asks, a traitor to her self-absorbed generation, asking a stranger about their problems. "What brought you to Luxor? It sounds like you've been at this hotel for a while."

"I'm a widow. I lost my Peter a few years back." I raise my hand before she jumps to the conclusion that he was an early victim of the plague. "No, it wasn't Covid. Peter died before that horror began. But I was just stewing around in our old house and decided to be bold. I bought a ticket, and here I am. I've been all over, but I will tell you, Tess—and they don't pay me to say this, I swear—I've been at the Royal Karnak for three months, and it's home!"

Tess smiles. "That's so impressive. I have a grandmother in Marin right outside San Francisco, and she refused to leave her room after my grandfather died. I mean, she's been in her own personal lockdown for years, long before Covid!" I give a self-satisfied grin, although, because Tess reminds me of Julia, I wish I reminded Tess of her mother and not her grandmother.

"I lost my daughter too," I blurt before I can stop myself. I don't like to discuss Julia, it fills me with too much heartache. "She was just a few years older than you when she passed. An adult with a whole life ahead of her. This was back in Wisconsin. None of us saw it coming." My eyes begin to tear. "I'm sorry . . ." I try to launch myself from the sofa, and Tess's hands work like a crutch to help me up.

"Oh, your daughter," she whispers. "That's terrible. Oh, Maggie."

"There's so much I didn't get to say to her."

"I'm so sorry. And here I am going on about my problems. There's too much loss all around these days, isn't there? Everyone's been hit. Whole families wiped out with this epidemic."

"Yes, too much loss," I repeat and turn away, not wanting to break down. I grab my umbrella and hold it tightly as I take a breath. Then I face Tess, trying to keep my voice strong. "I appreciate your sharing your troubles with me. It makes me feel useful to be a sympathetic ear." I notice that the daylight has disappeared from the window, replaced by a purplish dusk. How long have we been sitting here? "Tess, I have to go downstairs. Do you want to grab Otto and come enjoy the sunset?"

She shakes her head. "He's resting. And I think I'll just stay up here."

"I understand," I reply, even though I don't. There's an enormous orange gas ball dropping behind a mythic desert mountain embedded with ancient treasure right outside the front door, but Tess thinks she'll just stay up here in this hallway. "I'm looking forward to our excursion tomorrow!"

"Me too," she says with a smile.

I hurry down the hall, my hip prickling like a pincushion and my ankle palsying even before I punish them both by scrambling down the stairs. The lobby's garish electric lights have already been switched on, yellow filaments glowing from under magenta lampshades so dusty they look like they're ringed in volcanic smoke. There is hardly a trace of crimson sky in the front windows. Two maids stand forlornly by the door, and near them looms a gawky Finnish family that must have been notified of the evening tradition. Ahmed stands in front of the reception desk with the silver bell in his hands. He watches me descend with an air of disappointment—like it really is my job to ring the bell every evening. Like I've failed him for neglecting my duty this one time. Like he couldn't have simply rung it himself to call everyone together.

"I know, I know," I harp as I dash across the lobby, panting with effort. "Don't worry, there's still a little sunset left. Let's get everyone down here."

Ahmed doesn't extend the bell to me. Instead, he presses it against his stomach. "No, it is too late today."

"Nonsense," I cry, "there's still plenty of light left! I can see a trace of it!" I gesture to the window with my umbrella. "We just need to get everyone gathered quickly, *tout de suite*."

"No, Maggie. We wait too long."

The Finnish family has stepped outside, only to return, muttering in their elfin language. The maids are disbanding, heading back to their chores. A cook wanders in from the terrace, having taken the initiative to bask in the sunset alone. Ahmed dispenses a lipless frown at the cook. I'm guessing it worries him that the servants are starting to act like guests. It dawns on me that this is the reason he can't ring the bell. He needs me, as a paying guest, to be the instigator. I can invite whoever I want. "It is okay," he crows. "We try again tomorrow."

"Ahmed!" I grouse, yanking the bell from his unwilling fingers. He stares at me, startled, uncomprehending. I'm on the verge of begging his forgiveness. He's been such a wonderful friend. "Let's please try," I say. "If we skip a day, the guests will lose the habit." He gives a pained smile, but before he can stop me, I turn toward the staircase, away from the dark windows that confirm the sun is already gone. I clang the bell. "Sunset! Hurry, everyone! Sunset! It's almost too late! Catch the tail before it slips away!"

6.

Most nights I sleep like the dead. I click my bedside lamp off at 11:00 and enjoy seven uninterrupted hours of annihilating blackout. Every so often, though, dreams will creep in—or dream, singular, because it's always a variation on the same one. In this dream, a secret shares my hotel room. It's small and hairy, completely blind, smells of Wisconsin roses, and rasps when it breathes. Somehow the door has been left open, the secret has gotten out, running through the halls, shouting its existence to anyone who can hear it. I wake with my heart pounding. *You're fine. No one here knows or suspects. That's all in the past. Everyone at the Royal Karnak still loves you. Here, on the edge of a vast desert, you're safe.*

I rise at six and lug the desk chair over to the window to do my exercises, waiting for the birds to wreath the first light with their garden song. I think of Peter as I shower. After making a quick scan of my body to ensure it hasn't incurred any new spots or rashes that could wreak havoc on my skin, I slip into a kaftan and knock back my pills with a gulp of water. Then I move through the silent halls to be the first at breakfast. My right ankle is slightly swollen, from what minor trauma I do not know. At my age, injuries appear out of nowhere, like dangerous men on the sides of highways, trying to convince you to stop for them. The ankle doesn't hurt exactly—it's numb where it's usually cactus-prickly. I worry about my ability to keep up with Tess and Otto on the afternoon tour of the Valley of Kings. I don't want to be considered a burden, the old lady holding them back.

As I round the second-floor landing, I notice there are no discarded room-service trays left outside Tess and Otto's door. Last night they didn't join the rest of the guests at the "bistro" for dinner. At the time, I figured they must have turned in early, Tess taking the queen bed while Otto slept in a cot wheeled in for children. Unless they both share the bed. I didn't consider the other possibility, that they ventured out to look for a restaurant in town, a quest that can be daunting for those not initiated into Luxor street life. Most of the better restaurants require navigating the hub by the railway station, teeming with cars and brash young men freed from the supervision of their families for the evening. Tess's prettiness might have attracted unwanted attention, her light hair catching the headlights of cars, catcalls and come-ons trailing her down the dark streets. As is the case in so many places in the world, beauty is a liability here. I can't help but worry that Otto and Tess are frightened in their new home.

I glide my hand along the banister as I make my descent to the lobby. The tour guides aren't sitting on their usual sofa. I catch sight of them through the front windows, smoking cigarettes on the terrace, which isn't normally allowed. For a second morning in a row, the hotel's routine has fallen out of whack. I catch the glimmer of Ahmed's gelled hair at the reception desk and wait for him to scold me on my late appearance. But he seems to be in a mild state of distress, flustered by the papers he's rifling through. As I cross the lobby, I realize that someone is sitting on the sofa reserved for the tour guides. I didn't see him at first in the gloom because his head is hanging low, a bald spot at the top of his scalp the size of a silver dollar. He glances up, and I instantly recognize the slender nose bent at the bridge. Geoff Bradley looks as if he's been crying. For a moment, I genuinely can't fathom what could possibly be wrong with him. But then I see the yellow silk scarf, held loosely in his hand as if he's a magician who has conjured his last trick. His eyes don't linger on me. They only register that I'm not his wife, and he drops his head again and lets out a self-pitying moan. Ahmed peeks over at me and gives a tactful nod. "Good morning, Maggie! You're late." The joke is too half-hearted.

"Morning, Ahmed. Is everything okay?"

"Well, we've had a surprise departure this morning. But we're going to make certain that everyone's—"

"It's Shelley!" Geoff announces from the sofa. "My wife! She took off this morning, acting crazy. She didn't bother to say goodbye. Not even to her own daughter. Just packed her suitcase and off she went, she did. Says she won't be at home when we get back. She's gone completely mad. And all because some moron in housekeeping got another woman's undergarments mixed up with our bedding! I'm going to report—"

"Mr. Bradley, I'm certain it is all a simple misunderstanding," Ahmed promises, trying to console the scorned party from the safe remove of the reception desk. "Disputes happen among families. It is very stressful, vacations with this virus, even among loved ones, but please don't lose hope that Mrs. Bradley will return."

I nod in agreement, although I hope the very opposite, that Shelley is flying away from her cage as fast as she can, her face shearing the wind in her first whiff of freedom after twenty-three years of Bradley family captivity. Shelley is soaring. I'm so proud of her.

I'm headed toward the breakfast room when I happen to glance into the corner of the lobby underneath the staircase, where an old high-backed iron chair looms in the darkness, as foreboding as a suit of armor. Today, to my surprise, Otto is sitting in the chair, his bare legs swinging back and forth, his hands clamped on the ends of the armrests with a princely dignity. He offers me a smile.

"Hello," he says.

"Otto! My goodness, what are you doing up so early?"

He kicks his skinny legs twice more. "Seif promised if I woke up at dawn, I could feed the cockatiels their breakfast."

"That's very nice of him. And very nice of you to give up your sleep for the birds."

Otto doesn't respond verbally. But through his thick glasses his eyes latch on to me. After making eye contact, they flicker over to Geoff with the yellow scarf in his hand and then return to me. Again, more slowly this time, they travel to the scarf and back to me. A thin smile worms across his face.

He knows. He saw the tail of the scarf in my pocket yesterday as I left Carissa's room. He's put the puzzle pieces together. Clever boy.

For a moment I'm frightened that Otto is about to expose my ruse. Geoff would no doubt believe him, taking up the boy's account as an article of faith, this wicked old woman who, only days earlier, finagled time alone with his wife to put ideas about happiness into her head. I wait, not daring to breathe, as Otto's legs swing back and forth, stretching out the seconds of his verdict. Finally, his smile widens, showing off his crooked teeth.

"Are you headed to breakfast?" he asks sweetly.

"Yes," I squawk in relief. "Bright and early, as usual! Let me clue you in on a top-secret tip, Otto. Ask the chef for a plate of his special green cookies. Best sweets in town, even if they turn your lips green!"

I match his wide smile with my own, our eyes staring into each other's, neither of us wanting to be the one to break away first. I'm accustomed to hiding my pride in a job well done, swallowing it down the way a sword-swallower does his saber, all the way to the hilt. No blade in sight. But for once, matching the boy's gaze, I think, *Yes, I freed her, I was the one, Otto. I saw her sinking in quicksand, and I pulled her out.*

Right then, I know in my heart that Otto and I are destined to be friends.

7.

Are you absolutely sure, Maggie?" Ahmed frowns at me over the reception desk. His hair has lost the sleekness of its gel and has begun to kink, his side part no longer a militant border crossing. Sweat beads rise on his cheeks like blisters alongside the midafternoon shadow of his beard.

"I'm absolutely sure!"

"But you know that we"—he glances around the lobby to ensure that no other guests are within earshot. "You of all people know we don't encourage tours in the afternoon. You helped me write the warning sign! And you saw what happened to the Austrian woman last week who—"

I nod through his lecture. "I have my umbrella. And we won't stay long. I want to show the boy and his mother Seti. And maybe Ramses. I promise, those are the only tombs we'll visit. Well, they'll also want to have a gawk at Tut. But regardless, we'll bring extra water. And I swear, Ahmed, I'm sturdier than I look!"

Ahmed forces an agreeable smile, but I can tell he's unconvinced. Frankly, I'm unconvinced too. We shouldn't risk the afternoon heat. But as Otto's father didn't show up from Paris this morning, I feel I'd be disappointing mother and son by canceling the outing to the tombs. And I need to be the one who takes them.

Ahmed tries once more to dissuade me. "Maggie, I feel I must warn you, today is particularly bad, worse than usual in April. It's forty-one outside, or . . ." He needs to use his phone to make the conversion. I haven't acquired fluency in Celsius, even though I've been out of the land of Fahrenheit for five years. "That's . . . 107 for you."

A brutal number, 107, which will press down on us in the desert like a sweaty palm. The mere thought of that kind of heat causes my grip to tighten on my umbrella.

"Ms. Seeber and her son," Ahmed appeals, "they are young, but . . ." *Seeber.* I like my new family's name.

Right then, I spot Tess and Otto descending the stairs, right on time according to the double chime from the lobby's grandfather clock. Both are wearing canvas shorts and loose T-shirts, no hats or scarves or sunglasses. Did they even bother to apply sunscreen? I wave my arm as if I'm signaling from across a vast ocean. *Over here! It's me!*

"It will be absolutely fine!" I assure Ahmed, who still looks worried and, out of an overwhelming need to care for me, reminds me that it's time to refill my prescriptions at the pharmacy. But I'm not listening. Mother and son are crossing the marble hall, waving back. "We won't be long," I promise him. "Extra water. The boy needs to see the stars!"

• • •

We're off in the white hotel van, THE ROYAL KARNAK PALACE emblazoned in pink cursive along its sliding door. I'm sitting in the far back seat on plush blue upholstery. Tess and Otto have taken the row right in front of me, both turned around with their elbows on the seatback so that we can share the ride together. Our driver, along with a terse older guide that Ahmed cajoled into accompanying us, sits up front listening to Arabic talk radio. Out the window, the soupy brown Nile flows, the wind farther down the river tessellating the surface into a pattern of lizard scales. We are crossing the bridge to the West Bank.

"Now, you're sure it won't be too hot?" Tess asks. She's taken over the job of haranguing me about the heat. I don't remind her that it was she who insisted on the late start in case Alain showed up. I merely nod with a smile.

"You're both in for a once-in-a-lifetime experience."

Tess glances worryingly out the window. "Can we maybe stop at an ATM? I don't think I have enough cash on me unless they take—"

"My treat, my treat," I assure her with a pat on her hand.

"Otto, what do you say to that?" Tess prompts. Her son stares at me with his homely half smile. "Otto?" she scolds when he doesn't break into a song of gratitude on command.

"No need to thank me," I say with a wink to relieve him of the obligation. His mother doesn't know that we've already developed a special understanding. "It's really my pleasure. Thank you for letting me tag along. It's a joy spending time with you two."

Otto is fiddling with an American quarter. He tries various tricks with it, dancing it across his knuckles and hiding it in his palm until he feigns pulling it from his own ear for practice.

"Otto, can you make a quarter appear out of my ear?" I ask to invite myself into his game.

"Not yet," he says. "I need to get better. Soon I will."

I nod in agreement. "You'd probably only get a nickel out of me now. Maybe a few pennies. Better to wait until you can pull a whole quarter."

He snickers and looks at me again with his mismatched eyes, scrutinizing me with a bald fascination. He must be thinking of the scarf trick I performed on the Bradleys. *To be as good as I am, Otto, takes patience, dedication, and practice.*

The van veers onto a thin two-lane road that runs parallel to the river. While paved, it possesses all the jerky, pot-holed bumpiness of dirt, and we bounce on our seats, Tess's shoulder slamming repeatedly against the window. Otto's hand is latched on the seatback, and I tap on it as we drive past a row of squat trees lining the riverbank, their long branches shaped like candelabras. "Look, Otto!" He follows my finger and gazes out the window, where ibises nestle in the branches, their ivory-white feathers shining like angels on Christmas trees. The sight of them elicits a brief appreciation, "Oooooh!" His interest feels like a reward.

"And they're wild," I point out. "Unlike your cockatiels."

"I love the cockatiels," he says, turning away from the window as if loving one species means denying all others. "They're my friends."

"Do you have a lot of friends in Paris?" I ask him. Silence intrudes in the back of the van, the radio in the front playing tinny commercials, and I fear I've once again misstepped. Tess studies her son's reaction, which I can't see because he's staring forward now. But his little voice finally breaks the stalemate. "Grandma is my friend."

Tess winces, but I clap my hands at the adorability of this answer. "Well, isn't she lucky!"

"We can write her a postcard later, kiddo," Tess says, and turns to me with a cringe, as if a lack of friends is a family embarrassment. I don't have any friends back home either, not anymore. I used to have such a multitude in Klode Park that I couldn't walk half a block without running into one, but they've all disappeared. Otto and I have both been lonely, too lonely. "Because of the quarantine," Tess explains, "he hasn't been able to see many kids his age." She smiles at me, the excuse a paper plane she hopes will be sound enough to fly.

The van slows to avoid a donkey wandering through traffic. A military checkpoint looms ahead, soldiers drowsily leaning on their rifle butts under an improvised shed of corrugated metal. Small brush fires burn on the roadside, the black smoke beating against the van's closed windows. Out the opposite side, pastel-green fields of sugarcane and alfalfa stretch for miles, irrigated by the Nile on its journey north. Soon vacant lots cut up the farmland, with cinder-block houses set on acres of muddy hay. We follow the road into the foothills of the purple Theban mountains.

"Where are the tombs?" Otto asks. "Inside houses?" Before the guide can rotate in his seat to field the question, I rush to supply the answer.

"Deep underground," I tell him with eyebrows raised for added drama. "Like caverns underneath the mountain. They were built far below the earth in Egypt's Imperial Age, hidden from sight so grave robbers couldn't find them. That's why they were preferred to the Pyramids. You can't miss a giant pyramid if you're in the mood to grave-rob, can you?"

"How many tombs are there?"

"They've only discovered a dozen. But there are probably more out there, many, *many* more. Maybe you'll find one today! Keep your eyes out for any glint of gold in the ground!" Otto doesn't appear sufficiently awed by this offer of cheap adventurism. He continues practicing the palming and disclosing of the coin, and he's already become more agile with its choreography. Tess, however, tries her luck in entrancing him on today's field trip.

"How would that be, baby? If you found a tomb of a pharaoh? Would you like that?"

He pauses, taking the question seriously. "Yes, that would be nice," he says. "But, Mom, what about the game console? You promised!" He turns to look at me. "Mom promised we'd have one in the hotel room."

Tess and I exchange motherly glances. "Sorry, buddy," she says. "I was wrong about that. But you still like the hotel, don't you? You like the birds. And you made a sauna in the bathroom last night."

"A sauna!" I quack. "You lunatic! A sauna in the Sahara Desert?" But Otto isn't charmed by the off-compliment, and I try to lead his attention back to our outing. "You can buy that video-game console if you find some buried treasure. Nefertiti's tomb hasn't been discovered yet. Have you heard of her, Otto? A great pharaoh queen? We could be driving over her tomb this very moment. You know, a lot of the locals keep rabbits in their backyards, hoping they'll burrow in the dirt and find ancient relics to strike it rich."

His nose crinkles in disbelief. The van pitches as it maneuvers over small boulders, and Tess's turquoise pendant earrings swing violently, her shoulder knocking into the window again.

"Is that why you've stayed here for so long?" Otto asks. "To find treasure and get rich?"

I giggle. "Oh, no, dear. When my husband passed away a few years ago, he left me in very good financial shape, so that's one difficulty I don't have to worry about. But, take note, that's the reward you receive from a life of hard work and dedication. Although I'm not saying I would pass up a solid gold funerary mask if I found one out here in the desert. There's always room in my closet for one of those."

For the first time on the drive, Otto seems to take a genuine interest in the idea of finding gold. He hides his mouth behind the seatback, all nose and glasses, staring at me, one eye green, one brown.

"Do you miss your husband?"

"Honey!" Tess snaps.

"No, it's okay," I assure her, appreciating his curiosity. "I do miss him, Otto. So *very* much. There aren't many perfect humans in the world, but my Peter was close. I keep a lock of his hair to remind me, that's how much I miss him. When you love someone, you always want to keep them with you."

"Can I see it?"

"I'm afraid I don't carry it around, dear. It's safe back in my hotel room. Far too valuable. More valuable than gold!"

"Did you have any children?"

Tess nudges her son's shoulder and says, "Okay, honey, turn around now. You need to put your seat belt on." She flashes an apology to me with her eyes. I shake my head, *No offense*. The question doesn't hurt. It feels good, in fact. For once I want to remember her out loud.

"We did have one child, a daughter," I finally say, but he's no longer listening, dutifully buckling his seat belt. "She meant the world to me, the moon and the sun. Everything." Otto begins flipping the American quarter in the air, and impressively, even as the road narrows and grows bumpier, he manages to keep landing it on the webbing of his fist. Each time, tails, tails, tails, tails, tails . . .

We snake up the mountain to the beige gates with a metal "KV" sign on the front. King's Valley. The driver parks, and the touts come running toward us with a bounty of cheap trinkets in their outstretched arms.

8.

Once we clear the ticket office, Otto runs ahead to find a bathroom, his feet coughing up dust clouds. Every step since I left the van has been tantamount to walking through a four-alarm fire. My nylon umbrella blocks the sun but is useless against the heat, and the washcloth that I doused with cold water in the parking lot has already turned dry in my hand. Kindly, Tess is trudging at my snail's pace up the hill toward the mouths of the tombs. "Are you okay to continue?" she asks every twenty feet, and it takes all my strength to bestow an eager nod and quicken my pace for a few steps before sinking back into crippled lethargy. My right ankle is more swollen than it was this morning, but that's a minor complaint compared to the woolly torpor of 107, probably 108 or 109 by now, sucking up my wits. Tess is sweating too, a mustache of perspiration framing her lip. Her shirt collar sags in the back, revealing a dusting of faint blond hairs on her pale skin, which is sure to burn within the hour. The shadow of my umbrella falls on the ground ahead of us, accompanied by the thin black beam of Tess's body, these two incongruous shapes gliding smoothly over the rocky terrain. I would offer to share my umbrella with her, but it's a tiny nimbus of shade. Tess is fifty years younger than I am. She can afford a little sun damage—who knows where one blotch on an eighty-one-year-old body will lead? At least Tess had the good sense to buy a pair of sunglasses from the hawkers at the entrance gate.

"Are you sure you're okay to continue, Maggie?"

"Of course!" I wail through gritted teeth and grind the gears inside of me to accelerate on whatever spare fuel I have left. Along a shoulder of cordoned-off hillside, turbaned men in filthy sun-faded uniforms shovel heaps of rubble into wheelbarrows; other workers cart the wheelbarrows to buckets where a team of older men squat, sifting through the pebbles with mesh trays. Ben explained to me that these laborers are hired by the government to hunt for the tiniest fragments of ancient artifacts—a human tooth, a ceramic scarab, a precious flake of gold leaf. But even an expert like Ben couldn't decide whether it's all a show for tourists—the same piles of rubble sifted through every day to feign a fevered national commitment to archaeological exploration—or whether the government truly believes this ragtag crew might stumble upon a rare find in this oversearched *wadi*. No matter, even watching these men slave in the sun over enormous piles of dust is purpose-sapping, evidence of the eternal torment humans are forced to endure during their brief span on this planet. Out of some instinctual fear of backbreaking labor, Tess and I veer away from the dig, moving toward a meager line of shade at the foot of the mountains. Somewhere amid that thin, wavering band of darkness lies the entrance to Tut's tomb.

Before we reach this oasis of shadow, Tess glances around for her son. I decided to make use of his absence to test the extent of her marital heartbreak. "Did you hear from Alain?" I ask in a hopeful tone.

She doesn't look at me as she sighs. She pushes her hand through her hair, clamping onto the back of her skull as if to massage it. "No. Well, not directly. I heard from his assistant. 'Alain is very sorry'"—she uses a thick accent to suggest that the assistant either spoke to her in French or relayed the bad news in tortured English—"'but the shooting schedule has shifted, and he cannot leave set today. He promises to call you this evening.'" She shakes her head and hurries to cross the threshold into the shade first.

"You must be disappointed." I close my umbrella and waddle to the shelf of mountain rock, leaning against it to take the weight off my hip. I can't hide my panting breaths. My eyes scan the hillside for our tour guide, who I sent back for the bag of bottled water, which I "accidentally" left in the van. "Is Otto sad not to see his father?"

Tess snorts. "The better question might be, is Alain sad not to see his son?" She pulls off her sunglasses and gazes down at the desert floor.

The silver foil from a cigarette packet is peeking from the dirt, and Tess stares at it intently before nudging it with the tip of her shoe, as if she's put stock in my story about glints of buried treasure in the ground. Is that what she's hoping for, the miracle of money falling into her lap? Perhaps that's all she needs to get free. "Does Alain want to see his son anymore? I genuinely don't know the answer to that question."

"Oh, Tess . . ."

"He's been so difficult lately. Like, out of the blue, this monster I don't recognize erupts inside him, lashing out, making everything a fight. . . . It—well, I won't lie, it's been frightening. There are moments when I've felt scared for my safety around him, and then he'll be perfectly loving and sweet the next moment." Her voice wavers. The sweat around her eyes makes it hard to determine whether she's crying.

"That isn't fair for you to have—"

"Sorry," she interrupts. "I shouldn't be telling you this. Please forget I said anything, it's not fair to Otto. It's so unbelievably hot here, isn't it? We probably should have come this morning." She puts on a brave face as she beats the front of her shirt against her chest for air. *Forget it?* How could I? I'm here to work as her secret advocate, hers and Otto's against Alain. But I won't lecture Tess right now on the importance of escaping an abusive partner. I'm more curious about the grandmother who Otto claims is his only friend.

"Do you go back to the States often to see your mom?"

Tess shrugs, stares into the heat wafting up from the valley, and wipes the sweat off her upper lip. "Remember when I told you yesterday that Otto is a fighter?" I nod. "I wasn't exaggerating. He was so sickly when he was born, six weeks premature. He had everything wrong with him, underdeveloped lungs, sepsis, a blockage in his intestines. You name it. The doctors were basically taking odds on whether he'd make it a week. The nurses looked at me so uneasily, like which one of them was going to have to break the news when it finally happens. My god, all those sick babies in their incubators in that ward . . ." Tess shakes her head at the memory. "But Otto, you've never seen a being more determined to live. He had a will to survive and to just keep going, fighting through every setback, scraping by with his little lungs and his faint heartbeat. It took more than a year, and that was the worst year of my life, so many surgeries and trial drugs and bad news and 'it's time to prepare for the inevitable' speeches. I'm ashamed to say, there were moments I thought it might be more humane if we just let him go. For him, I mean." She shuts her eyes at that confession. "Alain was with me in San Francisco—he took off a year of work to be there with us. And by the time Otto made it through, we were just so beaten. Me in particular. A zombie, a ghost."

"I can imagine," I reply. But Tess wards off the sympathy, as if that isn't the purpose of the story.

"Alain had to return to work in Europe. We needed the money. And I decided to stay with Otto in California, because my mom was helping out, even though she and I didn't have the best relationship."

"It happens with mothers and daughters." Even Julia and I had our little spats and flare-ups, and we adored each other.

"Yeah," Tess agrees. "But then, it was like . . ." She pauses. "I never know how to put it . . . like I had delayed postpartum depression. Like I'd been holding my breath for a year and finally all the air went out of me. Something just broke inside. After a few months I needed to get help, psychologically, some space and time to heal. My mom was so good with Otto, and she promised to take care of him while I got my head screwed on straight. Alain was in Paris and . . ." A shivery breath erupts, but she swallows the pain back, pushing it down her throat. "I didn't come back for nearly two years, and by then my mom had gotten her hooks into Otto and wanted custody. So that was another fight, a very ugly fight between us. Eventually, though, I did get him back, because I'm his mother, and we went to Paris to start fresh. It was all going so well. Then the problems started, really awful problems with Alain . . ." Her voice rises toward a whine, like the helium in a balloon leaking from its rubber lip. She wipes her face. "God, sorry. Why am I telling you all this? The whole point of being here is not to think about my mother or Alain or Paris or how it fell apart."

"Don't be sorry." I want Tess to understand that listening is my talent, that I'm proud of her for raising her son to be a fighter, defying all odds to be with us at the Royal Karnak, to realize she can shed her old family for a new one. Instead, I simply offer her this morsel of advice: "I think your being here, away from Paris, away from Alain, is extremely healthy, for the both of you. You can relax at the hotel and get some perspective and see what the future holds. Listen to an old woman, will you, Tess? We all need to escape our lives every so often. To recognize the cage we've found ourselves in, the bars around us that we've accepted as normal because they've risen up so slowly and imperceptibly over the years. That's how life betrays you, day by day, when you aren't paying attention." I smile at her. "Do you know what the word *luxor* means? 'Many palaces.' It's a land of reincarnation, of second chances, of new homes. I promise this will be a good place for you and Otto." I worry I've oversold the inspirational tourist package.

"I think you're right," she says less dolefully. "Yes, you *are* right! My god, look where we are!" She begins to spin in slow circles and stares up at the limestone cliffs, as if she needs to perform a dramatic actor's flourish to fully appreciate her surroundings. "I wish our tour guide would come back so we could hear some of the history."

"We don't need him!" I say, tapping my temple. "I've got it all memorized."

She looks at me with astonishment. "Thank you for bringing us, Maggie! And for saying what you just did, for making us feel so welcome."

Otto is jogging up the path, the lenses of his glasses winking in the sun, a little V of sweat on the front of his T-shirt and his white socks stained terra-cotta from the dust. He's bought a candy bar from the commissary and swallows down the last of it, chocolate smeared on his fingertips.

Tess claps her hands with overzealous stage-mother excitement. "Are you ready to be a tomb raider, sweetheart?" Otto presses his chest forward as he reaches us, like a marathoner pushing through the ribboned finish line of shade. If only those doctors who predicted his death could see him now, running through the deserts of Africa. This darling boy.

"I'm ready, Mom!" He's gleeful, jumping up and down, possessed by the first pure bout of childish delight I've seen in him. I want to be a part of their joy. I want his energy, his stamina, his newness to the wonders of all things.

"Will you take a photo of us?" Tess asks, handing me her phone. She squats down next to her son, and I scan the vicinity for a friendly tourist or guard who might take the photo of the three of us, a portrait of our outing at the Valley of the Kings.

"Oh, let's see," I say, feigning confusion as I aim the screen, hoping Tess might notice me having trouble and suggest switching places. In truth, I know perfectly well how to snap a phone pic.

"A big smile, sweetheart," Tess instructs. "I want to send Dad a nice one, okay?"

Tess smiles. Otto does not. No smile for the abusive father he hates. I snap three shots before Otto wiggles out of the frame.

"Now it's time for the most famous tomb!" I vow. I'm determined to herd them toward the entrance before our guide stumbles into view. I'd be happy to pay the guide to remain in the van for the duration of our visit. "And then, on to my very favorite tomb, so special it requires its own ticket, which I've already bought for us!" I reach for Otto's hand, and while he doesn't open his palm, he offers his fist. Maybe he doesn't want the chocolate smears to get on my fingers. I happily hold his fist, squeezing it like a banister knob. "Let's go," I cry. "Tut, Tut, Tut, Tut!"

• • •

Peter and I always made a point of visiting museums. While we weren't prolific travelers, every few years his attendance was required at a renewable energy convention. We'd hire a babysitter for Julia, and Peter and I would fly off to a polite, wide-sidewalked city in the chubby midsection of America, the big-boned towns forever on the cusp of cosmopolitanism. As a ritual, Peter would skip out on the conferences for a single afternoon, and we'd sneak off to the city's art museum. Denver. Cleveland. Des Moines. St. Louis. No matter the city, the local museum always held a spectacular plunder—the *"creeeam* de la *creeeam,"* as my Klode Park neighbor used to say. We'd amble through the halls holding hands, our *awwwws* and *would you look at thats* contagious. Yet a secret part of me would stand in the midst of those opulent galleries and think, *These artworks, they're lovely, they're absolutely gorgeous, but when you really think about it, is this the best that three thousand years of human civilization could come up with to embody our time on Earth? Are these paintings and sculptures and silk-upholstered chairs the highest reaches of what the most talented of 117 billion people have managed to achieve? By that measure, what a paltry spread. This can't be our crowning glory, all we've managed to cobble together to represent our eminence.* I never shared that feeling of disappointment with Peter. He thought I cherished the medieval altarpieces and Impressionist picnic scenes, and we'd buy postcards of our favorite works in the gift shop and keep them in their crinkly paper bags in the kitchen cabinet back home. But often I left those museums with a mild depression that I couldn't shake for the rest of the trip. A hollow formed inside me, right under my heart. *What are we? So little when all the accounting is done. A few colorful paintings. A statue with missing arms. A hand-carved chair.*

Egypt, though. That's what I didn't know at the time. I hadn't seen Egypt, which cured me of this dismal appraisal of our collective brilliance. In Luxor I found a trove of masterpieces worthy of our wildest dreams and highest ambitions. The underground tombs at the Valley of the Kings are tattooed in vivid wall carvings that portray a royal journey through life and death; their caverns are packed with treasures that gleam like the eyes of crocodiles in the dark. A Renoir, a Degas, even a Matisse—as pretty as they are—they don't stand a chance next to a gold pharaonic death mask with its burnished lips and jeweled, unblinking eyes staring across a thousand centuries. The artisans and tomb builders of the New Kingdom were the alpha and omega of awe. They alone could make the gods jealous. No civilization has ever outshone them. Ironically, these underground chambers were never meant to be seen by human eyes.

Tut's tomb is lovely. Not my favorite, but definitely worth a visit. I let Otto and his mom run down the sloping subterranean shaft to the burial chamber. Not much is left in there—after its discovery in 1922, the treasures of the Boy King were boxed up and spirited away. But there is still the pharaoh's corpse, as well as some elegant hieroglyphic carvings, and as an additional perk, the darkness of the cavern offers a much-needed respite from the sun. When I reach the chamber, Otto is poised at the large glass case that protects Tut's mummified body, a thin, dry cadaver the color of a rawhide dog bone. Under a white linen sheet, Tut looks strangely peaceful—as tender in his bed as if he'd nodded off in it some thirty centuries ago.

I can't resist a bit of lurid gossip to entice Otto. After all, I am today's de facto tour guide. "He might have been murdered!" I whisper.

"No!" Otto turns to study my face. "But I thought he was king!"

"Kings can be murdered. Do you think they're immune to knives or poisons? No one really knows the reason Tut died so young. He was only seventeen, still a boy."

Tess gives me an aggrieved look as she palms her son's head, and I worry it was a mistake to introduce death into our excursion. And yet, how can we avoid death while touring an elaborate underground cemetery? Still I want to recover the lightness of a moment ago, and I list the royal carriages, the imperial furniture, and the gobs of jewelry boxes that were once crammed inside this tiny chamber like a New York City storage unit. "They took everything with them into the afterlife, an entire house of treasures. Even food. Even their servants! A house on the move, impermeable to death!" Two veiled women enter the room, dethroning Otto at the glass case, and the stale air doesn't accommodate all of us—especially during a contagion. We head up the long, steep passage toward daylight. I'll save my razzle-dazzle tour-guiding for Seti.

Tomb KV17. It's only a short walk through the valley. "Excited?" I ask Otto. "Eager for the showstopper? Seti's tomb is the deepest and longest in the complex. And you know what, Otto? It was closed for decades because of fear of collapse! But don't get scared that the walls might cave in when we're down there and that we're going to be trapped underground together forever!"

I get the reaction I want. Otto squeals in terrified delight. But Tess gives me another sour smile, which I deflect by dipping one side of my umbrella down to block her from my sight. It is only Otto who matters. The dust stirred up from our feet stings the eyes and grits the tongue, and for a minute I simply concentrate on not sneezing. At the tomb's gate, a sun-weary guard inspects the Seti tickets that cost me an additional two hundred Egyptian pounds. I retract my umbrella and follow Otto past the chain-link gate and into the narrow opening. Tess's cell phone chirps as she's about to enter. "Go ahead," she says. "I want to check the message. I'll be in in one sec." Otto doesn't hear her, his sneakers slip-sliding on the slanted wood gangplank as the limestone walls come to life around him, first with pale hieroglyphics nearest the entrance, faded like fabric left in the sun. But already figures of men begin to converge on all sides in bas relief. I want to explain the meaning of the scarab patterns to Otto, how the beetle symbolizes reincarnation because of the way it eats its own dung, forming a perfect regenerative loop. But the boy is descending too quickly, shooting past the spells of the dead and the pictographic triumphs of Seti's reign.

"Hold up!" I cry. "Wait for me!" But he either doesn't hear or doesn't want to stop. He's already a tiny shrinking blotch in the tunnel, hopping down the next flight of steps, past the point on the walls where the figures transform from mortals into gods, their bodies painted turquoise blue—the sun god, Ra, handing Seti the keys to the afterlife, the parade of gods with heads of ravens, jackals, and cobras celebrating the pharaoh's membership in eternity. "Otto? Otto, you're missing—" I had imagined us looking at these totems together.

My hip is on fire, and I clutch the banister as I make my way down the stairs, taking deep breaths through my mouth to beat back the pain. My ankle stings with each step. I can hear the whispering of Otto's feet farther down the tunnel, but it's too dark to see him. I hope he isn't scared. For a moment I lose my footing and feel like I'm falling, my muscles clenching in anticipation of a hard landing, but it's the trick of a glass floor that covers a pit. I remember from my previous visit that it's right at this spot, halfway through the tomb, that the original architects created a false dead end to trick thieves. The pit was a booby-trap to ensnare the undeterred before they could break through the artificial wall.

I can hear Otto, faintly, near or far, I can't tell. It is only the squeaking of his sneakers or maybe it's his voice, paper-thin, reduced to the quietest squeal. "Otto?" I cry into the darkness. "Are you okay?" There's no response. I'm breathing heavily, centuries of dust blowing in and out of my lungs. For a moment, I sense a dark presence racing up the cavern toward me, its sides scraping against the brittle walls, hungry to reach daylight, cold and unstoppable. I close my eyes to calm myself, waiting for the panic to subside, because of course nothing comes to swallow me on its way to the surface. How ridiculous I'm acting, like a child afraid of the dark. Did I forget to take my risperidone this morning? No, I'm sure I took it, right along with my other pills at the bathroom sink.

I force myself to continue, fighting through another wave of exhaustion. I can just make out the green glimmer of display lights in the deepest room. Why did Otto have to run ahead? Glancing back up the shaft, I no longer see even a pinprick of sunlight. There's also no sign of Tess. Only minutes ago, the three of us were together as a family. Now loneliness is gripping me in this crumbling tunnel. How strange to feel orphaned at eighty-one. As I hobble downward, I try to summon some maternal fortitude. *Be patient with him*, I remind myself. I'm not used to boys, and on top of it, Julia was such an obedient child. She never ran ahead, always trailed, serving as Peter's slouchy shadow; how many times did I have to yank her out from behind his legs, ". . . and this is our daughter Julia!" She was so shy, so timid, that for years she couldn't spend the night in her own room for fear of the dark and slept in a sleeping bag at the foot of our bed.

I pass through a succession of storerooms, each egress leading to a side chapel. I hope that Otto and I can tour these alcoves together on the way up and I can describe the treasures that once piled to the rafters. Anyway, it's this final room that blows every visitor's mind. As I slink down the last set of steps, I see Otto racing in circles around the burial chamber like a trapped bat. He stops when I enter, turning perfectly still, and he looks over at me. I'm startled by the coldness in his face. In the dim green light, I can't make out his mismatched eyes, but his expression contains a palpable anger, a throb that, if I didn't know better, nears violence.

"Where's the mummy?" he charges. For a second, I think he wants his mother, but he means the body of the king. I'm about to correct him—these pharaohs were anointed gods, not Saturday-morning cartoon monsters—but Otto steps up his demands, jumping in front of me with his hands on his hips. "Where's the sarcophagus? You said this was the best tomb! There's nothing down here! It's empty! Why did you trick me?"

I respond with a gentle laugh. He is such a boy, and boys are lovers of creepiness and death. Maybe Otto's fascination stems from his own close call with death as a sickly infant, some imprinted memory of how close to the dividing line he reached. "I'm sorry to disappoint," I reply before explaining that Seti's body was removed by priests millennia ago for fear of grave robbers. Then, after the tomb was rediscovered by an Italian adventurer in the nineteenth century, his alabaster casket went to the highest bidder. It currently sits in a rich man's house in the English countryside. "But, Otto, dear . . ." I press my hand on his tiny shoulder and pivot him toward the far wall. "It's the decoration that makes this tomb so wondrous. Not even decoration, but oracles of the divine." I point up to the carving of Nephthys, daughter of Nut, wife to Set, a woman spreading her giant feathered wings in a sign of protection. Death would never feast on the man buried beneath her. "She was married to the god of havoc. The god of deserts, and foreigners, and thunderstorms. But look, Otto, Nephthys's a bird, like the ones in the hotel garden that you love, sheltering us with her giant wings!"

I feel so close to Otto right now, like I'm his protector, spreading my own arms to shield him. He scantly notices Nephthys, and so I point up at the masterpiece of the ceiling. Across its vaulted blue dome, gold stars tremble and deities loom. "Look above us. It's even prettier than our own sky. Do you see, it's an astronomical chart! Doesn't it look like the heavens to you?" I hear Tess's feet pattering down the tunnel and, longing to cement our bond in our brief time alone together, I nestle Otto against my hip, squeezing his shoulder with one hand as my other hand waves across the constellations. "You see the hippopotamus with the crocodile on her back? The ceiling tells the story of the sun's renewal, eaten at night by Nut only to be birthed out of her every dawn—"

Otto mutters something up at me. My fingertips feel the blood coursing through his neck veins.

He mumbles it again. "You did that this morning." His twin lenses are tilted up at me, glinting green from the lights. "The man sitting in the lobby with the scarf." His tone isn't accusatory but neutral, establishing a fact. There might even be a hint of reverence in his voice. "You caused that to happen." I feel an instant sense of relief in hearing it spoken aloud and acknowledged. Finally, here is someone who won't misjudge me. Otto saw, he understands, he knows too well the torture of an unhappy family. He's a member of one himself. "I saw you take that scarf from the lady's room."

I nod. "It's very complicated," I tell him. But it really isn't that complicated. Otto gets it. A part of him understands, even if dimly, that he and his mother would be better off if his abusive father were cut from their lives. "What do you think the man's wife is doing now?" I ask him. I want him to dream Shelley on a safari or on a plane flying over a turquoise sea dotted with tropical islands. "I think she's—"

"I'm going to tell."

His homely face shrivels, his front teeth as crooked as old shutters, the light gone from his glasses, leaving only a flickering of his pupils underneath the lenses.

"What did you say?"

"I'll tell," he repeats, "I'll tell that man what you did." I'm assuming he means Geoff. Or Ahmed. "I'll tell that you sent the mom away."

"*Tell?*" I pronounce it like it's a foreign word.

His smile straightens into a proximity of sweetness, the bland innocence of an American eight-year-old, and he tries to push away from me, but my hand is pinned to his shoulder, and he can't wiggle free.

"No, Otto, you misunderstand. It wasn't for my benefit. I was helping her. She—"

"We have a bad room at the hotel," he blurts. "It's small, and it shakes all the time from the elevator. You said in the van that you have lots of money. I won't say anything if you get us a nicer room with a game system. It can't cost much for someone as old as you."

"Oh, sweetheart." I'm still holding him against my hip, and my voice quivers with pity and affection. "If you want something, you shouldn't threaten. Just ask me. I'm here to help you, like a member of your family. As good a friend as your grandmother. Tell me, are you lashing out like this because of your father? Because he hurts you and your mother?"

"I want Mom and me to have a better room!"

"Otto," I chide, reaching to stroke his cheek, "I'm sorry, but you have to ask nicely—"

He grabs his ear and squeals, even though my hand hasn't been near it. He pushes past me so forcefully I have to catch my balance on the back of my heels. He rushes toward his mother, who is standing in the passageway to the burial chamber. Otto's arms lasso around her waist, his wet eyes and smudged glasses pressed against her breasts. He's acting too babyish for his age, and Tess is slow to clamp her hands around his head, her eyes hanging on me in confusion as if seeking an explanation.

I try to get words out, but Otto is whimpering a message up at her, tightening his hold on her body, and Tess drinks him in with her attention. "She hit me . . ." I hear him say. "For no reason. She hurt my ear, Mom!"

"Otto," I plead. "That's not—"

"I want to go," he sobs. "She scares me. Please. She's not a nice woman."

The wheels of my brain are turning too slowly for me to make sense of his manipulation. In astonishment, I manage only a few sputtering consonants in my defense. Tess glances at me with another aggrieved expression, the third I've earned from her this afternoon. How can she believe her own son over me?

"I'll take him back in a taxi," she says calmly, trying to pillow the awkwardness of the situation. "You take the tour van. I think he just needs to get back to the hotel and rest." Does Tess really believe that I hit him? Does she imagine I'm capable of striking a little boy? Whether she does or not, the damage has been done. Otto pulls his mother up the steps, and I'm left alone in a hole in the ground.

9.

There's no sign of Otto or his mother when I emerge from the tomb. I was forced to take my time up the gangplank, keeping as much weight as I could off my ankle. The tour guide is waiting at the top, belatedly brandishing the bag of water. "Your friends, they leave," he notifies me with a self-satisfied grin, as if our rift might have been due to the lack of expert guiding. I grab my umbrella from the guard's chair.

"Would you like to visit Queen's Valley?" the guide has the nerve to ask. "It's where the wives are buried." I glare at him and point my umbrella down the hill toward the parking lot.

On the van ride back to the hotel, I decide to chalk up the confrontation with Otto to a misunderstanding. He was asking me for help in his childish way, trying to convince me to arrange a room upgrade for his mother's comfort, and perhaps, in a moment of confusion, my ring accidentally snagged his ear. I was sure my hand was at his cheek, but the encounter is already blurring in my mind, Otto's method of requesting a favor so off-putting that my hand might have hovered near the side of his face. Yet as the guide cranks up the music on the radio, spitefully blasting it through the back speakers, I'm reminded of the inexorable facts. Otto tried to blackmail me, and he used the charade of being hit to demonstrate how skillfully he could elicit sympathy and turn an audience against me, even if that audience consisted of his mother. Otto threatened to tell. And while there's no evidence for his claim—*Ahmed,* I begin rehearsing, *I don't have the slightest idea what this boy is talking about! Seen coming out of where? You mean that Greek woman who wears the bikinis? What on earth would I be doing in her room? I don't understand*—nevertheless the suspicion would stick to me, the first stain on my spotless reputation.

The Royal Karnak is the place I've been happiest since Peter's death, and it's allowed me a fresh start after the disaster in the Alps. I won't risk the home I've made here. Where else would I go? *Ahmed, I don't have the slightest idea what this boy is talking about! Seen coming out of where? You mean that Greek—*

"Ma'am?" The guide has lowered the volume on the radio and is staring at me from the passenger seat. "What did you say? About a boy?"

"Nothing," I reply. "Just take me to the hotel please." I strap a mask over my mouth to discourage further conversation.

Out the window the late-afternoon sun is still strong, blasting the Nile, turning the river into a flat sheet of copper. It won't be too long before sunset. Otto betrayed me—I take a deep breath—but a fix is feasible, a reparation that isn't beyond my financial means. How long are the Seebers staying? No checkout date, no return flight booked, and queasily I recall only two hours ago encouraging Tess to stay in town indefinitely.

The van pulls into the U of the driveway, and I struggle out of the back seat, refusing the help of the guide's hand. With my umbrella open, I hurry up the horseshoe steps and circle through the revolving door. Ahmed is standing at reception. He points to the bell on the desk when he sees me as a reminder of my nightly duty. It feels like an invitation to atone for yesterday's mishap, and it warms my heart to be needed. I scurry over to him.

"Ahmed, I need a favor."

His eyebrows dip. "Did something happen on the tour of the tombs? The mother and son came back a half hour ago."

"The boy was tired and threw a tantrum. You were right. The afternoon sun in the desert is too intense. Frankly, Ahmed, you should have stopped us from going."

He laughs. "Well, Maggie, you are a hard woman to stop. 'The boy was tired.' That's what his mother said too."

I lean over the slab of bloodshot marble. "Listen, the favor." Even though no one else is in the lobby, I speak in a hushed voice. "I feel a bit guilty for taking them out there in the heat, and they are sweet, aren't they, Tess and Otto?"

"Oh, yes," he agrees, "the boy is very sweet." I resist the urge to correct that impression.

"How long are they staying? Not more than a week, right? Maybe less?" Ahmed shrugs. There are so many vacancies, guests are no longer required to set strict departure dates. "Well, I'd like to upgrade them to a nicer room. My treat. I'm aware they're staying in that horrible room next to the elevator." Ahmed rushes to defend the sanctity of room 201, but I shake my head. "Could we find them a nice double so they both have a bed. What about a room on the 05 line?"

"We have a medical convention scheduled for the end of the week. Very busy. Doctors from Belarus. I pray they do not cancel."

I want to ask about the Bradleys' room—the husband and daughter can't possibly be staying on without Shelley—but I don't want to link myself, even indirectly, to their misfortune.

"We do have the Royal Suite, 211, that's free. But it is quite expensive, Maggie. Nine hundred US dollars a night. And if they don't leave for—"

"That's fine!" I chirp. "Let's take it. Can you move them this afternoon?"

"It's sunset in just over an hour. Will you not ring the bell?" Ahmed sounds worried. The ritual has come to matter to him. It binds him to the happiness of his guests. I am needed here, expected to perform my chores in my new home.

"Of course I'm ringing the bell! I promise I'll never be late again. Just let me go freshen up." I rap my knuckles on the desk, the problem of Otto and his bad-tempered fit of prepubescent selfishness solved. "Charge their room to my card. But, Ahmed, don't tell them I'm paying. Make it seem like a free upgrade from the hotel. I don't want Tess to feel indebted."

"You are too generous, Maggie! What an angel you are to be so kind. I will move them right away." He smiles at me with his round brown eyes.

...

I ring the bell through the halls. "Sunset! Gathering time!" On the second floor, the door to 201 hangs open, allowing a glimpse into the Seebers' old room, which is now deserted but for a balled-up towel on the floor. The door to the Royal Suite farther down the hall is closed, but an empty luggage cart is parked next to it, evidence of Tess and Otto's move. I shake the bell with extra fervor in front of 211, hoping that they will appear, and I can be assured that peace has been restored.

Outside on the front terrace, the maids stand in a cluster by the balustrade, their faces shimmering as they watch the giant red orb skirting the mountain peaks. Ben and Zachary don't always attend the sunsets, but today they've come, arms interlinked, marveling as the last of the rays torch the sails of the Nile boats. One of the gardeners has even defied Seif to pause with his rake at the bottom of the steps. I catch sight of Geoff Bradley, head bent in the realization of his failed marriage, no doubt missing the wife he for too long ignored, and pudgy Stella beside him, scrolling on her phone, paying zero attention as her world crashes down around her. Out here on the terrace, there are faces I recognize and ones I do not, some covered in masks that obscure all but their eyes. We're a small, eclectic group gathered here to say our goodbyes to the day. To my great disappointment, Tess and Otto are not among us.

Zachary gives me a playful wink. Yasmine waves to me.

"There's just a sliver left." "No more than a fingernail." "I can still make out a tiny piece of gold." "Don't leave. Come back!" "Going, going, going . . ."

...

That night, I lie in bed with the covers pulled up to my neck. In the patch of ceiling above my bed, two perpendicular cracks make an accidental cross. After a childhood programmed by Catholic school, I feel the automatic urge to say a prayer at the sight of any cross. Usually I pray for Peter, asking God to conjure more untapped memories of our fifty-four years together, fresh Peter material for me to consume—the joy of Julia's first breaths on my chest in the hospital, Peter racing around the bed suggesting girl names until we hit on the perfect one, our first dinner together with Julia asleep in her crib, the way he kissed me and asked if we should start making another baby, and we both laughed and shook our heads no. Tonight, though, I lodge a different divine request. I ask that my small act of generosity for Otto and his mother proves sufficient, that my altruism settles any brewing hostility that has come between us. I end with an "Amen," but my brain isn't ready to let the boy go. That child, his cleverness, his different-colored eyes, they glow in my mind as I lie in the dark, and the uneasiness he stirs in me transforms into worry. What is he thinking? What will he do next? Fear is more unshakable than love, and to my irritation, instead of Peter, I think of the boy as I try to find sleep, even as I try *not* to think of him, to excise him from my head, one eye green, the other brown.

I hear the bats fluttering in the palm trees out my window. Somewhere in the garden a Spanish couple is arguing in a duologue of drunken hisses. I don't register falling asleep, but I'm rocked awake by a crinkling sound coming from somewhere in my room. I click on the bedside lamp, expecting I'll find a mouse darting into a corner. There's nothing except for a pink sheet of hotel stationery that's been shoved under my door.

I stagger out of bed, dizzy with sleep and fighting sore muscles from the day's excursion to the tombs. My balance fails me, and I pause at the corner of the bed until the spell passes. At the door, I anticipate the strain on my hip as I bend down to pick up the paper. Unfolding it, I find a stew of blue pen marks underneath the floral-wreathed RKP hotel crest. I don't have my reading glasses on, but Otto has kindly scrawled his note in giant print.

Thank you for our new room. Mom and I each have our own bed with a balocy and a view of the Nile! We are so much happyer here!

This message heartens me, the lost art of the handwritten thank-you note, a measure of courtesy that I used to badger Julia into penning a week after birthdays and Christmas, chasing her around the house with her box of monogrammed stationery, following her room to room like some yapping dog of etiquette.

Don't forget the XTMegaBox with the Vrroom Nigel game. There is an electronics store in town that sells them. We saw it in the windo yesterday. Bring it to me by noon tomorrow, I also want some things for Mom and will make a list.

Otto didn't sign his name. Why should he bother? There is only one guest at the Royal Karnak currently blackmailing me. I wonder whether he's still standing out in the hall, a tiny troll of a boy looming on the other side of my door. I quietly turn the door handle before yanking it open in a surprise ambush. The hallway is empty, only the cool night air running down the marble corridors. He must have returned to the sanctuary of the Royal Suite.

Had Otto asked me nicely, in the tenor of a favor, I probably would have bought him his XTMegaBox. But I'm already shelling out $900 a night for his luxury suite with a balcony, and now he's upping his demands with promises of more to follow: *I also want some things for Mom.* I would love to spite him with an unexpected plot twist: moving to a new hotel in the middle of the night, canceling my credit card, and leaving the brat and his mother to pay for their stay. But that's a careless, pyrrhic fantasy. The Royal Karnak is my home, my refuge. Why should I be the one to leave?

I return to bed, click off the light, and sink into the mattress. It occurs to me once again that Otto has no proof I was the one to plant the scarf under Shelley's pillow. The little fool has overplayed his hand. He's an eight-year-old boy, of weak eyes and bad teeth, barely a survivor of his infancy, his only friends a religious nut of a grandmother and a cageful of exotic birds. He doesn't seem to realize the vulnerability of his position, threatening me in my own home.

At my bank job in Milwaukee, I was mostly shielded from the fallout of unpaid mortgages. By the time borrowers forfeited their payments and foreclosed on their loans, their cases had been turned over to collection agencies and all I witnessed was the paperwork in need of a final executing signature. Peter, however, experienced the intensity of human desperation first-hand. His acquisition of natural-gas deposits was not universally heralded as the savior of local economies. Lawsuits and protests ran rampant as soon as his team of orange-vested survey crews rolled into tiny rural towns. But over the years, Peter learned one vital lesson: the communities that are the smallest, the weakest, and the most geographically isolated, those lacking a town square and controlled by outmoded zoning laws, can always be counted on to break. The residents' dependency on their full-time jobs will eventually erode the head count at protests, and the money required to retain lawyers for costly, time-sucking court cases always runs dry. The small and frail can be conquered—that is an American fact. It was only the sad circus of waiting for them to realize that they'd lost the minute Peter hovered his finger over their houses on a map.

Otto must assume I've already been defeated, a lonely, elderly widow isolated from her family without much fight left in her. There he's wrong. As I count backward from one hundred to try to fall asleep, I stop at eighty-one, considering Otto's reaction when he doesn't receive his game system by noon tomorrow. I also wonder when the Bradleys will cut their vacation short and return to Manchester. With them gone, there will be very little gunpowder in the boy's ammunition. No one will care about a scarf when Geoff and Stella vanish with their luggage out the front door. *You sent the mom away. I'll tell.* Tell who? Who's going to listen to a little boy?

Still, I don't want Otto making a fuss and raising suspicions about me. Even unverified, such claims could open the door to the darker secrets in my past. Maybe I should buy him his precious game system to shut him up. The inclusion of a mandatory deadline, by noon tomorrow, is laughable, almost adorable, as if the boy were a Lindbergh kidnapper; he must have learned the lingo from violent video games or his father's television shows. I happen to know the electronics store he mentions; it's in the center of town, its front windows epileptic with strobe lights even in the sunniest hours. It can't cost that much. Buy it for him and tell him it's his last present and make him think he misunderstood what he saw. I realize that a part of me still covets the boy's friendship, still wants to earn his respect and maybe even his love. But it's the threat of the last line in his note that stops me. *I also want some things for Mom.* The demands won't cease. Tomorrow will bring more requests, and eventually Tess will notice. It's one thing to be discovered taking pity on a woman and her child by quietly paying for a more comfortable room. But to be caught showering a strange young boy with expensive gifts . . .

On and on my thoughts churn through the night hours, my brain litigating arguments, adopting new strategies, weighing pros and cons, forecasting potential outcomes that factor in even the most ludicrous possibilities. In the past six years, I've lost my most cherished possessions—a husband, a daughter, a house, a country—but it's the tiniest concerns that keep a person tossing and turning at night. I watch the five o'clock hour on its relentless spin-cycle toward six, the time I'm supposed to be out of bed performing my morning stretches. Finally, hoping to seize the smallest scrap of sleep, I manage to drift off.

· · ·

I wake to sharp daylight and the echo of the touts shouting from the corniche. For the first time in my stay at the Royal Karnak, I've slept until nine a.m.

I don't exercise. I don't think of Peter. I splash cold water on my face, gulp down my pills, and quickly dress in a wrinkled kaftan. I hurry into the hallway, where the room-service trays have already been collected. I've never been this late to breakfast, and I'm witness to the peculiar sight of families leaving their rooms, already dressed for a morning of sightseeing, perhaps having already dined on Hamza's buffet, nodding to me with knowing smiles as if they sympathize with my bedraggled hair and puffy eyes.

I descend the stairs as fast as I can. On the final turn of the staircase, I glance out the window and spot Otto and the gardener, Seif, walking back from the aviary. They must have just finished feeding the cockatiels, and Otto has clearly said something amusing because Seif's shoulders are quaking in laughter. I've never seen Seif smile, let alone laugh. The fact that the boy has managed to endear himself to the only hotel employee impervious to my charm is nothing short of a provocation, a little Otto flag planted on my turf. He is bouncing along the path next to the gardener in his neon sneakers and electric-blue shirt, his twiggy arms flailing at his sides. I have the sudden vision of snapping one of his arms in half, and then being the savior who rushes him to the hospital so the doctors can set it with a cast before I carry him back to the hotel, *He's fine, everyone! He just needs to heal. I'll take him up to his room! No, no, I can carry him. I've come this far! I'm old but I'm sturdy! We need to get him into bed!*

As I reach the lobby, the touts' chanting funnels through the open front doors. Luggage is being carted in for the morning's check-ins. New guests rush into the lobby like bank robbers with masked faces and bulging eyes. Ahmed, consumed with the fresh arrivals, still manages to notice me. He steps from the reception desk and glances at his wristwatch in astonishment. "You're late this morning, Maggie!" For once, he's not joking.

"I, I . . ." I can't summon a funny excuse. Or even a truthful one. Instead, I feel my face burning red, and Ahmed heads toward me with a frown of concern.

"Are you okay?" he asks, his eyes roving my face as if searching for Covid symptoms. "Are you not feeling well? That excursion to the tombs yesterday afternoon was not wise."

I clasp his forearm softly. "No, no, I'm fine. I just slept in for once. I probably needed it. But thank you for worrying about me." My eyes begin to sting, on the brink of tears. Such a paltry amount of tenderness has been directed at me since I left Wisconsin, it means more than it should that Ahmed looks after my health. "I promise, I'd tell you if I were sick."

"It's another strange morning," he confides with a tense laugh.

"You wake up late. Yasmine has misplaced her keycard. The Bradleys change their mind. And half the doctors from Belarus cancel for the upcoming convention because one of them tested positive. I appreciate their caution, but . . ."

"The Bradleys?" My hand slides down Ahmed's arm and grabs his wrist. "Changed their mind?" My stomach begins to roil. "Did the wife come back?"

He shakes his head. "Sadly, no. The daughter wanted to leave right away, but the husband was determined to stay on for the remainder of their trip, I think to prove to his wife that he wasn't fazed. But this morning, he decides maybe it is smarter to go home. They leave this afternoon." Ahmed leans in conspiratorially. "It must have dawned on him that his wife might be packing up all the valuables at home!"

My lips flutter into a smile. Ahmed's news is the reassurance I need. The trifling detail about my holding a scarf in the upstairs hallway two afternoons ago won't matter once Geoff and Stella are sealed inside a plane heading toward England. In the bright daylight of the lobby, I can't comprehend the reason for my spiraling insomniac worry. All my anxieties about Otto melt away like ice. Why did I even bother to upgrade them to a suite? I have half a mind to ask Ahmed to return them to their original room by the elevator shaft. But no, better to chalk that decision up to a good deed and from here on leave that woman and her hornet's nest of a son alone. My mistake was being too kind, wanting more from them than they were able to give.

"I wasn't honest with you," I confess to Ahmed. "I didn't sleep well last night. Maybe I felt a bit sorry for the Bradleys. It's sad to see a family fall apart right before your eyes." Ahmed nods compassionately, a cascade of wrinkles falling over his chubby cheeks.

"You care too much," he tells me. "Take my advice, Maggie, because I have learned over the years. These guests and their problems, they are not your burden. You must let them make their choices and live their lives. We can serve as a sympathetic ear. We can help in small ways when asked. But we can't fix the things that don't work inside them. We are but temporary friends."

"You're right," I reply with a dipped head. "You're absolutely right, Ahmed. The Bradleys aren't our problem anymore. And speaking of . . ." I lift my eyes to his. "I do want to make Tess and her son feel at home. But I can't possibly pay for any additional charges they accrue. Only the room, not a single soda from the minibar more. You'll tell them that? Maybe later on today? I see that you're quite busy this morning."

"Of course," he says. "I'll let them know."

I head past the trophy cases stocked with silver chalices and porcelain dishes. In the dining room, I find, to my delight, that Hamza has reserved my table for me in the corner, leaving a plate of pistachio butter cookies on it to ward off any short-term guest's claim. I scramble to my seat and raise one of the cookies toward the chef, who is slicing roast beef at the carving station. "Thank you, dear Hamza, for remembering me!" I bite into the cookie with joy, and an avalanche of crumbs falls down my chest.

10.

Each morning at eleven, the garden's brick walkways are swept and hosed. By noon, as I stroll toward the pool, the sun has already sucked them dry. Along with my umbrella, I've brought my canvas tote bag with me. I'm planning to spend the afternoon at the market—an elaborate shopping trip to buy everything except an XTMegaBox. Otto's strict deadline for his precious game system is right now at this very minute, and initially I considered sitting in the lobby as the noon chimes sounded, gloating in my invulnerability to childish threats. But I'd rather be off the premises for the day, and Ahmed has reminded me for a second time of the need to refill my prescriptions at the pharmacy. Happily, the Bradleys' suitcases are already stacked in the lobby, waiting to be loaded in the airport shuttle van.

As I pass the section of the garden devoted to Seif's meager rosebushes, I spot Tess sitting alone on a stone bench surrounded by the budding pinks and reds. She's holding a paperback novel in her lap but stares gloomily up into the trees, a furrow between her brows. The definition of a short attention span, she gets to her feet and paces in the direction of the iron gates that separate the garden from the city streets. Her hands tighten into fists, only released when she distractedly peels bark off a gum tree. Not for the first time, it dawns on me that Americans are the least at home of any people in the world, never quite able to settle into their surroundings, a part of them always off somewhere better or worse in their heads. I feel the urge to comfort Tess and be an ear for her problems, but I remind myself that it's in my best interest to leave the Seebers alone.

Easier said than done. Turning down the path to the pool, I catch sight of the boy. He notices me at the same moment, his face and shoulders covered in the blue shade of the cypress trees. He's lingering in front of the aviary. Seif must have leant him a pair of work boots because he's standing in dirty yellow rubber up to his knobby knees. The boots are starred in white cockatiel crap. One of the birds, the largest, with its yellow mohawk and orange cheeks, sits outside the cage on Otto's shoulder. I have always assumed the birds would fly away if let out of their enclosure, but maybe their wings are clipped and they can only hop around from branch to branch like primates.

Our eyes lock, mine and Otto's, almost like they fit together, like they belong to the same set of plates, and he gives a faint grin, not wide enough to be interpreted as either kind or conciliatory. The skinny pink lips still manage to hint at a question just for me. *Will I find my game system waiting in front of my room? Now is your deadline. Remember, if it's not there, I'll tell.* I picture Geoff Bradley at the reception desk studying the printed-out tally of his family's minibar purchases and handing over his credit card, Stella in her crop top and tight denim shorts snapping selfies with peace signs to post for her twenty followers. Any minute they will be stuffed into the hotel's airport shuttle van. I know what Otto's thinking, but does he know what I'm thinking? I pause for a moment and smile back at him, the giddy smile of an old woman feeling victorious. I want to advertise that I'm in no rush to fulfill his demands. When the tiger-striped cat scurries around my ankles, I bend down to pet her matted fur. My hip shoots with pain, but I keep my smile wide as I make exaggerated strokes along the backbone.

"Good kitty." The cat skitters off into the bushes. Rising with my smile starched on my face, I continue toward the pool, making a show of waving to Ben, who is slumped at a table with Zachary next to him on a teak lounger. "Hi boys! I'm hungry for once! Don't order lunch without me!"

As I make my way around the pool, Ben wrinkles his nose suspiciously at my uncharacteristic enthusiasm for the lunch menu, but his husband, shining like an opal in all his suntan oil, nods as he reaches for the laminated menu below his lounge chair.

"I'm trying the burger," he announces.

"Maybe I will too!" I realize that I'm not simply performing a rendition of blithe happiness for Otto's sake. I genuinely do feel happy, as if I've managed to sidestep some impending threat of banishment from the Royal Karnak, and the close call has renewed my devotion to the hotel. In fact, I feel so ecstatic about this safely averted disaster that I find the courage to stop in front of the gigolo on the way to my friends.

"Hello," I chirp at his feet. He's sitting on a lounger, one hairy leg bent around an ashtray. He squints up at me, perplexed, a few bare traces of stubble on his cheekbones glinting gold in the sunlight. "Hello," I repeat. "I'm Maggie."

He finishes sucking on his brown cigarette, biting down on the smoke before it escapes his mouth, his pectoral muscles flexed, his nipples narrowing into winks. In a higher octave than I would have assigned to this young man in his prime, he says "Hel-lo." Suddenly, out of nowhere—*Forgive me, Peter*—a wave of desire races through me. Physical contact is a habit, and after enough years alone, you eventually lose the craving. One day you forget it was the reason you left work early and drove straight home, hoping to find your husband's car in the driveway. But I suppose I'm not entirely cured of the need. Right now, I wouldn't mind the gigolo's slim, muscular body on top of me for a half hour, our lips and hips kissing, his penis sliding in and out of me. *Will I ever know that feeling of pleasure again?* I almost laugh at this unfamiliar urge purring in my veins. I wonder how much he'd charge for a half hour with someone as old and out of practice as I am.

"Can I help you?" he asks, staring at me curiously when I don't move. I remember both Ahmed's and Yasmine's advice to steer clear of this young delinquent, but I'm in too good a mood to resist a one-sided flirtation, especially with the boys watching.

"Well, maybe you can!" I reply coyly. "Luxor is your hometown, right?"

He nods before taking another drag off his cigarette. The smoke wafts from between his teeth before he sucks it back into his mouth. "You like my city?"

"Very much. I'd love any insider suggestions you might have."

"Suggestions," he slowly repeats in his high-pitched tenor, running his hand absentmindedly over the muscled grooves of his abdomen. "It depends on what you want."

"Yes, I suppose it does. What do I want? I'll let you know if anything comes to mind."

He nods gamely. "Yes, okay, you tell me"—and adds with an impish laugh—"I will help if I can."

I turn and slink toward the boys. Both Ben and Zachary are gawking at me. My smile is a brag, a sign of triumph. We do have fun here at the Royal Karnak; we act like clowns from time to time to entertain one another. I duck under their table umbrella, close my own, and take the empty seat.

"You bold floozy," Zachary exclaims as he rotates onto his stomach. "I didn't count on you as my main competition."

"Someone had to break the ice," I retort. "And now we know he's definitely a local."

"Did he just proposition you?" Ben asks. *It depends on what you want? I don't think he was talking about restaurant recommendations."

Catching the gigolo staring over at us, no doubt gauging whether our gossiping involves him, I loudly change the subject. "Boys, I'm going to the market this afternoon. Do either of you need anything? My treat. Mom's feeling generous today, so don't be bashful. I'd surprise you both with gifts if I could think of anything you don't already have."

"Ben," Zachary prompts, "show Maggie what you want more than anything else in Luxor." Zachary casts his eyes back on me. "Not exactly something you can pick up at the vegetable stalls. Although, according to Ben, that's where a lot of the best relics end up."

Ben gives his husband an icy glare. "You're not supposed to yell it from the mountaintops, Zee. Learn to keep quiet."

"But it's Maggie!"

"Yes, Mags is fine. But I didn't want to show that kid, and you forced me."

"What kid?" I demand, my heart on alert.

"Tess's son." Ben rubs his wispy mustache. "When Zachary feels the need to impress someone, even a ten-year-old boy will do!"

"He's eight!" Zachary retorts. "And he's a sweet kid. Jesus, Ben, you're an Egyptologist. It's a career invented to impress little boys."

"What did you show him?" I ask insistently, and Ben offers another wrinkled nose at my sudden hysteria. He reluctantly shoves his hand into his shirt pocket. He withdraws a tiny gold figurine, only slightly taller than a cigarette lighter, which he stands on the table, holding it up because it can't balance on its own. Even in the shade, the precious stones embedded in it—jewels of dusty orange, sea blue, and silvery yellow—gleam as if lit from their cores. The figure's arms are crossed over its chest, its legs are banded, and I make out the miniature face of a jackal covered in tiny blue rosettes. This figurine far exceeds the caliber of the previous artifacts that Ben has smuggled out of the museum during lunch. Even to my untrained eye, it possesses all the radiance of a priceless icon.

"It was cataloged wrong," Ben explains, staring down at it with pride. "I found it wedged in the back of one of the museum's storage drawers. The tag on it identified it as a relic from a minor priest's tomb. Not a chance. It's pure New Kingdom Empire, the height of its expression, and judging from the jewels, definitely pharaonic." Ben taps his own front teeth. "I even bit it to be sure."

Zachary fans himself with the menu. "The old teeth test never fails."

"Which god is it?" I ask.

"Set." The god of havoc, of disorder, of foreigners and storms. I recall trying to tell Otto about this god in the tombs.

"I thought Set was a malevolent god," I say. "Isn't it strange that a pharaoh would be buried with him?"

Ben gives a coy smile, like a grad student feasting on a basic 101 misconception. "Don't be a victim of dichotomous Western thinking, Mags. The ancients didn't see gods as either good or bad. Set was beloved in some ways because he kept life interesting. Always throwing in an invasion or a hailstorm to break up the desert monotony. Plus, when the sun god Ra sails through the sky at night, he needs Set to fight off the serpent Apophis, who also happens to be a god of chaos."

I nod as if it all makes simple sense. "So it takes one agent of chaos to defuse another."

Bingo, Ben mouths as he lifts the figurine to his eyes.

"Stop drooling," Zachary snipes from the lounger, and his eyes catch mine. "I can tell when Ben is smitten. I swear, Maggie, I won't gasp in shock when I discover that figurine on our mantel back in Boston in a year's time."

"Shut up," Ben snaps. "Although, honestly, it would be safer on our mantel in Boston." He eyes me wearily. "You wouldn't believe how many fakes there are in the museum collection. Who knows when the swap occurred. It could have been seventy years ago or seven months ago. All it takes is a greedy curator or a visiting scholar or an opportunistic janitor to seize the chance to replace an ancient scarab for a facsimile. There are zero security precautions. It's a looter's paradise."

Zachary sits up, eager to add his voice to a scandal. "The fakes in the market are super convincing. Right, honey?" His husband nods. "After they're mass-produced in a factory, they're rubbed in dirt to give them the look of an authentic archaeological find. It's the one economy where grime adds thousands to the price tag. Ben, tell Maggie what happened to your assistant when she came for a visit last year." The invitation for Ben to recite the anecdote is rhetorical. It's Zachary's story now, and likely will be for the rest of their marriage. "Ben's assistant bought a little ceramic ankh for, like, ten dollars from a tourist gift shop around the corner. When she's flying back home, she gets stopped at airport customs, and they find it in her bag and accuse her of stealing a national treasure. It was so cheap, even I could have told them it was a reproduction. But they held her for hours while waiting on the phone with the Minister of Antiquities who wanted to inspect the little tchotchke with his own eyes. She was on the verge of missing her plane, and they warned her she'd have to spend the night in a cell. Finally, she just said, 'Take it. Keep the thing. Whatever it is, I don't want it.' I bet that same ankh was for sale the very next day at the same shop, waiting for the next dupe tourist."

Ben grunts. "They're always suspicious of thieving foreigners, and I can't say I blame them. Yet try alerting anyone on the museum board about possible fakes in their own collection, and they treat you like you've insulted their mother." As if reminded of museum protocol, Ben quickly tucks the figurine back in his shirt pocket. "Zee, don't get angry if I do keep this one up on the mantel in our hotel room. At least for a few days. Promise not to alert the Minister of Antiquities."

"There are very few crimes I would report," Zachary says before turning his attention to the menu. "Signal the waiter. Maggie, do you want a burger?"

I glance beyond the pool and spy two spindly legs, free of rubber boots, running down the garden path toward the hotel. He must be heading up to the Royal Suite, which once hosted movie stars and prime ministers, to find no gift waiting for him at its front door. Well, that's not entirely accurate: disappointment can be a gift, absence, loss, humiliation—that's a gift you never stop opening.

"Should we order some wine?" I find myself suggesting. "Ben, I know you're going back to work, but what about half a glass? We're so lucky not to be under lockdown in some morgue of a city back in America. We're alive, my darlings, if only for this day, and I, for one, feel like celebrating."

11.

In spring, the sun sets later each day by an increment of half a minute. When I began ringing the lobby bell in January, I needed to assemble the guests by 5:15. Now we don't gather until well after six o'clock. As full-time residents of Earth, we're all keenly aware of the lengthening days after the winter solstice. And yet to celebrate the sun's disappearance each evening is to watch a ballroom extend right below your feet, the band playing one more encore, the bartender carrying out a fresh box of champagne. It's like discovering a new subspecies of butterfly that lives underneath your porch step. Our terrace sunset ritual is the closest I've ever come to beholding the miracle of time in its purest form. In this season, the mouth of the day ever widens, its upper and lower jaws opening farther around us, and we, the happy guests of the Royal Karnak, are dancing on the edge of its teeth.

I return from the market much later than I'd intended. It's nearly five by the time I ascend the horseshoe stairs from the corniche. The white wine at lunch with the boys—three glasses each—delayed my start. Perhaps the hawkers sensed my splurging spirit, because I was trailed for blocks by two horse carriages as their drivers took turns shouting at me: *Madam, I bring you. It is too hot to walk. Very bad men around the corner. I charge only two hundred pounds? Okay eighty? Okay thirty-five?* I shopped for an hour in the bazaar, until my ankles ached and I was tired of bartering for souvenirs that I'd never end up purchasing. Souvenirs are consolations for lonely travelers, a reminder that there's someone at home eager for your return—and I have no one back in Klode Park waiting with open arms for me. A scatter of friends and family tried calling or texting me after I left for Europe. That was followed by the explosion of concern in the first weeks of the pandemic, when the guilt-ridden felt the sudden need to check on any neglected seniors in their lives. I never once picked up the phone, never answered, never read a text, never responded with a thumbs-up emoji. They'd had all the time in the world to be concerned for my welfare when I lived in Wisconsin. After the market I made my monthly pit stop at the pharmacy.

Diclofenac for my sciatica. Diltiazem for my blood pressure. Celecoxib for my arthritis. The list goes on. There's barely a muscle or joint inside me that isn't sponsored by some multisyllabic wonder drug. Due to the pandemic's havoc on the global supply chain, it was hard enough to get my prescriptions in Europe. In Egypt refills are dice throws, and I'm required to come into the pharmacy in Luxor to beg and plead and flaunt my octogenarial feebleness as the pharmacist pecks away at his keyboard to track down each medication. Risperidone, needed for my sanity, has been the hardest to secure, and each batch arrives in some new pill form from a different European or South African supplier: a chalky white pellet, an orange-and-red capsule, a mauve-coated tablet the size of a pea. It's the equivalent of the random candies filling the glass bowl at the Royal Karnak's reception desk. Still, as I pace the tiled pharmacy floor, the white wine wearing off and the night without sleep starting to show its teeth, I'm grateful when a spare dose is found in the town of Marsa Alam, two hundred miles away. "Thank you, thank you, *shakran lak!*" It's a full-service operation: the pharmacist's son will deliver the prescriptions to the hotel by motorbike when they're ready.

After the pharmacy, I stopped into a restaurant by the train station known for its filtered water and English-speaking waiters. At a table in the walled courtyard, I accidentally dozed off for half an hour, slumped against the cool ceramic tiles. I fell into such an abyss of sleep that when the owner shook me awake, I had no idea where I was—which country, or restaurant, or century. Taking a new route back to the hotel, I happened upon a shop selling high-quality reproductions of ancient artifacts. Inside, among the gilded merchandise, I spotted a tiny brass figurine that held a shoddy likeness to Ben's Set relic. This garish facsimile couldn't touch the original's beauty, the jewels were colored glass, and yet I couldn't resist buying it as a gag gift for Ben. He could take this ersatz jackal god back to Boston to display on his mantel. As I went to pay, the shop clerk gestured toward a curtained doorway behind the register. "We do have," he said discreetly, "some *rarer*, more *valuable* items, not advertised, for the discriminating collector . . ." I declined the invitation, but that tiny glimpse into Luxor's black market recalled the gigolo's offer to facilitate any unorthodox requests. I wondered how far the young man's criminal connections extended. What could he get me at a moment's notice? What would be the price?

Back at the hotel, I find Ahmed smiling up from the front desk, relieved that I've returned in time for my sunset chore. In the late afternoon, the slant of light through the front windows makes the polyester sheen of Ahmed's suit more pronounced. I wish I could have used the money I'm spending on the Seebers' Royal Suite on a tailored suit for him. There's not a single gray hair on his head, and I wonder if he dyes his hair black, just as I do mine. Leaning against the reception desk, I ask whether the Bradleys made it to the airport.

"Checked out and gone!" Ahmed replies with relish. "They did not tip the housekeepers or the bellhops."

I'm glad the Bradleys aren't Americans; for once I don't have to apologize for the rudeness of my people. "Disgusting," I croak.

"Mr. Bradley still blames us for that scarf his wife found in their bed." Ahmed shakes his head. "He makes a big scene before he leaves."

"Thank god he's gone!" I intone. "And the daughter too, with her skimpy clothes."

"Mr. Bradley threatens to lodge a complaint with headquarters."

I roll my eyes, calling Geoff's bluff. "About what, getting caught cheating on his wife?" I want to reassure Ahmed that in my checkered experience with Richesse Resorts, the hospitality chain has more taxing problems on its hands than mistakes in laundry service at a moldering, underperforming hotel in southern Egypt.

"It could reflect very badly on us if he raises a fuss," Ahmed says. He then clears his throat and straightens his shoulders, as if to reestablish a guise of professionalism. I, too, prefer to put the matter of the Bradleys behind us. "By the way," he says, "I told Ms. Seeber that she would be responsible for any additional charges, including the room service that the boy ordered for the past two days. Of course, I didn't mention that they had a secret benefactor."

"Thank you."

Ahmed laughs. "It was funny. Little Otto was not pleased to hear it! I'm afraid he threw a tantrum right here in the lobby."

I can't control my mirth. "Poor thing. And let me guess, the mother just stood there and let him rage. You know, in my day there was such a thing as discipline."

"It's a difficult age for boys," Ahmed says too forgivingly. "Ms. Seeber certainly has her hands full. And yet Seif told me how gentle the boy is with the birds."

"Then maybe he should sleep outside with them." Triumphant, I grab the bell on the desk, eager to put Otto's brattiness behind me. "I've been thinking, Ahmed. We should reopen the terrace bars. We have plenty of people for it, and I have no doubt serving cocktails will lure the Russians as well." I give him a wink. "Things are getting back to normal, aren't they?"

I ring the bell and patrol the halls, calling to warn of impending night. "Sunset! Time to gather! Get your fresh, hot sunset! It's happening live right downstairs, and it waits for no woman or man!" Nearly sixteen of us congregate on the terrace to watch the day die, a purple-red wash coloring the faces of the guests and staff, and I'm thankful that Otto and his mother aren't among us. It might be the most beautiful sunset I've witnessed yet, and when the last sliver drops out of sight, we all let out a collective gasp.

Most of us head directly from the terrace into the bistro for dinner. I sit with Zachary and Ben, who admit to also having taken afternoon naps thanks to the wine—Zachary by the pool, Ben in the museum's break room. "No bottles tonight," I decree, although the boys order Negronis from the bar. It's a lovely evening, and I don't once think of the Seebers enjoying their free $900 suite only one flight above us.

In the evenings, the temperature drops, and the dining-room windows are opened, bringing in a cool spring night. No one seems ready to go to bed. Carissa, the Greek divorcée, offers to play the piano. According to Ahmed, she was mostly unfazed by the news that one of her scarves ended up in another guest's bed linen. True to character, she used the opportunity to announce her imminent departure for Athens, although none of us believe she'll actually leave. Ahmed promised to have the scarf dry-cleaned and sent up to her room with a bottle of champagne. Tonight, Carissa attempts a few choppy melodies on the untuned baby grand. I sing along to the opening bars of each standard, until I realize that no one else knows these songs. I was the only one alive when they were popular.

It's nearly ten thirty by the time I climb the two flights and wobble down the hall to my room. Did I expect to find a note from him? Maybe in the back of my mind, I did. Still, the sight of the pink paper sticking like a tongue from my door pricks me with dread. Otto has no right to hold such power over me. He's been in this hotel for a total of three days. I've built a life here. I unlock my door, consider ignoring the note, stomping on it as if it were no more than a paper scuff mat from a car wash. The room is dark, the air stuffy with the trapped smell of old carpet and sour waterpipes. I flip on the switch. The bed is made, the comforter so smooth over the mattress there's not a single ripple—such a lovely life raft after a long day. As I shut the door behind me, the pink stationery flutters into the room, landing on its side by the wall. I decide that I won't read Otto's note filled with insipid, eight-year-old-boy demands until morning.

Then I see my pink-and-red-striped cosmetics bag sitting on the desk below the flat-screen. The zipper is open. I am propelled toward it, even as my mind makes no sense of what it's doing on the desk instead of the bathroom counter, where I always keep it. As I reach for it, I recall Ahmed mentioning this morning that Yasmine had misplaced her master keycard. My jaw tightens in the realization that I'm no longer the only guest who has access to every room.

My fingers fumble over an old lipstick, three tubes of concealer, a pair of tweezers, and an eyebrow comb, until they finally locate the Ziploc. I yank out the plastic bag, partly relieved to find it still in its hiding place but already knowing it shouldn't be unrolled, because that isn't how I protect Peter's lock of hair.

My heart doesn't want to believe what I see when I hold the bag up to the light: a clear pane of plastic. There are only two stray silvery white hairs at the bottom of the bag. Peter's hairs, from the lock I clipped on his hospital bed, which very soon became his deathbed. Later I wished I'd clipped more of him, his fingernails or eyelashes or the whiskers growing along his neck. How much would they have let me take? That lock is all that I have left. The wrenching in my chest is so sharp, I recoil from the desk and trip over the chair, falling backward and hitting my good hip against the floor, the wind knocked out of me. I'm still clutching the plastic baggie as I crawl toward the pink paper by the wall.

I thought you were sorry.

This boy can't possibly understand what he's taken from me. He's only eight. He can't know that all I had left of Peter sat inside that paltry plastic Ziploc, tied with a blue ribbon and rolled up like bad marijuana. He's not old enough to comprehend the kind of annihilating loss I've suffered, and he didn't mean to rip the last remnants of my husband away from me. I tell myself this as I run down the hall, the baggie in one hand, the note in the other, making involuntary guttural noises from my mouth. The sweat is soaking my neck, and I count backward through the hours of the day—when did he break into my room? How long has Peter's hair been out of my possession and in his careless little-boy hands?

The stairs are a blur. I don't remember taking them. I'm already racing down the second-floor hallway, first heading in the wrong direction, and when I realize it, I spin around to sprint toward the Royal Suite. Two oh eight, 209, 210 . . . there it is, with a gold plaque on the wall. On my dime! He is staying in this room on my and Peter's money, our decades of hard work and scrimping, of not taking vacations or going out to dinner or buying new winter coats. All our sacrifices! I pound on the door, my fist beating against the wood, sweat now streaming down my face. After thirty seconds, I finally hear footsteps. The door opens a tentative inch, and Tess's face appears, her brow furrowed, her hair stringy with post-shower dampness. She takes me in with her big green eyes, and whatever she sees causes her to keep a firm grip on the door.

"Maggie?" she asks in a tone of bewilderment. As if I've shown up unannounced to her apartment in Paris. As if the Royal Karnak isn't my home.

"Tess," I gasp. "Where is he? Where's Otto? I need to see him this instant!"

This urgent appeal for her son tenses her face. The toughness of her beauty comes out in sharp relief. I hate her, but only because I despise her boy, and she gave birth to him.

"What . . . ," she stumbles. "What do you need Otto for? He's asleep. He went to bed an hour ago."

"Please. I must . . ." But threatening to snap her son's neck isn't going to convince her to open the door to me. I know from my own experience as a mother that accusing her son of breaking into my room and stealing a priceless possession will only rouse her defenses. All that matters is Peter's lock of hair. "Please, Tess, can you wake him right now. Tell him I'm sorry. Please!"

"Sorry? Oh, I see." She thinks I'm admitting to striking him in the tomb. I nearly show her the note he slipped under my door, but I don't want to open myself to questions.

"I mean, I want to apologize in case it was an accident. I feel terrible about the confusion. I really don't think I hit him, even by mistake, but it was so dark down there, maybe I was turning and my arm swung . . . Anyway, I feel awful. I'd like to see him. I'd like to tell him in private, just the two of us, that I'm his friend. Would that be okay?"

Tess doesn't look convinced, staring at me with exhaustion, her forehead still tensed.

"That's very sweet of you," she replies, "but it's eleven at night. Otto's bedtime is nine thirty. Could your kind words wait until the morning?"

"Of course!" I cry. "Of course they can! I'm sorry. I was in bed myself and had a terrible dream." This cover story spills out of me before I have time to approve it. "I was dreaming about my daughter, Julia. I told you about her, how she died when she was about your age. Almost your age exactly, maybe just a few years older. And I woke up feeling like . . . well, like making amends with your son. It seemed so important to me. I'm sorry to bother you."

The pity works. Tess's eyes absorb me lovingly. "I'm so sorry, Maggie. They haunt us forever, don't they, the people we've lost? But I always remind myself that in the midst of suffering . . ." I don't want to hear Tess's platitudes on overcoming anguish, or what a mere thirty years of life has taught her about grief. I want my husband's hair back, and I want the Seebers thrown out of my hotel. I want them tossed down the horseshoe steps until their necks break as they land in a pile on the sidewalk.

I nod appreciatively. "Exactly! Exactly that, Tess. You said it. I'm so embarrassed to be down here." Before I turn, I catch a whiff of something putrid, a substance burning or burnt, emanating from inside the Royal Suite, blowing into the hall from a current of air off the Nile. My lips twist in repugnance, and Tess guesses the reason.

"I know. I opened the windows, but the smell is just terrible. Otto bought a bundle of herbs off one of the street vendors this evening. It's supposed to clear the air of dead spirits. He insisted on burning it in the ashtray, but it reeks, doesn't it? It smells just like—" Like hair, like burnt human hair. That monstrous child burned my precious Peter. Tess is babbling on, ". . . marble ashtrays all over the place. We got this room for free, I think because the manager figured we'd complain about the noise of the elevator. It kept both of us up the first night, howling through the wall, and poor Otto was so tired the next day, I think that's why he had that fit in the tomb. This new suite is so much nicer, except for all the shouting on the corniche, which . . ."

I turn mechanically. "I need to lie down," I mutter and stagger along the hall, my foot tripping against a discarded food tray. Otto burned Peter's hair, that soft bundle of curls that I would rub against my lips to bring his face into focus; after six years, I find I'm already losing a solid image of Peter's bent nose and gray November eyebrows and the pink hue of his cheeks in winter. That lock of hair reliably brought his face back to me. And Otto took it from my room and set it on fire in an ashtray simply to increase my suffering. I'm standing by the stairwell, my hand clasping the iron post and my eyes fixated on the bordello-red swirl of the Murano chandelier. I want to hurt Otto. I want to make him suffer. Therefore, instead of heading up the stairs to my room, I descend.

12.

I wake at my usual hour of six. The room has lost its darkness; already the air is a soft mineral blue, drifting in from the open windows. I rise while appreciating the delicious quiet of the morning. Ten minutes of exercises with the help of my desk chair—knee bends, "tornado arms"—and a little prayer to Peter as I step into the shower. *I love you, sweetheart.* Toweling off, I check my skin for any unwelcome blotches, swallow my pills, dress in my favorite black-and-yellow kaftan, and strap on my Velcro sandals. It's 6:40, a touch too early for my purposes. I want to hear the moment of discovery and then hurry down the stairs to witness my masterpiece.

I lie back down in bed, place my hands on my chest, cupped over my heart, close my eyes, and wait. I am drifting, as if on a raft in a swimming pool, like the kidney-bean pool we dug behind the house in Klode Park. I rarely used that pool, except for the summer when Julia went to sleepaway camp, and it seemed such a waste to keep it cleaned and chemically balanced without anyone enjoying it. That single summer—Julia was thirteen and had just finished seventh grade—I would spend a few hours on hot afternoons floating in the deep end. Peter called the backyard my "Mexico" every time he saw me grabbing a towel in my red sunglasses. "Off to your Mexico. Don't forget to send a postcard." At that point, we still had Chloe, our sixteen-year-old pug, a gray pudding dollop of a dog who howled hoarsely at the edge of the pool as I floated in the center. We kept trying to put Chloe down, and several times we made the "final appointment" with the vet, but Julia would grow hysterical and beg us for another few months with the dog. Who could blame her? That pug was the mascot of her childhood; it represented the breadth of her history as a person, and no one wants their childhood mascot euthanized. We finally made a pact to wait until Julia got back from camp. (She wouldn't last one month, as it turned out; bullied because of her fear of the dark until she wet her bunk bed, she refused to return to camp ever again.)

Why didn't Peter swim with me in the pool? He loved swimming in the lake with Julia—for hours and hours they'd explore the marshy coves and inlets—but he never took to the tameness of the backyard pool, always treated the few times he braved the shallow end like a chore, a pained smile on his face. He loved my tan lines, though, kissing where they crossed over my shoulders and along my upper thighs. That summer, while Julia was off at camp, Peter experimented with growing a beard. His stubble tickled my skin as he kissed me. He shaved it off the morning he went to pick up Julia. I asked him to keep it—I loved the sandpaper of his face on my skin—but he didn't want to scare our daughter. "Kids," he said, "get upset when their parents change. And you know Julia, it will be too much of a shock for her." Of course he was right. Peter was always right about parenting. I was so lucky to raise a daughter with him.

Right now I am floating on a blow-up raft filled with Peter's breath in our backyard in Klode Park. I'm drifting under a clear Wisconsin sky, tinted brown through my red sunglasses. I am waiting for Peter to kiss me with his scruffy face. What did that face look like? I can almost see it.

A scream erupts from the garden. It's a piercing shriek, the unmistakable reaction to a violent shock. I leap from bed, the nerve endings in my body blossoming with tiny buds of excitement. For the first time in so many months, my body doesn't experience its usual aches. I grab my umbrella and hurry down the hall, skirting the steps so quickly I'm astonished I don't lose my footing. Other guests have heard the scream too. They open their doors hesitantly, neither dressed nor caffeinated enough to react quickly to this emergency. I am circling around the chandelier's chain, taking the stairs as fast as I can. In the lobby,

Ahmed has already left his post at the reception desk, no doubt running toward the cry. I yank open the heavy doors to the backyard and struggle with my umbrella. A tiny crowd has already gathered around the aviary. *Act surprised*, I remind myself. *A hand over your mouth in horror.* I'm eager to see his face.

Seif stands by the aviary door, shouting at an underling gardener, his arms shaking in angry grief. Ahmed is trying to calm him, the gel in his hair shining in the dawn light.

"What's the matter?" I exclaim as I approach.

Through the cage's thick mesh, I see the remains of the slaughter: three slain cockatiels, what's left of them, two reduced to a mere pulp of feathers and bone, the third strangely intact but for its chewed-off head. The tiger-striped cat, that high priestess of the garden, sits in the aviary's far corner, her tail beating back and forth, her yellow eyes innocently observing the fallout of her nighttime feast. I sensed her immense gratitude last night when I unlatched the aviary's door for her. After all, she'd been hungering for those birds her entire life.

Seif looks like he's on the brink of throwing a punch. I feel terrible about his distress, but it was his choice to befriend the wrong guest. Anyway, it's not the gardener's reaction that interests me. I glance past him and find Otto sitting on a stone bench, his face buried in his hands. He's sobbing, his whole hairless, fatless body quivering like a bow. "Oh dear," I groan. "What on earth happened to our beautiful birds?"

Ahmed turns to me to report the obvious. "The cat got in and killed them. A catastrophe! These birds were the symbol of the hotel." Just like Chloe the pug, I think, our incontinent, blind Burkhardt mascot. "Those cockatiels have been with us for more than twenty years!" Ahmed's eyes are glistening, and I feel another throb of remorse for the hurt I've caused. I would never want to upset the staff. They are family. But I shove my guilt aside.

"How could that happen?" I cry. "For twenty years they've been absolutely safe and suddenly—" Am I overdoing it? I don't think so, especially since I've caught the attention of my nemesis. Otto glares up, his hands still cupped below his face, his expression an intoxicating mix of devastation and self-pity. He's taken his glasses off, and the folded pair are wedged in his crotch, sticking up like a little erection.

"Mr. Otto found the cat with the birds this morning when he came to feed them," Ahmed explains.

I stare at Otto, offering a look of compassion. "Oh, Otto, I'm sorry. How awful. Did you forget to secure the door properly yesterday? Is that what happened?" My intention is to increase the decibel level of his agony. I won't be satisfied with loss. I want him to feel blame. At my insinuation, Seif's eyes venture accusingly toward the boy on the bench. It's a sad end to their short-lived friendship.

"I latched the door!" Otto swears in teary appeal. "I wouldn't leave it open. I promise I latched it yesterday!"

I consider adding *I'm sure you thought you did*, but it's better not to push too hard.

Tess is running across the brick path in a pair of flip-flops. She's wearing a bikini underneath a waffled hotel robe, a flash of mint-green Lycra against pale, smooth skin. She must have been dressing for a swim when she heard her son's scream. She tears through the crowd, her mouth twisting when she sees the bloodbath in the cage, and kneels before her precious child.

"Honey, are you okay?" She pats his face and body, searching for an injury or scratch, as if Otto had been trapped in the cage along with the birds. The tiger-striped cat wants to slink from view. Her fur is covered in linty white feathers, and she paws at the door to be released. Instinctively I inch forward to free her, but I catch myself. I can't be seen aiding and abetting the predator.

Instead I step back from the group, holding my umbrella over me. Otto is hugging his mom tightly, his chin nestled on her shoulder, his cheeks swollen with tears. I can't stop looking at his face, mesmerized, like staring into a fire, the power and force of it. When he lifts his eyes up at me—I can't help it—I smile.

13.

In the breakfast room, the news of the massacre has already reached the kitchen staff. I have greatly underestimated the Royal Karnak's devotion to the cockatiels. Hamza looks particularly sullen, his meal service clumsy and distracted. Catching my eye, he pads over to a section of wall across the room and points up at the mural. Right next to a beige water stain, three lutino cockatiels are perched on a painted branch with their long Elvisy faces, cresting mohawks, and orange beaks parted in song. Hamza touches his heart, and I nod sympathetically. No green cookies arrive at the end of my meal.

I plod down the hall toward the lobby. There's a tiny in-house gift shop halfway down the corridor no bigger than a coat closet. It's never been open during my stay, another casualty of lost tourism, and its lights are off. But as I pass, I notice for the first time that a few of the ceramics in the cases are decorated with likenesses of the cockatiels. A queasiness descends on me at the sight of those cheap birds collecting dust behind glass. I wish I could remove them. Even the most trivial reminders of loss are enough to wreck a house.

The lobby is eerily quiet, and for a moment the reception desk looks unattended. But Ahmed is merely resting his forehead on his folded arms, trying to collect himself. I hurry over, desperate to offer my support. I don't bother to circle around to the opposite side of the counter like a formal guest, but step inside the galley-sized staff area. My hand is on his back.

"What's the matter? Is this because of the birds?"

He lifts his head, his face a brutal moon of wet eyes and tired pouches. In fairness, I want to point out that if the birds had meant so much to the hotel, perhaps a sturdy lock on the aviary door would have been advisable. Really, it's a miracle that the cat didn't gain access sooner.

"Yes, the birds," he replies. "They were very important to the soul of this establishment. And very important to our new owners, Richesse Resorts. The new emblem they were designing for the hotel had a drawing of the cockatiels in the center. Now I must report that they were killed. All three of them."

"Can't we just order . . ." I temper the suggestion. "Is it possible, Ahmed, despite this horrible loss, that we could replace them with three new cockatiels?" Perhaps the birds are rarer than I suspected, especially during the current collapse in global trade.

Ahmed shakes his weary head. "You see, Mr. Bradley *did* file a complaint yesterday with headquarters. And now these birds are also killed because we forgot to secure the cage. It all reflects very badly on me and my team. This Belgian company, they are my new bosses, and they doubt my management skills. This morning already the Belarus medical convention canceled because of more sicknesses. Too many rooms empty."

"But that's not your fault!" I interject. "My god, Ahmed, a plague is sweeping the globe, killing a war's worth of people. They can't expect you to keep this hotel at maximum capacity. You're doing your best!"

"But we are a new acquisition, and they are looking for reasons to bring in a fresh team. So these incidents, one on the back of another, this madness, it doesn't look good. They have scheduled a Zoom meeting with me tomorrow about lax policies. And I haven't even told them about the birds yet."

I let the quiet wrap around us. It is utterly selfish, I know, in light of my dear friend's troubles, to tap the knife a little deeper into Otto's chest.

"That boy," I whisper. "Maybe I shouldn't have splurged on a nicer room for him and his mom. If they had just left, if that abusive husband had come and collected them, if Otto hadn't been so careless as to leave the aviary door unlatched . . ."

Ahmed squints skeptically at me. "The French husband is abusive?" he scoffs. "I do not believe that. He is very nice, very concerned about his wife and son. He calls every day to ask me how his family is doing."

"He does?" The news doesn't track with the picture Tess painted of a violent, volatile cinematographer. *There are moments I've felt scared for my own safety around him, and then he'll be perfectly loving and sweet the next moment.*

Ahmed nods. "Mr. Seeber asks about their well-being, particularly the boy's. You see, every morning I receive a phone call from him."

A red-leather-bound phone log lies on the desk. It once belonged to the concierge, before the official concierge was dismissed during the bookings drought and Ahmed became the de facto representative. He opens the log to reveal a list of calls from a +33 number, "Alain Seeber" scribbled next to them in blue ink. "I hope you don't mind, Maggie, but I told Mr. Seeber that the hotel gave his family their complimentary suite. I know, I know, and I don't like taking credit for your kindness, but . . . ."

I smile indulgently, although this news stings. I'd hoped to mount a case for throwing Otto and Tess out of the hotel due to the slaughter in the garden. Now their continued comfort and happiness are points of hotel pride.

"Still, though, the slain cockatiels, simply because of the boy's carelessness! You're right, Ahmed. It's not a minor episode right before your big meeting with headquarters tomorrow. The entire staff at the hotel will probably turn against Otto for his mistake. Those cockatiels were our mascots!"

Another dubious squint of Ahmed's eyes, and I worry he might be catching on to my darker intentions, laying all the blame at Otto's feet. He turns to face me. He's only an inch shorter than I am. Would I find Ahmed attractive if I were forty years younger? He has an earnestness and warmth about him that attracts me. His face begins to redden, and his lips stumble over each other in a prelude to sharing his thoughts.

"Maggie, I hope this isn't inappropriate to ask. I hope you won't take offense . . ." For a second, I genuinely can't tell if he is going to accuse me of killing the birds to frame an eight-year-old boy. "To-night is the start of Ramadan. Which means that tomorrow, from sunrise on we fast, but at sundown we have a special meal to celebrate. My wife, she has heard so much about you, about our friendship over these months." The blush deepens. "She asks me to invite you to our house for the dinner. Would you like to join us?"

"At sundown? Your house?" I take a deep, relieved breath. "Yes, Ahmed. I'd love to be your special guest."

14.

Tit for tat. In my mind, all I've done is even the score. The bird sacrifice for Otto's far more atrocious violation.

Yet after I leave Ahmed at reception, it occurs to me that Otto might view this morning's tragedy differently—as me nosing ahead. Worse, I fear he might use his keycard to take revenge, and that fear holds me hostage in my room, holed up against any further incursions. A security safe the size of a toaster oven sits on a shelf in the closet. I've never felt the need to use it, but now I load the safe with personal items that Otto might deem valuable to take: my passport, insurance cards, and $2,000 worth of cash in Egyptian pounds. It takes me nearly twenty minutes to figure out how to use the safe's electronic touch screen. An hour later, I add my wallet, filled with credit cards and now mostly useless American IDs. After another hour ticks by, I include my diamond wedding ring, my blue sapphire ring, the pearl earrings that Peter gave me on our thirtieth anniversary, and some of my dwindling, harder-to-replace medications. I consider alerting Ahmed to the fact that Yasmine's misplaced card could lead to a crime wave. Can he really afford another managerial calamity right before his big Zoom meeting with headquarters? But resetting the housekeeping cards would delete my access too, and I can't help but wonder which favorite items an eight-year-old boy might possess that are consequential enough to steal if the need strikes.

Through the early afternoon, I keep guard, pacing in circles, hurrying to the window to spy guests passing through the garden. At two thirty, I catch a break. I spot Otto running into the hotel from the back patio, only to reemerge a few minutes later in fluorescent-blue swim trunks. His scoliosis-bowed back and bony shoulder blades disappear under the canopy of trees. I'm disappointed to see him returning so casually to the scene of the crime, no sign of sulking or feeling chastised by the morning's incident. Yet his trip to the swimming pool temporarily frees me from the prison of my room. I quickly change into the black kaftan I usually find too grieving-Italian-grandmother to wear, tie a wide-brimmed hat around my chin, and grab my umbrella.

To avoid any unnecessary interactions, I take the elevator down to the basement and slip out the service door. Right by the dumpsters, one of the gardeners is clicking his tongue and calling for the orange cat. She must have sensed her plummeting popularity at the hotel and wisely fled the scene. I slink past him and circle around the garden's perimeter by following the hotel's iron gate. A hose is running full blast inside the bird aviary, Seif cleaning away the gruesome remains. The bleach he's using stings my sinuses, and stray hose spray creates minor rainbows under the trees. The garden is eerily silent, no other birds whistling, as if in deference to their fallen comrades.

Soon, though, as I wind around the back of the fitness center and trudge along an open patch of muddy driveway reserved for service vehicles, I hear splashing in the pool. I sneak through the thicket of trees and emerge near one of the pool's hidden coves, removed from the main stage of sunbathers and lap swimmers. Pinkish hibiscus flowers the color of waterlogged teabags hang over tranquil water, disturbed only by the filter's gurgling bubbles. These quiet coves must have been designed as a rendezvous for lovers in a more romantic, less family-friendly era of international tourism.

I creep around the edge of the pool toward the Olympic rectangle. I don't want to be seen; I'm merely here to observe the boy, to take his temperature and determine the severity of his disposition. Through a patch of ficus plants drowsy with bees, I peer out to find Otto soaring through the air over the water's flat blue belly, flying in a bottle-rocket arc. He lands with a splash in the deep end. To my irritation, Zachary's head bobs up from the launching point. Otto resurfaces, giggling, and sharks his hand through the water to generate a sizable splash toward his new playmate. His joy is infectious, the roughhousing so fun it's as if three innocent birds had not been killed a few hours ago for his benefit. Yet some of my wrath is reserved for my friend, the former corporate lawyer, now entertaining my enemy. My eyes scan the umbrellaed tables for a sign of Ben, but he must have already finished lunch and gone back to the museum. Ben wouldn't betray me. Ben would hate the boy too.

Otto dog-paddles toward Zachary, eager to climb back onto his shoulders for another rocket launch. I've never actually seen Zachary swimming in the pool, using his waxed, gym-built, protein-shake body for physical activity. I've always thought of his muscles as ornaments on an idle man of fifty, but now he lowers himself to let the scrawny brat mount him, like an obedient pony. For once he pays no attention to the sexy, chain-smoking gigolo sitting at the far end.

Otto flies through the air, screeching in delight, and Zachary's balding head returns to the surface to appraise his skills in the art of boy tossing. I miss a single poolside lunch, and this boy has eclipsed me in the heart of my friend.

A bee wafts near my face, attempting to land, and I step farther out from the bushes than I'd like to escape it. But I'm such an invisible entity that no one notices my presence. Who would bother themselves with the sight of a depressing old woman in the midst of so much pooltime fun? On the other side of the pool, Tess walks to the edge in her green bikini, her posture shy and shoulders hunched despite her enviable body, all ribs and unwrinkled skin. Otto climbs onto Zachary's shoulders and signals to his mother to join them. "*Saute! Saute*, Mom!" And then he is shot skyward like a cannonball. Tess doesn't dive. She squats down, palms flat on the concrete, and slips into the water, gone from sight until she surfaces next to Zachary, her hair fanning down her face as she pinches her nose to clear away the snot.

Otto, Tess, and Zachary form a giddy circle in the pool's center, drifting in an intimate ring, warm smiles on all of them. If I didn't know better, I would mistake them for a happy family. On impulse I pull my cell phone from my kaftan pocket and snap a few photos of them. Otto encourages his mother to use Zachary as a human launcher, and reluctantly she is coaxed onto his shoulders. I take more photos as she falls, giggling, into his muscular arms.

Zachary dog-paddles in my direction, perhaps trying to flag a passing waiter for a drink. I retreat into the leafy camouflage of the ficus grove, but I'm not fast enough, and his eyes fall on me. At first, he isn't sure who he sees and focuses his stare before lifting his hand in a tentative wave. Silently, before he can get a word out, I sink back into the shadows and disappear from sight.

15.

At six in the evening, I stand at my bathroom mirror, applying sunscreen to my face. I refuse to let the threat of Otto keep me from my job as sunset hostess. For safe measure, I've added my old plane tickets and a charm bracelet that belonged to Julia to the safe along with my other belongings. I rub two fingers of rose water behind each ear and practice a smile in the mirror. That's when I hear it, the faint tinkling of a bell in the distance, emanating from somewhere far down the hall.

At first I assume it must be the elevator alarm, someone stuck again. But as the rings draw closer to my room, the dread begins to descend. I step out of the bathroom, concentrating on my ears. The clangs of the bell, of *my* silver bell, intensify as they advance down the hall.

"Sunset!" I hear the boy cry, plaintive and urgent, as if warning the guests of wolves. "Sunset downstairs. Everyone gather! Get your fresh, hot sunset before it's gone!" Otto has stolen my job. The little shit is trying to make me redundant; that's his revenge. *I* who invented this ritual, who coined the very words he's now aping to lure guests down to the glory of *my* dying day. Children aren't the world's inheritors, they are its thieves, skating by on the hard work of generations that came before them. "Sunset! Catch it by its tail! Don't miss the final act!"

His voice trails down the hall, escaping down the steps. I hear doors opening, the tourist lemmings following him more readily than they ever followed me. Ahmed will set this injustice right. Ahmed will see that a spiteful impersonator is ringing my bell, and he will pluck the instrument from the boy's grip before offering it to me like a rose. *This is a job only for Maggie. She is still needed.* I leave my room and rush down the hall, which is now filled with the day's fresh arrivals, new people who aren't familiar with our customs. A family of blond Swedes eagerly follows the clanging down the staircase. There are seven of them (what couple has five children anymore?), which will make for an infuriatingly robust addition to Otto's terrace body count. Of course a child can appeal to the public in a way that the elderly cannot; there's a reason little girls sell cookies door-to-door and not the old hags who bake them. What if I showed up, fingers ropy and withered, trying to entice harried fathers into buying coconut-covered biscuits?

"Sunset! Sunset! Watch the sun go down the drain!" he improvises, now just an echo as he wanders along the second-floor hallway. I dash down the last flight of steps to beat him to the lobby, excusing myself as I slip past the Swedes, holding up my black kaftan at the knees as if it were a ball gown. Ahmed is already waiting for me at the bottom of the stairs with blushing embarrassment, his wide brown eyes taking me in. He waits until my feet reach the last step before addressing me.

"You heard the bell?"

"Yes, I certainly have!" I restrain my fury because Ahmed has acknowledged the transgression.

"What do you think? A good idea, no?"

My jaw clenches. "What idea?"

"That Mr. Otto rings the bell for sunset. He asked me this afternoon if he could try it. Isn't that sweet of him, trying to make up for the accident with the birds? I remembered what you said this morning, Maggie, about how he might feel as if the hotel has turned against him over it. And I knew you wouldn't mind . . ."

"Of course not!" I belch. "Why would I mind?"

"I thought it might give Otto some confidence that he is part of the Royal Karnak Palace family. And you shouldn't have to go up and down all those steps ringing it every night! Let the little boy do all that strenuous exertion. You should stay down here enjoying the sunset."

I try for a smile, its phoniness so heavy on my face, it feels like a prosthetic, like holding a barbell between my lips. "That was awfully considerate of you."

"There is no use having the boy feel guilty if he forgot to shut the aviary." Ahmed studies me for a second, as if to gauge the sincerity of my response. "You're okay with him ringing the bell, yes? I didn't think you would mind. Plus, he can take over tomorrow evening when you come to my house for dinner."

I'm thankful that Ahmed doesn't wait for an answer. I don't think I could have faked enthusiasm about being forced into early retirement. Too many guests are pouring through the lobby, and Ahmed races to open the front doors to beckon them onto the terrace. Zachary is descending the steps, his blue eyes blazing through a fresh sunburn. My initial instinct is to turn my back on him, but I manage another forced smile. I can't afford to lose a friend. He heads toward me, swigging a beer from his minibar.

"Was that you creeping around the pool today, Maggie?" he asks humorously. "Is my vision failing? Or were you *malingering* in the bushes this afternoon?"

"I was just passing by. I wanted to get some fresh air in the garden," I manufacture. "I'm sorry I missed lunch."

"Don't worry. Ben did too. Some bigwigs from his Austrian sister university are in town, and he was stuck at the museum showing off his 3D renderings. He's at dinner with them now. I refused to join. If you think finance meetings are snoozefests, try academic dinners. All that pompous intellectual doubletalk through three courses, and then everyone bickering about how to divide the bill."

"You were quick to find a replacement to amuse yourself this afternoon," I say coolly, and avoid his eyes, glancing at a herd of guests advancing toward the front door. I am unable to relinquish my job as hostess, guiding them with an outstretched arm as they pass, muttering "Welcome, welcome, it's right outside."

"Otto?" Zachary snickers. "Poor kid. He felt terrible about the birds. I was trying to cheer him up and babysit so his mom could relax. He's quite good at magic tricks. He pulled a quarter out of my ear. By the way, I don't know if you're aware, his father is still MIA."

"Missing in action? Isn't the poor man working on a television series?

My god, during a pandemic, risking his own health to put food on the table, while his wife and son do nothing all day but float around in a pool at a luxury hotel . . ." Zachary's face tightens, and I realize that in defending Alain, I've accidentally insulted him. Zachary, too, is a hotel freeloader, living off his partner's paycheck. "Oh, you know what I mean," I say with a sigh as I grab his biceps. Zachary pulls his arm away to take a swig of beer.

"I think I'm being rather charitable in looking after the kid. I even promised I'd give him swimming lessons at the crack of dawn tomorrow when the pool's empty. Don't think for a second that I'm a lenient coach. I take fitness seriously. I'm making Otto swim five laps of the pool, including those side arms. No cheating." He smiles wickedly at me. "Care to join? You could use some exercise too."

"I have no interest in racing a boy around a pool."

"Scared of a little eight-year-old competition?"

I grunt. "I used to beat my daughter when she was eight, and she was an exceptional swimmer." I remind Zachary about Julia, who was not much older than Otto when we lost her. I tell him about our pool in Klode Park and about Peter teaching Julia to swim in the lake at our weekend house and how they would race out together while I waved goodbye from the dock. Julia was mopey on land, but graceful in the water. Her favorite stroke was the butterfly. . . . I realize I haven't been saying any of this aloud to Zachary. He isn't even paying attention to me, his eyes already turned toward the terrace.

"Should we head outside?" he asks.

It is my habit to be the last person to step outside for sunset. "You go ahead."

The ringing bell echoes from the upstairs hallway. Otto is being exceedingly thorough in his duties. I linger by the reception desk, waiting to be the last, when I catch sight of Tess through the front window, already standing on the terrace with the others. I didn't see her go outside. She must have circled around from the back garden. I slip outside to stand next to her, scurrying along the marble wall as I thread past unfamiliar guests.

"Hi," I rasp when I reach her. She offers me a furrowed brow and a mouth hanging slightly open, as if caught between opposing reactions, a greeting and a reprimand. I beat her to whatever she's going to say. "I'm sorry I bothered you last night, knocking on your door. I've been having terrible dreams."

"Don't worry about it," she whispers tersely, as if we're in the middle of a church service.

"Any news from Alain? Is he coming?"

She tightens her mouth and shakes her head. I expect her to share her misery with me, but her eyes avoid mine, watching as Ahmed snakes to the front of the group, his heels daring the edge of the horseshoe steps as he faces us.

"I've been thinking," I persist in a whisper, "maybe I gave you the wrong advice about staying on here, away from your husband. Perhaps it's wiser to return to Paris and try to work things out with him, for your sake, for your son's. You mentioned that you had already abandoned Otto once when he was a baby, and now with Alain—"

"I didn't *abandon* him!" Tess wheezes in defense. "I only—"

"Needed time away," I correct to soften the sting. "But maybe removing his father from his life has been triggering for him. Something tells me"—I don't mention Alain's daily phone calls to Ahmed—"that your husband is concerned about your well-being and wants you back."

Her lips attempt a response, but Ahmed begins his speech before she can piece any words together. The manager takes the opportunity to inform his guests that the holy month of Ramadan begins this evening, and starting tomorrow many of the staff will be fasting. "Please don't take it personally if we are a little grumpier than usual," he quips, "it is simply due to our grumbling stomachs!" Cue canned laugher. He waits like a professional comedian for it to settle. "I also want to thank this evening's volunteer bell ringer, Mr. Otto Seeber, who has kindly done the honors of leading you all down here to our spectacular terrace. Please give a round of applause for Mr. Otto?"

Clapping erupts from the crowd to prompt Otto into accepting the limelight. The guests turn, searching for a little boy in their midst.

Even Tess is straining her neck in an attempt to find him. My eyes hunt the waistlines of adults, looking for a set of glasses, a pug nose, apricot ears, and gapped teeth. Where is he? Did he even come outside? The last I recall of him, he was ringing the bell from an upstairs floor. Alone upstairs. What if he never came down?

"Excuse me, I forgot something upstairs . . . " I mutter inanely to Tess, already launching myself from my spot. I shove past guests in panic, knocking through the Swedish family that refuses to disentangle, all of them too lost in the beauty of the sun dipping behind limestone peaks. "Move! Coming through!" Finally I reach the front door and tear into the lobby, clawing my way through the maze of toe-stubbing furniture. I'm certain that Otto has orchestrated this ploy to purge everyone—particularly me—from inside the hotel so that he can activate whatever special torture he has planned. By the time I reach the second-floor landing, my ankles have seized up on me. Groaning in pain, my face washed in sweat, I pull myself up the final flight, hand after hand along the banister. I bolt down the third-floor hallway, desperate for my room. My heart sinks when I see my door hanging ajar. My lungs are making a dying-possum sound as I push the door wide into the room. Only a faint trace of window light makes sense of the interior, where not a single item appears out of place. He hasn't touched a thing. Is that his trick, to make me paranoid for no reason, to go mad combing through everything I own in the search for what's not there? As my breathing softens, I hear the sound of water running in the bathroom. I walk with cautious steps toward the open bathroom door.

I pause at the threshold, where the carpet meets the marble tiles. "Otto?" I call through the loud gush of the tub faucet. "Otto, please! Stop this foolishness." I decide to lie, which is all adults do to kids anyway, lie to them viciously about the benevolence of the world we're passing on to them. "I had nothing to do with the birds. Are you sure you didn't leave the aviary unlatched?" My heart is pounding in fear of what the boy might be doing in my bathroom. But why should I be scared? There's nothing left in my room to destroy; everything of value is stowed in the safe.

I lurch into the bathroom, forcing my feet to commit to the tiles. The only person I find there is myself, reflected in a mirror slowly being consumed by steam. My arthritic hands are bunched at my chest, my face fissured with lines. Otto isn't in here. Cautiously I move toward the tub. The bath is only half full, but even at a glance I know he's left something in it because of the water's rosy tint. It takes me a second to discern the creature sunk under eight inches of bathwater. Its wings are spread out, as if flying, which it never got to do in its caged life. The yellow feathers are stained with blood. But the reason it takes me so long to identify it is because its head is missing, the one slain cockatiel that the cat didn't fully devour.

This gruesome act of retaliation is almost laughable. Does he really think he can frighten me with a mutilated bird? It's a sick, twisted prank, but one I can stomach. Once again, Otto underestimates me.

I flip the lever that opens the tub drain, and the water begins to swirl away. But as I reach to turn off the tap, I notice a strange wispy substance sticking out of the bird's decapitated neck. Some of it even floats on the water's surface, like the willows that drifted on the shallows of the lake back in Wisconsin. I clamp my hand over my mouth as I spot a fragment of blue ribbon at the neck. It's Peter's hair, not all of it burned like I thought, but whatever he saved now jammed in the decapitated body, right where its head should be. I fall to my knees and try to gather any wet strands I can salvage with my fingers as they spiral down the drain. As I flail my hands through the water, the bathroom goes pitch-black and the door slams shut. The boy must have been hiding behind it, waiting until I got on my knees before flicking off the light switch. I'm left kneeling and groping in the darkness. Beyond the suck of the drain swallowing the last of the water, I hear a child's laughter and the sound of feet fading down the hall.

16.

At precisely 5:45 a.m., on the cusp of first light, when darkness still envelops the Nile Valley, the pool cleaner casts his net into the water. Like a gondolier, he's sublimely agile with his pole, fluid in his strokes as his net collects leaves, insects, and plastic debris. With a shake, he dispenses the refuse into a bag hooked to his belt. He performs this predawn chore at the same time every morning—in a sense he's the twilight counterpart to my sunset bell ringing. I've never been down to the pool this early to witness his unappreciated craft. Today I wait in the shadows of the trees for him to finish his task, unhook the bag from his belt, and carry it off to the dumpsters. When I'm certain he's gone, I slink to the pool's edge in my bathing suit, a blousy black one-piece with a frill at the waist, which I last wore in a jacuzzi in Sils Maria, Switzerland. I endure the shock of the chilly water and sink to a squat in the shallow cove under the low-hanging hibiscus branches. Here, in the dead hour between the shifts of bats and birds, I press my back against the side of the pool, hidden from the Olympic rectangle of teak loungers and mosaic tables. With my mouth under the surface and my nose taking in air, I wait.

My intention is not to kill him. That is what I tell myself: I'm not going to murder Otto. I simply want to scare him with the possibility of death, to shake his unearned sense of invincibility so drastically that, perhaps for the first time in his eight years of life, he truly feels the flimsiness of his mortality and understands the pecking order of the planet. I was here first. I want to take him to the border of death without crossing it. A scare, you might call it. An education.

Last evening, I did not run screaming from my room with my composure cracked, putting on a floor show of the crazy old woman in 309 for the guests returning from sunset on the terrace. Nor did I call down to Ahmed or alert housekeeping to the dead animal soaking in my bathtub along with my husband's last remains. No, instead I collected my wits and went to work, grabbing a laundry bag from the closet and donning the plastic gloves that come with my hair-dyeing kit. There was no salvaging Peter's hair; by the time I turned the light back on, the drain had taken all but five strands. I carefully collected those five last pieces of him, stained pink by the foul water, and returned them to the Ziploc. That left only the bird, which, even waterlogged, was surprisingly light. I could have thrown it into my trash can. But I didn't want Yasmine or her flock of maids to discover the mutilated creature. I skipped dinner at the bistro—I had no appetite. In the middle of the night, I carried the carcass in the laundry bag down in the elevator and tossed it in the dumpster.

My motivation for keeping quiet wasn't merely to show the boy that I wouldn't cower. I had other reasons. Ahmed would surely have added this incident to his growing list of calamities, and I can't risk attracting the attention of the management of Richesse Resorts. They need to stay in far-off Belgium, out of Egypt. Leave the Royal Karnak to us.

On my way upstairs from the dumpsters last night, I rooted through the lobby's lost-and-found bin and pilfered a pair of plastic swimming goggles. Crouching in the pool, I now slip them on, their lenses turning the first morning light a thunderstorm gray. When a groundskeeper appears to arrange the teak loungers, he doesn't notice me lurking in the shadowy water underneath the flowering hibiscus branch. Invisibly, I wait.

I must have dozed off, my head thrown back and resting on the pool's edge, because I awaken to a brighter morning, my body cold, my hands pruned, my neck aching. The sunlight is strong in the center of the pool, but that only amplifies the darkness of my alcove under the branch.

"Get in, I'm starting the stopwatch!" Zachary shouts with exhilaration from the giant rectangle of the pool. I can't see him from my hiding spot. He's modulated his voice into a coachlike baritone, as if he's committed to his new role as surrogate father. I don't allow myself to consider the guilt Zachary might feel were Otto to drown while his stopwatch counts the boy's last seconds. Soon I hear a cannonball splash, and after a moment of silence, Otto is asking about the starting line. "By the steps in the shallow end," Zachary says. "But you have to swim the entire perimeter, *including* the arms. No cheating, you hear me?"

Does my little boy cheat? He's so many awful things, but I hope he isn't a cheater.

"Ready?" Zachary asks.

"You don't want to race me?"

No, I pray. *No, Zachary, don't.* "No, I'm the trainer. You're trying out for the Olympic team. Ready for the countdown? No floating on your back to rest. Three. Two. One. Go!"

I freeze, mouth underwater, nose creating tiny ripples with each exhale. I hear Otto's messy stroke, like a handsaw cutting through a log. I picture the stopwatch on Zachary's phone, and I'm rooting for Otto to break all records, to get to me as quickly as possible. The length of the pool is agonizingly long, too much time to reconsider my plan. Finally, though, I hear him tearing closer through the water. He reaches the corner, where the pool bisects into its private coves. As his flailing arm flies into view, I lift my mouth above the surface, take an enormous breath, and go fully under. The rushing silence fills my ears, the liquid blue absorbing all sound, my pale feet dancing on the smooth floor as I squat down and wait. Suddenly there he is, soaring over me like a scrawny superhero, relaxing his speed just a notch because his coach can't see him. He is cheating a little bit, freestyle kicking in a straight line down the center to complete this section rather than swimming dutifully along its sides. But that only makes my job easier, keeping him in the deepest water. He touches the end of the pool right above my head, swivels his tiny body around, his legs nearly brushing against me as they rotate behind him. He struggles to reverse course. He's so close, I can make out the three-inch scar on his abdomen from his intestinal surgery as an infant. He's not wearing goggles, thank god, his little eyes as tightly closed in the chlorine. Otherwise he might find an old woman with streaming black hair smiling up at him from the deep.

He's faster than I expect, a silvery minnow already speeding toward the main stage where his coach waits. In a flash I propel myself up, my hand reaching out desperately, and I just manage to get my fingers around his left ankle. I squeeze tight. He senses the sudden restriction and lets his leg go slack as if it's merely caught on floating debris. But as he loosens his muscles, I give a hard yank, pulling him under by the leg, his whole body sinking before he has time to take a solid breath.

I just need to keep him far enough under that his arms and mouth can't breach the surface to make a sound. A jolt of panic brings his leg to life in my grip, and he begins kicking frantically to be released. I tighten my fingers on his slippery ankle, using all my hatred of him as the stimulus to hold on—Peter's white hair burned in an ashtray, the rest of it disappearing down the drain, the boy sleeping in a king-size bed that I pay for—and wrench him farther down into the water as I sink to the bottom.

His shoulders wheel around, his face red as precious bubbles escape from his mouth, his short brown hair standing on end. He's semi-blind without his glasses, but his wide, frightened eyes seem to take me in, and he tries to reach his hand to his ankle to pry my fingers loose. I grin widely, in case he sees me, and yank him harder, sending his little body straight as it arrows downward. Now he's bucking, every muscle in him rebelling, fighting with clawing limbs to reach the breathing world only a few inches above him. But I won't let go, not for a few more seconds, this moment so pure and satisfying that I want to extend it for as long as possible. His eight-year-old body is jerking into exhaustion, his arms and legs starting to lose their struggle, turning gluey in the water. I know I should let him go now. *Let go!* a voice in me cries. *Let him go so he can drink the air and live.* But I want another minute with him like this, holding onto him without any resistance from him, the two of us together in perfect unity and stillness. He's floating like a starfish, utterly untroubled. I begin to loosen my fingers around his ankle, and in a sudden jolt, his foot comes alive. It shoots toward me, the heel hammering into my left eye so violently I'm stunned into letting go of his leg. My vision fizzes with tiny red stars as I rise involuntarily to the surface, coughing and sucking in air. Otto is swimming for his life, with little gasps of oxygen between his strokes. Somewhere beyond the turn, Zachary shouts, "Otto, no resting! You lost a whole minute being lazy back there. You still have another arm to do!"

Why do I feel like a failure? I only wanted to scare him, to bring him close to death, and I succeeded in that goal. So why do I feel panic surging through me, dread and sickness tangling together as I struggle out of the pool, the skin on my hands almost peeling from being so pruned? I scamper into the shade of the trees and listen for any sound from the pool of Otto crying about what happened. I don't hear anything, not Zachary's coaching orders, not even the splashing of his swimming.

I'm wet and freezing, although it's already a boiler of a morning. I left a pile of towels behind the hibiscus tree, but the groundskeeper must have cleared it away. I need to get back to my room, as an alibi, as protection. I run as fast as I can around the fitness center. Pop music blares through its open windows, but no one seems to be working out inside. I hit the stretch of driveway used for deliveries. It's a long, open expanse of dirt, the sun beating directly down, with no shade to block it for a dozen yards. Fearing exposure, I return to the garden's shadowy trees, fighting through a cluster of bushes to reach the brick path. I duck under the branches of an olive tree, and as I do, my foot stirs up a cyclone of flies. Right below my foot, splayed on its side in the mulch bed, is the tiger-striped cat, sphinx of the garden, now a feeding ground for maggots. I gag at the sight of her, the orange fur matted with blood, teeth shattered in her mouth, her bludgeoned body left to rot in this neglected patch of the garden. I despise Otto all the more for carrying out this unnecessary execution. Poor beauty, punished for doing only what came naturally to her.

But I can't linger. I'm desperate to get to my room. I step over the dead animal and cross another hedge to reach a brick path leading to the hotel. An older couple passes, and I manage a sugary hello. Finally, there is nothing between me and the hotel's back door but twenty feet of unshaded brick. I wait until the coast is clear, and bolt across it. I make it six feet into the hot shine, when I hear my name being called behind me. "Maggie? Wait!"

I turn to find Zachary standing far down the path with his hands on his hips. "Have you seen Otto? He was in the pool, but then"—he laughs at the absurdity of the situation—"he just disappeared on me."

"Sorry, I don't know." I pivot around to continue my escape into the hotel. But, looking up, I spot Otto, his shivering, furious face in the stairwell's second-floor window. Glaring down at me, his eyes tighten, and I fear what he might be seeing. Then I glance down at my body and see it too. A green blotch on my chest, the size of a half-dollar, and another on my thigh that seems to be growing darker by the millisecond. For five years this hideous skin condition has been in remission, thanks to my vigilant avoidance of chronic aggravators. For five glorious years, blotch-free and nothing to worry about as long as I kept calm and stayed out of the sun. Gone until this very moment, as Otto stares down at me in the hard daylight, his eyes taking in the shame of an old woman in a bathing suit, dripping wet, black hair ratting down her checks, left eye swelling into a bruise, her body speckled with welt-colored blots.

The boy is the aggravator. He's the allergen that's poisoning the house. No more half steps. He must be gotten rid of.

17.

_____

For a long time, I only saw a monster. Tiny blood-black spots dappling my arms, putrid-green bruises dotting my stomach and breasts.

When did these symptoms first appear? Was it right after Peter died? Or did it wait until Julia passed? I truly don't know the answer. In that year of traumatic losses, I spent so much time inside my house, alone with the lights off and the curtains drawn, a prisoner to other people's shadows, I barely paid attention to my own body. My lungs went on breathing, that much I knew, and my heart continued to beat. But this affliction of my nerves and skin? Maybe it was due to losing Julia so soon after Peter. The erasure of your entire family can induce any number of unexpected side effects.

I probably didn't notice the first blotches. You bump your shin against a bed corner or knock your elbow on the refrigerator, and voilà, a bruise. You develop a chest rash from a discount laundry detergent. Your burlap skin decides to add a few showier age spots to its ample collection. After age seventy, you develop a businesslike relationship with your body, a chilly nod at the mirror in the morning will suffice. Thus, my condition could have been developing unchecked for some time.

First it was a series of purple marks running along my hips. I assumed it was a reaction to my heating pad, and sure enough, they soon faded. Then I noticed five bluish quarter-size spots along my rib cage. After that, blotches on my breasts appeared, such a vibrant green they looked biohazardous, like a comic-book humanoid post–nuclear meltdown. They disappeared, only for the purple marks on my inner thighs to return en masse. To stand naked at the mirror with the overhead lights on was to behold a torso speckled in the colors of violent injury. The blotches weren't painful. They came with no fever or cough. In fact, I felt as physically hearty as I always had, my appetite even coming back. But I looked like I had been beaten, attacked, thrown from a car, maybe even dropped from a plane. Dressed, I appeared the same old Maggie, the daughterless widow haunting the windows of her blue Tudor Revival, the one house on the block no longer decorated in Christmas lights. I'm not ashamed to admit that a part of me hoped these strange marks were the early warning signs of a terminal disease. Standing naked at the mirror, I often thought, *Yes, of course, it's my turn. How perfect. First my husband, then my daughter, now me.* I wanted to lie in bed and accept whatever death was coming. Instead, I made an appointment with my doctor.

Dr. Reiselman examined me from hairline to toenail with the care of a jeweler appraising a gemstone. "I see a few irregularities, one or two bruises, some minor blotching for sure. But that's to be expected at your age, and it's nothing to worry too much about. Otherwise your skin looks fine. That mole on your back could use a biopsy." I contested, argued, described the gruesome splotches that turned the color of sunsets and came and went like thunderstorms. It just so happened that my condition had improved on the day of the appointment.

Dr. Rieselman nodded like he was accustomed to the ranting hypochondria of the over-seventy set. He ran some blood work and referred me to a dermatologist who likewise found no reason for alarm. She said that fleeting skin flare-ups were routine among the elderly, with their thinning skin and weakened immune systems, but the lion's share of blame was reserved for the sun. "Take skin cancer seriously, Mrs. Burkhardt. The sun will aggravate *any* condition. At your age, it's best to picture the sun as an apex predator licking its lips right outside your door."

I returned home, where my affliction greeted me the next morning in the mirror, worse than ever, nearly covering my entire body. Maybe I was losing my mind. Or maybe it was just another ordinary humiliation that came with old age, and I was obsessing over it for lack of any other distraction now that everyone I loved was gone. After Peter and Julia died—his end as drawn-out as hers was violent and sudden—I didn't have many friends to whom I could turn. But it was just as well: no one to hide from; fewer excuses to make for the bizarre alterations in my behavior—avoiding the sun, wearing bulky clothing, hiding under an umbrella. In the end, it was easier not to leave the house at all. Klode Park loves to gossip, and I didn't want the news of Maggie Burkhardt's freakish condition to contaminate the memory of my loved ones. Mostly I lived with the lights off. I've found that the best way to hide a secret is to keep it from yourself.

Eventually I returned to Dr. Reiselman for one last shot at a cure. He asked me point-blank whether I was lonely, and I said of course, desperately so. "It might be that your depression and nerves are aggravating your skin problem." That's when he prescribed risperidone. He also recommended a vacation. "You've had a terrible year, Maggie, the kind that would smash anyone to pieces. Why not get away for a while and see if there's any change? Honestly, at this point, what have you got to lose?"

After a year alone in the Tudor Revival, I left. I flew to a continent where no one knew me and checked into gloomy palaces in the mountains, the Dolomites and Alps, where the rooms were built for shade and darkness and the shifting cloud cover muddied the sunlight. In these hotels I felt safe and at peace. Sometimes, out of pure greed for beauty, I would risk venturing to the grand hotels of southern Italy, but that boldness for strong sun was rare. Mostly I kept to the shadowy corners of Europe, and the pills began to work their magic. Slowly I was freed of my affliction. The splotches disappeared, until there I was, just another elderly American, utterly fine, as normal as could be. Naturally, I worried about a relapse. But thanks to my prescription, and the distraction of my fellow guests, I found I could leave those fears behind. Still, never did I dream I'd end up in a desert in Egypt, a land sculpted entirely out of sun. But we live in astonishing times.

To my own surprise, I love it here in Luxor. A home. A family. A fortress of protection. A few cherished friends. No outward indication that anything is wrong with me. At least not until the boy arrived. Here's a warning to keep in mind for your own future disasters. You can only withstand losing everything in your life once. There can be no second time.

18.

"Maggie, your eye!" Ahmed is dressed in his usual navy suit, although today's fabric is of a finer material, not prone to a synthetic sheen in the last of the lobby's sunlight. He's staring at my eye with a grimace, as if it hurts simply to look at it. The bruise rose quickly after Otto's heel clobbered me in the pool, the skin a phosphorescent purple and green, with a corona of yellow skirting the socket. But at least this bruise has an unambiguous source. After returning to my room and peeling off my swimsuit, it was the marks on my chest and thigh that stole my attention. Blessedly, there weren't any others. My breasts and stomach looked perfectly normal. In fact, out of the sunlight, the two blotches were far less noticeable. *These will not spread*, I promised myself. *A minor flare-up from too much sun, that's all.* I swallowed down a second risperidone, the last of my supply, and called the pharmacy, begging for my refill order to be rushed. I tried covering the eye bruise with concealer, but the lid was still too swollen, and the makeup only called attention to the injury. Best to cover it with an excuse.

"Oh, it's no big deal, Ahmed. I just tripped over my desk chair and knocked it against the doorknob. I promise, it looks a lot worse than it is."

He frowns as he concentrates on it, ignoring the rest of my face. "Maybe you don't feel up for coming to dinner tonight?"

"Don't be silly, I'm fine!" I do an impression of a hale midwesterner, huffing at the notion that a black eye would stop me from a dinner party. Although perhaps Ahmed doesn't want to bring a beaten old woman to his home to celebrate Ramadan with his wife and kids. He might be horrified if he got a peek at the rest of my body. Or maybe he'd be sympathetic, put his arms around me, understand. "Unless you'd rather I . . ."

"No! You are our special guest. My wife is excited to welcome you." He examines his watch. "And she expects us soon. If you're ready . . . ?" I brandish my umbrella to confirm that I am. In a half hour, Otto will ring the bell and gather the guests for sunset. We won't be here, and I'm grateful for the excuse to be absent. I don't want to see the boy, nor do I want to cower in my room, dreading the revenge he has in store for me.

I start heading toward the front door, but Ahmed signals for me to follow him down the hall to a set of side doors whose signage promises—falsely—that emergency alarms will sound upon opening. Down a side staircase and we're outside, crossing the mud driveway behind the fitness center, my umbrella carefully tilted westerly above me. I think of the bludgeoned cat in the hedges and wonder when the gardeners will discover it. It would be wise to implicate Otto in its death, to commit his atrocities to record, and I'm still formulating the right words when Ahmed smiles over at me with his eyebrows lifted.

"I usually take the bus home," he explains, "but since you are a hotel guest, we have the pleasure of using the company car tonight!" This extravagance seems to buoy his spirits, and it feels wrong to the specialness of the evening to mention the slaughtered cat. Ahmed whistles for a few steps as he leads me up the driveway past the pool and the ficus grove. "In better times, I'd have taken the afternoon off to get the car washed, but we are too understaffed as it is."

"Oh, I don't mind a little dirt. You should think of me as family," I say buoyantly. "Speaking of family, Ahmed, I'm thrilled Otto could fill in tonight for sunset, even if he's a little off-putting with all his shouting and childish jokes. I think I should resume my duties tomorrow so that guests know it's a venerated tradition. I mean, let's face it, the Seebers might leave us any day."

Ahmed offers me an enigmatic smile and points our way down the dirt drive. I've never been this far back in the garden, in the remote hinterlands reserved for maintenance. Beyond a stack of plastic trash cans, two wheelbarrows of moldy brick and a pile of mulch bags looms the vague shape of a car, covered by a giant bolt of striped fabric. Ahmed grabs a corner of the fabric and pulls it back, sending up a cloud of dust and leaves, peeling off the soft epidermis to reveal the black shell of an old-model Peugeot. A few spots of rust bullet the doors, and one of the back tires looks semi-deflated. But Ahmed gives me a proud wink before squatting by the front fender. He reaches under the chassis and removes a tiny magnetic box hidden there, flips the lid open, and shakes out the car key.

"Aren't you worried someone will steal it?" I ask.

He laughs at the idea of theft as he jogs to unlock the passenger door. "Steal it? We are very safe inside these gates. Don't tell me you worry about crime at our hotel?"

After I climb in, he gallantly shuts my door and hurries around to the driver's side. I wait until he settles in behind the wheel to respond.

"I feel perfectly safe at the Royal Karnak. As safe as I did in Milwaukee. Although didn't you mention that Yasmine lost her master key?" I've decided it's in my best interest for Ahmed to deactivate the housekeeping cards. Whatever I gain by having access to the rooms pales beside the fact that Otto has free entrée into mine—especially after our morning pool time together. "I guess I do feel a little unsafe, knowing her card is floating around somewhere."

Ahmed revs the engine, wrestles with the stick shift, and steers around the wheelbarrows to take us down the drive. We leave the gated hotel grounds, turning into stewing late-afternoon traffic, the rows of dirty windshields glowing purple, the red brake lights beginning to flare in the falling light.

"Do not worry, Maggie. I took care of it this afternoon. I reset and distributed brand-new cards to housekeeping. At least I managed to put out one fire today." Ahmed seems to be alluding to his morning Zoom meeting with the Richesse Resorts bosses in Belgium. I stare out the window, waiting as patiently as I can for him to volunteer the details of the call—I don't want him sensing how important it is to me. We pass green fields of budding okra and wheat, followed by asphalt lots on which entire living- and dining-room furniture sets sit out for sale, rightly unafraid of rain. Military checkpoints dot the borders of each village we enter, the shoulders of machine guns used as headrests by soldiers dozing on patrol. We drive south for twenty minutes, the sun now so low on the western horizon that I swing my visor against the side window to block its rays from my eyes. Soon we are speeding through miles and miles of farmland. I hadn't realized Ahmed lived so far from the hotel.

"How in heavens will I get back tonight?" I ask him. "Is there a taxi I can—"

"I will drive you. I have to return the car to the hotel. I am not allowed to keep it out all night. Then I will go home again by bus."

No amount of arguing convinces Ahmed to forgo this inconvenience, and I find myself begging to sleep on his family's sofa so that we can take the car back in the morning together. He laughs and changes the subject, listing the dishes that his wife is preparing for tonight's feast. He tells me the names of his two sons: Ahmed and Hussein, ages six and four. "My family is very excited to meet you! What an honor to have you in our home. You know"—he blushes—"I have never opened my house to a hotel guest before."

I smile, slightly in love with this man. "Before we arrive, Ahmed, I do want to ask, how did your conversation go today with your new bosses? I hope you convinced them what an amazing job you're doing, and that the last thing we need is outside interference."

Watching his expression fall is like watching a tire blow out, the buoyant roundness turning to limp rubber.

"Oh, Maggie, it is not good," he says. "They are sending someone from Brussels down to spy on us. 'Just to ensure proper procedure,'"— he mimics in an unconvincing Anglo-French accent. "But I know they are looking for a reason to replace me."

Before I can respond, before I can even ask the name of the person from the corporate office in Belgium who is coming to eavesdrop on us, Ahmed rotates the wheel and turns into a cinder-block driveway lined with a thicket of overgrown cane. Two little boys run like comets toward the car.

19.

The next morning, I only want peace.

I wake in my hotel bed with such an overwhelming desire for a truce, I nearly break into tears. Ahmed's spartan dining room, its walls a war of floral wallpaper patterns, held us in a tight embrace through the holiday dinner, with the two children sharing one side of the table to make room for me across from them. Ahmed's wife was shyly welcoming. She looked a few years older than her husband, fine lines cobwebbed around her mouth, and I could see the silver of her hair peeking from beneath her headscarf whenever she bent her head to eat. She'd prepared a feast of date jellies, spiced bean dishes, and a thick yellow soup whose ingredients flustered me with each spoonful—*Is that lentil? or cheese?* Her name is Bahiti, and while she didn't speak much English, she gave the impression of listening intently, nodding to every anecdote and raising her fine eyebrows when Ahmed and I drew our rosy portrait of hotel life. "I suppose I'm the wife of his *other* family!" I joked to Bahiti. "The thankless matriarch of the Royal Karnak!"

It was the two boys, though, who proved the evening's primary delight, dressed in matching beige suits that reminded me of sailor uniforms. They were fascinated by my lightning-quick English and wrinkled white skin, and they were too well-mannered to stare at my black eye. They sat through dinner utterly still from the waist up, while their legs fidgeted hyperactively below the table. The eldest kept swearing he was *starfing*—he loved to use this new English word. Their brown eyes, fringed with thick black lashes, were so much kinder than Otto's miscolored set, and every time the thought of that evil boy popped into my head, the circuits in my brain misfired, and I'd forget where

I was in the story I'd been telling. At one point I had been relaying a funny remembrance of Julia, but couldn't recall what. The family stopped chewing on their bread and waited in silence for me to continue. My hatred of Otto was so strong, it wiped every other detail out of my mind. I reminded myself that Otto was only two years older than sweet Ahmed smiling across from me, a boy so adored he'd been given his father's name. Meanwhile, Otto's father didn't even want to see his son. I thought of Julia at age six, at eight, and I tried to picture her face across the table from me at our own holiday dinners. I could recall her smell of strawberry soap and her tuneless whining about eating so late, even though she was insufferably picky about what she'd put in her mouth. And as I sat there, amid the warm cheer of Ahmed's dining room, I was struck with horror by the fact that I couldn't recall the color of my daughter's eyes. They were grayish blue. I could name the color, but what they had looked like, the precise shade of them, I couldn't summon.

"Maggie, more *ful*?" Ahmed asked, holding a plate of mashed magenta beans.

I climb out of bed. Do my stretches, and take my pills, minus my now-depleted risperidone, which I pray arrives from the pharmacy today. I shouldn't have greedily swallowed down a second dose after the pool yesterday, but when I undress at the mirror, I'm relieved to find that the blotches on my chest and thigh are all but gone. Almost invisible in the bathroom light. Just as the dermatologist predicted, it was the result of too much sun. I turn on the shower and think of Peter.

No more fighting. The evening with Ahmed's family reminded me that peace is always the preferred answer. Act dignified. Be the less petty person. Forgive, forget, start over. Last night, after Ahmed drove me back to the hotel in the dark, I helped him cover the car with the thick fabric. Like a mother and father tucking in a worn-out child, we each grabbed an end and spread it over the old Peugeot. When we were finished, he returned the key to its hiding place and offered me a handshake to say good night. Instead, I hugged him. I wrapped my arms around his shoulders and held him tight. "I had such a wonderful time," I said. Ahmed slowly slipped from my embrace, explaining he had an hour-long bus ride home ahead of him. "Why don't you stay here?" I suggested. "It's nearly eleven, and you'll have to wake up so early just to come right back. Why not sleep in one of the vacant rooms? Or, if that's not allowed, my sofa is available. Or, heck, I have a queen bed, and I don't snore!" The quiet of the night pressed between us, and I worried my invitation had been misconstrued. Ahmed whispered in resignation, "No, Maggie. I must go back to my wife and sons."

It's 6:40 a.m. I wonder whether Zachary is continuing with the swim lessons, if the boy is avoiding the pool because of the incident yesterday morning between us. No, I refuse to obsess over Otto's movements. After dressing, I descend the staircase to the lobby, where Ahmed's gelled head bobs at the reception desk. I pause, but he's on the phone and merely waves to me. The wave is friendly enough, accompanied by an exasperated smile, but he doesn't drop everything to step from the desk, look at his watch, and tell me I'm late coming down to breakfast. I sense a slight distance in him. I worry he regrets inviting me over last night and introducing me to his wife and children. Moments of extreme intimacy can often result in the drawing of colder boundaries. When I try to sustain eye contact with him, he quickly shifts his eyes back to the desk.

I won't hassle Ahmed this morning. Surely the poor man is exhausted from a night of three commutes to and from home—four if you count his bus ride to the hotel this morning. I amble down the hall, past the glass case of ceremonial swords and the herringbone ballroom that should be packed with Belarusian doctors discussing bone density. As I near the breakfast room, I hear Ahmed calling, "Maggie!" and all my worry evaporates. He hasn't forgotten me. He wants to thank me for coming for dinner and share greetings from his family. I turn with a relieved smile to watch him sprint down the carpet with the pharmacist's bag in his grip. "They dropped it off last night when we were out," he says curtly, and waits only for me to grab it before he hurries back to the desk. No salutations from Bahiti or the boys. No mention of our warm hug in the garden. I unfold the bag to make sure they've sent the risperidone, now in the form of a blue liquid capsule. I can take one at breakfast. I'll need all the sanity I can muster to forge a ceasefire with Otto. The Royal Karnak is my home, not his, but I can share it for a little while.

As I enter the breakfast room, I hear the shrill yap of a lapdog. The Yorkie belongs to a middle-aged Indian man who sits alone at the table next to mine. I try not to be irked by this new arrival who has beaten me down to breakfast, apparently an even earlier riser than I am. The terrier jumping around its owner's ostrich-leather shoes is tied to a chair leg by a long pink leash. I overdramatize a pained expression as it yaps, but the man doesn't bother to apologize. He simply leaves his chair and wanders over to the buffet to inspect the selection of cold cuts.

A plate of Hamza's green butter cookies is already waiting for me at my table, marking it off from any interlopers. The chef's thoughtfulness, going out of his way to make me feel at home during his busy morning, lifts my spirits. Typically, I don't indulge in the cookies until after breakfast, but I want to show Hamza my appreciation. As I break one of the cookies in half, I feel the softness in the center from where the batter hasn't fully baked. Oh, Hamza, you rushed your recipe this morning. Still, it has a crisp snap that attracts the Yorkie's attention. It drags the chair with it as it scurries to my table and paws at my calf for a bite. When it yaps, I give another dramatic flinch out of principle, even though the owner is preoccupied at the buffet. There used to be a strict policy against pets at the Royal Karnak, but like so many other restrictions, the rule has been relaxed during the pandemic; the hotel will accept anyone with a credit card and no symptoms of a cough or fever.

"No barking," I tell the yapping dog.

I lift the butter cookie to my lips, and a bitter odor catches in my nostrils. The cookie's underbaked soft spot has also left a sticky residue on my fingertips. I study the cookie, its pistachio-green hue and lunar dough, and bring it to my nose to take a cautious sniff. The acrid chemical reek doesn't seem altogether foreign. It takes me a second to recognize the smell of the disinfectant that Seif used to clean out the aviary. It can't be that. The Yorkie paws at my leg, yapping for the morsel. Checking that its owner is still preoccupied, I lower a piece below the table, just to be safe, and let the dog hoover it up. I know I'm being paranoid. I'm not listening to my own promise of an armistice. From this morning onward, peace will reign at the Royal Karnak Palace, a rapprochement to the days of escalating violence.

I wait for Hamza to emerge from the kitchen, carrying a silver terrine of cooked mushrooms. More guests have funneled in for breakfast. Two young couples are arguing about the latest round of restrictions in their home country, vitriolic about the policy of remote schooling, with one woman—German, from the accent—complaining that the entire pandemic has been mishandled, prioritizing the elderly while robbing critical years from the young. "What's a year or two more of adult diapers anyway, to someone in their eighties? These children are going to be impacted for the rest of their lives!" When she catches me watching her from across the room, she stares mutely at her eggs.

As Hamza circles the buffet, I jump from my seat to wave him down.

"The cookies! So kind of you, my dear. Thank you for my surprise at the table this morning!" I desperately want my version of events to be verified. Peace depends on it. Hamza rumples his forehead.

"The cookies?" he wheezes. "I have not forgotten you, Maggie! But I have not yet brought my treats out for you today."

I glance back at my neighbor's table. Below it, hidden behind its master's feet, the Yorkie is convulsing, foam bubbling from its tiny mouth. I don't wait for the owner to make the gruesome discovery. I take the remaining cookies from my table and dump them in the garbage before retreating down the hall.

Tit for tat. Attempted murder for attempted murder. Although I only meant to scare the boy, to bring him just short of the threshold, he was willing to carry me across it. It's clear a more definitive action will be required to dislodge Otto from my house.

20.

At 1:30 every weekday afternoon, the hotel workers congregate for a fifteen-minute staff meeting in the "business center." The small windowless basement room was once an annex of the hotel's wine cellar, and now, befitting its modified purpose, is furnished with retina-frying fluorescent lights, a cluster of linoleum tables, a printer, a fax machine, two antique desktop computers, and a nest of outdated chargers. The room reminds me of the sad basement meeting rooms full of anonymous strangers to which I routinely dragged Julia in her early thirties when her drinking became too unmanageable. At this hour the heat of the day is at its most oppressive, creating a lull between checkouts and check-ins, and the front desk is temporarily manned by the head bellhop, Karim, one of the few Copts working at the Royal Karnak. If you try to speak to Karim too quickly in English, he stares at you with the serene gaze of total incomprehension. Karim is lovely. Whenever we pass each other in the hallway, he greets me with an extended *Hiiii, Mees Bur-har.* As I approach the reception desk, I know I can use his bumbling, good-natured confusion to my advantage.

"Karim, hello, no problem, Ahmed wants me to have a look, okay, Karim? I need numbers, just to see for a minute, bubbles, chewing gum, antelope, for my room upstairs, Karim, tapioca, apocalypse, okay!" The English gibberish lulls Karim into a bout of polite nodding, knowing his job is to keep guests happy, and I quickly swivel the red-leather concierge log around on the marble. I have my pen and pad of pink hotel stationery at the ready. It only requires flipping the pages with a gleeful giggle to convince Karim that this elderly guest is enjoying herself, and then to copy down the eleven digits that comprise Alain Seeber's French cell-phone number. I close the log and spin it back around, returning it to Karim's elbow. "*Shukran.* Have a wonderful day!"

My plan isn't without its flaws. If I were more technologically savvy—as I'm sure Otto and his whole generation of future AI bride-grooms are—I might wait until the business center is empty and use one of the computers to create an anonymous email account. But I don't have time for such methods. I want the boy and his mother out of the hotel before the representative from Richesse Resorts arrives. It is imperative to restore our happy, peace-loving kingdom, free of any red flags, by the time HQ sends its scout on a welfare check. Instead of an untraceable email account, I will simply use my cell phone. Alain won't recognize the American number, and the content will overshadow the question of its sender. I used this tactic to dazzling effect two years ago in a hotel overlooking Lake Maggiore; it saved a life, cured a woman of her unhappy marriage, and no one ever bothered to ask whose phone number planted that fly in her ear.

I return to my room to find that Yasmine's battalion has already vacuumed and made my bed. They may occasionally forget to restock the soap, but they're experts at small, life-affirming touches: they've left fresh fruit in a bowl on the table and two chocolate squares on my bed pillow. I collect all the food and dump it into the trash can. None of it can be presumed safe until Otto is on a plane back to Paris.

There are moments I've felt scared for my own safety around him, and then he'll be perfectly loving and sweet the next moment . . . Alain is a jealous, hot-tempered Frenchman. In his more remorseful moments, he phones the hotel to check on his wife and son. I am banking on rousing the first Alain, the meaner one, the Alain who Tess felt desperate to escape. If I can ruin a marriage with a single text message like I did on Lake Maggiore, perhaps I can salvage one the same way. What will prompt Alain to jump on a plane to Luxor to collect his wife and child?

I'm not the most talented cell-phone photographer. I once owned a Pentax 35 millimeter that I was good at working, and Peter loved to use his camcorder, especially on Christmas, its cumbersome attachable spotlight so blinding that Julia often looked like she'd been pulled from bed in her nightgown and was being interrogated by the Gestapo while opening her presents. I don't know what became of all those VHS tapes that I once labeled by holiday and year. Honestly, even if I had them now, I couldn't bear to watch the grainy, color-saturated documentation of a world that no longer exists. If the dead came to life again, even for a second on a screen, I would die of heartbreak.

The photos I snapped from behind the ficus bushes are blurry. Zachary's biceps get lost in the splash of the pool water. But his sculpted back and bleached lifeguard teeth make for a convincing composite of a hunky suitor holding a wiggling Tess in his arms. In the next shot, I managed to get Otto in the frame, his ugly mouth open in a frozen laugh as his mother slinks her arms around Zachary's neck, their fit, nearly naked bodies pressed in an adulterous embrace. I wish I could put my fingers inside Otto's mouth, curling them around his lips, and open it wide until his throat becomes a giant pit so I could reach into him, up to my elbow, and take hold of his beating heart.

Now how do you create a new text message? Ah, yes, here we go. I type in Alain's phone number, attach the three most salacious photos of Tess, Otto, and Zachary, and add a short anonymous note: *They don't need you. Stop calling. Look how much fun they're having. God, does he know how to fuck.* Send.

On Lake Maggiore, I set a young couple free. Here in Luxor, I will bind a couple back together, condemn them to each other, strap them to the handcuffs of a little boy. *Delivered*, my phone reads with a satisfying blue check mark. I think of Alain on set, actors in period costumes ruffling around him, long hallways full of mirrors where the nobility get corralled and beheaded. As his phone vibrates in his pocket with an incoming message, he lifts his eye from the viewfinder of a camera. The message has reached him. A blue check mark.

The poisoned cookies that Otto left at breakfast make me worried for my safety in the hotel. Now my life is at stake. At four o'clock, I open the door and listen to a vacuum running at the opposite end of the hall. There is no other sound, and no sign of the boy, although he's far too smart to show himself so easily. He's more inclined to be hiding, lying in wait. I creep down the hallway, my sandals cushioning my footsteps. At the stairwell, as a safety precaution, I hook my ankle around the railing's wrought-iron bar before daring to peek over the edge—I imagine an ambush, an attack from behind, a sudden push that sends me tumbling to my death, my hands trying to grab the Murano chandelier as I fly past it before splattering on the marble. But no shove sends me sailing, only a gust of stale air breathing up the stairwell. Unhooking my foot, I slowly descend, my back firmly sweeping along the wall to keep away from the drop. A figure looms amid the second-floor shadows, but it's merely a short-stay vacationer reading a brochure on boat departures. He smiles at me, and croons something in what sounds like Czechoslovakian. "Very much," I agree and continue down the steps.

From the lobby, I pass along the main hall, into the side corridor that leads to the bathrooms and kitchen. Here the walls are covered in vintage posters for Cook's Nile Steamer Tours and art-deco advertisements for Egyptian cigarettes. Hamza keeps his kitchen spotless, the afternoon light bleeding over stainless steel prep tables and racks of iron pans. I try a few utensil drawers before I locate the knives. I have confidence that Alain will do the right thing, and in a wild fit of jealousy race down here to reclaim his wife and son. But in the meantime Otto might redouble his efforts with an even more brazen act of revenge. Nothing too large or unwieldly. The cleavers are out of the question, as are most of the carving knives, egregiously long-handled, with curved blades that make concealment impossible. Finally I choose a butcher knife with a seven-inch blade, just small enough to tuck into the front pocket of my kaftan. My intention is not to stab Otto to death (despite such a lovely daydream). No, I need the weapon for protection, in case the boy doesn't stop at poison.

I test out the knife's grip, holding it first like a mugger, palm-side up, blade tilted outward, then like a serial killer, handle smothered in my fist, blade pointing down. If Peter could see me, he would howl in laughter. *Don't laugh, Peter! This is happening, the world has lost its mind. It's not like the old days, where we could count on our home alarm system or the Klode Park police. I'm all alone with a monster, and I need to protect myself!*

Madness too is a kind of protection, a suit of armor to ward off calls for reason and proportion, and so too is talking to a dead husband. I slip the knife into my kaftan pocket, happy with my selection, and slink down the corridor to the outer hall.

"Mags?" I glance up to find Ben, wearing a hunter-green shirt and matching linen pants too loose for his spindly legs. The outfit is very veteran-Egyptologist. Despite this adventurer's costume, exhaustion radiates from him, his eyes bleary and his jaw slack. As he walks toward me, he notices my black eye.

"Doorknob," I say before he can ask. "Blame my feet for not paying attention around my desk chair." I'm fascinated by the alarmed reactions to the bruise, and I wonder how everyone would respond to a body covered in blotches if my condition kicks into full gear again. Ben nods at the credibility of my excuse.

"You look as beaten-up as I feel," he says with a weary smile. "You know what's funny? I keep getting emails from friends and colleagues back home, whining about this gift of boredom that the pandemic has given them, locked in their homes learning how to churn butter or spending their afternoons binge-watching reality shows. Some of these people are quite literally the most educated people on the planet. All of them griping about taking two naps a day because they don't know what to do with themselves. And here I am, working nonstop!"

"Zachary mentioned that you've been playing tour guide to some visiting colleagues?"

"Colleagues!" Ben huffs. "Does Zachary ever listen to a complete sentence? These 'colleagues' are the gatekeepers of my grant, which means it's their money that funds my research here. Thus, for the past two days I've been serving as full-time ancient Thebes scholar, as well as restaurant critic and papyrus-shop barterer." He taps his forefinger to his temple. "Wisely, I told them that the Royal Karnak is a dump, so they booked themselves into that new mega-hotel across town."

"Good thinking," I say with a laugh, "although don't tell Ahmed you drove away business. Are you finally free of them?"

"Only for the afternoon. Thank Ra for their desire to take a hot-air-balloon ride over the tombs. They'll be out of reach high in the Saharan sky for at least five hours. I told them I had an unshakable fear of heights." Ben gives a snort of self-satisfaction. "Sorry I missed you at lunch the past two days. I didn't figure my husband would notice, but I thought you might."

"I'm afraid I haven't been down to the pool for lunch either."

Ben crosses his arms. "Is it because of the new companion my husband is courting? Let me guess, you can't stand the boy either. *Otto.*" Ben groans out the name as if it were a roller coaster that's supposed to be fun but induces vomiting. I'm pleased by his open disdain for Otto, although I'm careful to couch my own hatred.

"No, no, it's not because of Otto. The boy seems like a perfectly nice—"

"Oh, cut the crap, Mags," Ben says. "We both can recognize an unbearable brat when we see one. Look, I'm married to an unbearable brat!"

"Zachary seems like a perfectly nice . . . ," I tease.

"Don't ask me why Zee has this sudden craving to play surrogate father. This from a man who was more heartbroken to learn that dogs could catch Covid than babies. I mean, he always said he wanted to be a father, but *abstractly*, like wanting a million dollars or universal health care or to sleep with an Armani model. But lo and behold, yesterday afternoon, I come back to the hotel to change my clothes, completely exhausted, and sitting on the floor in our suite is that boy, sifting through my archaeology research with Zee. Mind you, I'd just spent the past seven hours singing about the wonders of *Tu-tankh-a-moon*"— Ben pronounces the pharaoh's name with the exaggerated syllables of a professional—"because, let's face it, Tut's the only pharaoh anyone wants to hear about, with occasional unprompted questions about Cleopatra's sex life, although thankfully that woman is not under my purview. Anyway, Zee glances up from the floor and volunteers me. 'Here he is, Otto! Ben can tell us all about the treasures you visited on your trip to the King's Valley with your mom and Maggie! He'd love to go over each and every wall symbol with you personally.' I swear, I could have shot Zachary."

"There is an irritating lack of loaded firearms on hand in this country."

"That's when I see my precious gold Set figurine in the boy's hand. He'd grabbed it off the mantel and was marching it around like a Star Wars action figure. He asked me"—Ben claps his hands together, appreciating this particular morsel of indignation—"the little punk has the nerve to ask me, 'Can I have this?' It's worth a thousand Ottos, but he actually expects me to say, 'Yes, of course, put that right in your pocket! By all means, take it!' Zachary was grinning like it was adorable. I snatched it out of the kid's hand and returned it to the mantel. '*Ne pas toucher!* Don't even think about touching it! *Tu comprends?*' "

"Again, there is an irritating lack of loaded firearms on hand in this country."

"I told Zee later, nope. My supper-singing stops with the Austrians. I'm not razzle-dazzling some nightmare eight-year-old on the wonders of ancient Egypt."

"You know, Ben, your husband is right. If you hate children so much, you really picked the wrong profession."

"I know," he groans. "Sometimes I dream of being an expert on fourteenth-century Prussian enamels. The glorious freedom of a public's complete disinterest in, nay, resentment of, your little niche of expertise . . ." But even an exhausted Ben can't keep up the cruel sarcasm for long. His face softens, and he rubs his tongue over his dehydrated lips. "God, I'm awful. I should be more understanding. Zee gets the chance to play father for once, and, let's face it, the kid's clearly troubled . . ."

I'm heartened that at least Ben sees Otto for the terror he is. The boy has hoodwinked everyone else but the two of us. "Troubled how?" I ask.

Ben tilts his head. "When I came back from my hosting duties last night, Zachary was having a drink with Tess at the bar. I think he'd worn her down on gin. She was on a little tear about Otto being kicked out of school in Paris. That was back in the normal times, when there were still schools with in-person classes to get kicked out of. Honestly, can you even be a truant when school is a Zoom call? Anyway, I got the feeling Otto did something bad at the school. And then Tess admitted that full-time quarantine home life with the boy's father was a disaster."

Ben smirks. "Covid has really been a redemption for the barren, don't you think? Finally we reap the rewards of our refusal to procreate. What family locked in a house together for months on end doesn't end in disaster?" Ben suddenly realizes who his audience is and winces in apology. "Sorry, Mags. That was too harsh of me. I know how important your family was to you."

"I miss them so much. But don't worry, not even Peter and I would have enjoyed being locked inside our home twenty-four hours a day with our Julia." It's a lie. What I wouldn't give for that prison sentence. I'm so envious of families forced to spend a year together under one roof without interruption or any chance of escape. Would we have been safer—the three of us—if we'd never left each other's sight? What if Covid had crashed down around us years ago, when I still had a family? Would it all have ended differently?

Ben tries to stifle a yawn. "I should take advantage of Zee's absence and grab a nap. He took Otto and Tess to the market for the afternoon. The kid wanted to buy his grandmother in California a souvenir."

"Oh yeah, the famous grandmother, his only friend." I roll my eyes. "I'm sure the three of them will be mistaken for a family of gullible idiots and be harassed to no end." I'm teasing, but Ben eyes me oddly, having clearly lost his thirst for vindictiveness. Maybe it was the mention of my dead family.

"Oh, Maggie," he says reproachfully. "Let's hope only for good things going forward. There's been enough of the bad." He pats my shoulder and disappears up the steps for his nap.

I wait in the hall for a few minutes, drifting around in the dust and Lysol fumes, enjoying the peace of the hotel like it was before Otto arrived to ruin it. I glance down at the knife handle poking from my kaftan pocket, and for a second, I have no idea what it's doing there. Do I really need to carry a butcher knife around with me? Is that what my life has come to? I, who once helped organize benefits to stop street violence and who volunteered at the children's hospital in Milwaukee? I consider returning the knife to the kitchen, but I remember the Yorkie seizuring in the breakfast room. Did the dog survive? I didn't wait around to find out, and I've heard nothing about the incident. Like the bludgeoning of the cat, there's been no word circulating about any of the recent disturbing occurrences. Perhaps, because of the impending visit of Richesse Resorts, Ahmed and his staff have learned to keep news of calamities away from the guests.

I take the elevator to the third floor to give my ankles a rest. As I reach my room, the landline phone is ringing on the bedside table. I hurry over to answer it and am relieved to hear Ahmed's voice. A part of me hopes for an apology, or at least an acknowledgment of his chilliness to me this morning.

"Maggie," he says with hesitation. "There was a call for you from an outside line. But they just hung up."

"Well, it's nice to hear from you," I reply. "I had such a delightful time last night." I'm desperate for him to confirm that I'm still his favorite guest. "Please thank Bahiti again for dinner. I can't get over how delicious everything was! Those sauces . . ."

"Yes, I will tell her." His voice is rigid. I worry he harbors the wrong impression about my invitation to sleep in my room.

"And thanks for the medication today. You keep my head screwed on, Ahmed! I'd never remember unless—"

"Ahhh! Here is the call coming through again. Hold on, Maggie." I'm put on hold, subject to a crackly arrangement of Brahms strings. My cell phone vibrates on the bed. With the room phone to my ear, I pick up my cell and find a text from Alain at his +33 number.

Who is this??? he writes. I wonder whether he means me or the man in the photo holding his wife.

Ahmed returns to the line. "Your caller is back. It is a child, I think. I'll put it through. She says her name is Julia?"

All I feel in that second is the blood pumping through my temples. I press the phone to my ear, as if straining to hear a conversation through a thick wall. Julia is no longer a child. My daughter is dead.

I hear the click of the call being connected. Static-filled silence.

"Who is this?" I demand. "Who are you?"

There's a long exhale on the other end. Then the line goes dead.

21.

For an hour, I hear nothing further. I ring Ahmed at the reception desk and ask him, as calmly as I can, where the phone call originated. "Outside the hotel," he says. "Maybe from Luxor?" In the background, a nagging guest is demanding information on water transport. "Although I suppose it could have been international. The number didn't come up on the screen. Is everything okay?" There's a tremor of kindness in his voice, but I'm no longer in any mood to receive it.

"Yes. Headache, that's all." Does Ahmed know my daughter's name? He knows I had a daughter, but did I ever mention her by name? Did I let that detail slip in the early days of our friendship? Or did I mention it last night at dinner with his family? Three Percocets. That's all the sleeping pills I have left, because I haven't needed to refill that prescription. How short-sighted of me to neglect the one medication that promises blackout sleep. The pills expired four years ago, jangling in a slender lozenge-orange tube warning of overdoses. I swallow two down, close my shades to the late-afternoon light, and lie in bed sobbing into the pillow.

The phone rings to life, the volume amplified by the room's darkness. The display reads *Fitness Center*. This time it's not an outside call coming through the reception desk. It's the phone I used to dial Shelley a few days ago.

"Hello," I answer.

A pant of quiet, then the caller hangs up.

It rings five minutes later. *Pool Grill*. In my state, I misread it as "Poor Girl." I answer. Another hang-up.

Three minutes. *Lobby 2*. "Hello!" I yell into the receiver. A voice whispers, but I can't hear what it's saying. Babbling words, like water boiling in a pot, and then *click*.

Six minutes. *Staff kitchen*. Three minutes. *Housekeeping 2*. Eight minutes. *Bar*. There is the sound of a voice speaking, but never clear words, like echoes driving up a deep well. Finally, seven minutes later, I pick up the ringing phone and shout at the top of my lungs, "Stop!"

A pause. "Mommy, it's Julia." A child's voice, the sweet minor key on the far right side of a piano that no adult could mimic. I know it isn't my daughter, and yet to touch the illusion, to put my arms around a phantom, would mean so much to me, would be enough.

"Julia?" I beg to propel the illusion onward. Give it bone. Skin. Life. Let this lie go on forever. "Oh, honey. I miss you."

"Where am I? Why didn't you protect me? Why did you let this happen?"

Those accusations crack the dream. I refuse to answer such insidious questions. I scream into the receiver, "How do you know my daughter's name?"

The voice answers, no longer in the tone of a little girl, screaming: "Sunset!"

The connection goes dead. Only silence fills my ears, the ghosts of the hotel all mute, and my eyes fall upon my own blackened reflection in the room's flat-screen. Then faintly, as softly as a moth moving through the folds of a curtain, I hear the clang of the bell from three floors down. Otto is ringing it in the lobby to call everyone together for the day's end. It's his bell now.

Slowly the ringing grows louder as he climbs the staircase. He doesn't stop on the second floor but continues directly to the third. I stare at the door, with its plastic sign instructing me on the best escape routes during an emergency. The bell is clanging in even strokes, with school-principal precision. I stand stone-still watching the door, unable to move, as the bell begins its march in my direction along the hallway. I can't hear voices or footsteps, nothing but the clanging in the outer hall, increasing until it stops in front of my door. Otto's there, on the other side of the wood, ringing the bell as violently as he can. Time, that's what he possesses, and what I don't. He has all the time in the world.

"Stop," I whisper. "Stop ringing." But it continues, coming through the walls to attack me right along with Julia's memory. My fingers curl around the knife handle in my pocket. The butcher knife will stop the ringing. That is the reason I stole it from the kitchen. But as I take my first step toward the door, the bell's tongue falls silent. A scuffling of shoes and friendly whispering replace it. I hurry to the door and yank it open. Guests are flowing toward the staircase just in time to celebrate sunset.

A large-breasted woman I've never seen before with brown eye-shadow and maroon hair smiles at me. In a thick Polish accent, she invites me to join her on the front terrace. "It is ritual here at hotel, we gather for the end of the sun. Very beautiful, you will see. The boy does it for us every night."

I slam the door shut.

22.

What is a boy? A boy is a bomb ticking in the basement while women practice piano upstairs. A boy is a loaded gun, sitting within reach on a kitchen table. Is a curse word carved into a church pew. Is the menacing crunch of footfall to which deer lift their heads in danger. I never wanted a boy. I was so happy that our baby was a girl, and Peter felt the same—we admitted that to each other the day we brought her home. A baby girl, ours to love, nothing beastly about her. We named her after his grandmother, a tough, determined Wisconsin-ite who was one of the first women to work for the state lumbermills. Julia Elizabeth Burkhardt. In the years since Julia's death, I have asked myself many times, would she be alive today if she had been a boy? Boys are exceptionally hard to kill.

I skip dawn, skip breakfast, sit on the corner of the bed, no stretches, no strength even to take a shower. I'm scared to leave my room, scared what Otto might have in store for me. I dreamed of Julia last night, tornado dreams with no reason or plot, just a strange sense of her nearing me, the burning outline of her face flickering through riotous scenes that made no sense. I won't let the boy use her against me. I won't let him bring her back to life simply to kill her again.

But I must be careful. *Be careful*, I tell my black reflection in the flat-screen. *Remember what happened in Sils Maria. But that was different. That wasn't your fault!* I struggle to my feet, taking deep breaths as I head toward the bathroom. The face in the mirror looks visibly older than it did yesterday. Aside from the discoloration of my left eye, it's a sickly wax yellow. Already I feel fatigue weighing on my body like so many heavy coats. I quickly check my skin, and to my horror, three fresh purple welts star my hips. Thankfully, the splotch on my chest hasn't worsened, but I notice a faint dime-sized red mark above my collarbone, not dissimilar to the hickeys that Peter used to give me back before we had Julia. Instinctively I cover it with my palm, as if it were a burst artery or a bullet wound leaking blood, and I paw through my cosmetics bag for a tube of concealer. The red isn't too deep. A dab of makeup should temporarily hide it. But I don't forget that the boy has brought my affliction back to life. Too much grief, sleeplessness, and stress, all due to an unwanted squatter inside my home.

Peter believed it was best to take the high road during a crisis, infuriate your enemy with your civility. Show the brutes your unwavering dignity. I think of that advice as I finish applying the concealer to my neck and swallow down my morning pills, adding a second dose of risperidone for good measure. Calmly I walk to the closet, tap in the code to the safe, and withdraw the $2,000 in Egyptian pounds. I place the money in a canvas tote bag and slip the butcher knife into my kaftan pocket.

Peter also believed that if you're absolutely forced to do something unpleasant, make it someone else's job. I am too old and slow to kill him. But there are other methods.

• • •

Breakfast is already over by the time I descend the staircase. It's so late in the morning that the first tour groups are already returning from the nearest wonders. The Colossi of Memnon, which once whistled in song at first light from the strong Saharan winds. The Temple of Amun, with its stark corridors of sandstone columns. Its sister temple, Luxor, lined with stone sphinxes guarding the entranceway. As the tourists enter the lobby, their faces are drenched in sweat and they have the dazed expressions of students who have just weathered an intensive history class—centuries explained in minutes, whole civilizations summarized in a few short hours under a burning sun. Ahmed steps from the desk and heads toward me with a raised finger. No, he isn't reprimanding me about being late to breakfast. Nor is he going to tell me what I've done to turn him cold and distant. (I suppose it's an American trait to expect people to point to the wound that needs to be treated.) I'm too frazzled to attempt a reconciliation.

"Maggie," he says, "Tess was asking if I'd seen you. I believe she's sitting in the ballroom."

"The ballroom? No one ever sits in the ballroom." The chairs are gold-painted faux Louis XIV thrones, and sitting on them feels like perching on a pile of wire coat hangers. The only sitting that takes place in the ballroom involves the collapsible chairs set in rows during medical conventions.

Ahmed nods. "I believe that may be why she chose the ballroom." He extends his hand down the hall, as if I'm not familiar with the lay-out of the hotel. I give him an offended smirk, but the smirk immediately drops to a pleading frown. *Be my friend again, Ahmed. Invite me to dinner with your family. Don't treat me like a paying guest. What have I done to upset you?*

Tess is sitting in one of the two chairs by the ballroom's vast picture window. A tattered Persian rug covers the herringbone, and in the late morning a beam of sunlight slants between the chairs and turns the yellow rug a golden oatmeal. Even though Tess sits mostly in shadow, she's wearing giant black sunglasses. It's a theatrical touch reminiscent of an abused wife attempting to hide her bruises. But, in all fairness, isn't she an abused wife? Had the situation been different, I would have loved to help her out of her prison. As it stands, I'm disappointed that Alain hasn't appeared to whisk her and her son out of Luxor.

As I cross the room, Tess notices me and gives a shy wave. I'm fascinated by the sharp pink lips and the high cheekbones of her un-dernourished face. Does she realize that the words she's about to utter might change my mind and spare her son's life? I check that the knife is hidden in my kaftan pocket before taking the seat next to her. The tendons in my lower back spasm as I try to look comfortable in the car wreck of a chair.

"I'm so glad to see you," she breathes. "I asked Ahmed—"

"He told me," I say and pat her chilly hand. She stares out the window, or at least I *think* she does. It's difficult to tell through her enormous sunglasses. Then she slowly rotates her head as if absorbing the ballroom's elegant decor for the first time. Despite the beautiful oak floors and crystal chandelier, most of the furnishings—a mahogany armoire that no longer opens, a cluster of music stands, an empty silverware display case with the bowed legs of a newborn gazelle—are unwanted leftovers from other rooms. Otto's life hangs in the balance, but I let Tess take her time in bringing her attention back to me.

"I wanted to talk to you," she finally concedes, "because you've been so kind and supportive to us since we arrived. And I feel like I've been avoiding you because I was embarrassed about the incident in the cave."

"The tomb," I correct.

"Yes." She blushes. "I want you to know, I don't believe you hit my son." I don't rush to convince her that she's correct. I merely watch her with cool detachment and let her continue. Tess rubs her temple in slow circles, like a commercial for migraines. "It's something I believe that Otto does for attention, for *my* attention. It's my fault, and I'm sorry about that. The funny thing is, Maggie, and I know this sounds crazy, he really does like you. He seems to pick on the people who are the most kind to him." She shakes her head. "Like his grandmother."

"His best friend?" I reply.

Tess nods. "Yes, my mom. When I left him to get help for my depression, despite all her born-again mania, my mom was very good at raising him. I can't take that away from her. And Otto was so well-behaved as a baby. He hardly ever cried. It was only when I came back to San Francisco to get him that he started acting out. He'd only just grown out of his toddler stage, but we still thought of him as frail and weak from his sicknesses, so maybe we forgave too much. Or weren't strict enough. You see, he'd fought so hard to live . . ." She takes a deep breath. "As I told you, my mom demanded to keep custody, and when our arguments grew too heated for even a four-year-old to ignore, Otto began lashing out. Therapists, no surprise, have blamed me for leaving like I did. *Abandoning him*, as you said."

I won't apologize. I could never have abandoned Julia as an infant. "I'm sure you didn't intend to abandon him."

"I was so young and drained. And with Alain off working in Europe, unreachable most of the time . . . I'll always feel guilty for that decision, and I've done my best to make it up to Otto. To tell him I love him every day, to put him first no matter the price." She stops rubbing her temple, staring down at her lap as if her many mistakes have collected there. "Anyway, once we were deep into the custody battle, and it looked like I really might lose him to my mom, Otto started exhibiting some objectionable behavior. I think he feared I might leave again. You could say he began a campaign against his grandma. Kicking, biting, screaming, calling her names. I took it as a sign that he wanted to be with me. To go back to Paris, mom and son. So at first I guess I didn't discourage it strongly enough."

"How bad did it get?"

Tess's mouth shrinks. She turns away and forces herself to face me again. "I mean, he was four years old. Almost five by the end of it. He didn't know what he was doing. And he was probably traumatized because of what I—"

"How bad?"

"He started breaking things around her house, mistreating her animals, causing trouble at her church, asking inappropriate questions during their services. I told you, my mom's a lunatic about heaven and hell. Honestly, in my heart, I still believe it was an accident."

My eyes narrow. "What was?"

"Tell me a five-year-old understands allergies, okay? I'm sure my mother just said she couldn't eat it, not that it would make her so ill that she needed to be taken to a hospital . . ." Tess sighs, purposely eliding the details of Otto's poisoning. I could clue her in on his penchant for poisoning old women. "A total accident. Even the doctors said it happens more than you'd think."

"What did the judge think?" I ask.

"It never got that far. My mom withdrew her claim. I was free to bring my boy back to Paris. And it was all going so well, really, *really* well. We got past that ugliness, chalking it up to post-toddler tantrums. But then the lockdown happened, which drove all of us mad, and the trouble with Alain started . . ." She drops her head in defeat. "Anyway, I'm sorry about the cave. Otto didn't mean it." She keeps her head dipped, as if she's studying the thousands of threads that constitute the Persian rug at our feet. But even lost in despair, Tess can't resist the lure of her phone. I can tell from the way she angles her head that she's glancing at the screen sitting on the radiator for a sign of an incoming message.

"Thank you for apologizing," I reply. "And I like Otto too, very much! I know that boys can be handfuls, even bullies, at his age. I'm sure it's just a phase."

"I hope so," she says in a strained whisper. The tip of her nose is peeling. It must have gotten burned during her afternoon in the pool with Zachary. "When we got back from the Valley of the Kings, my first thought was to pack up and go. If not leave Luxor, at least find a new hotel. But then I remembered what you said about the Royal Karnak being a safe place, a home, for us. I decided you were right, that Otto needed some stability where he could be out in the fresh air and sunlight." She waves her arm toward the window light. "You don't know what it's been like during this pandemic, stuck in an apartment in Paris for months on end, the three of us confined to three small rooms. We could only leave once a day to buy groceries. We had to carry a card, an *attestation de déplacement dérogatoire*, that the police would check. Otherwise, we were locked in place. And with Alain stuck at home too, it was so cramped and claustrophobic, and all our nerves were frayed. At least here at the hotel Otto can run and swim and play, just like you said."

I nod in understanding, hating myself for my incurable helpfulness. Why did I tell her that the hotel would be a safe and loving home? I promised when I left the Alps that I would keep my distance from the problems of strangers. I didn't realize how difficult that promise would be.

Tess lets out a choking breath, her hand pressed against her chest, and once again, I feel tormented by my urge to help her. "I also want to thank you, Maggie, for suggesting that it was an accident that the bird pen was left open, Otto simply forgetting to latch the door. Because"— she pulls off her sunglasses and pinches her eyes—"God, am I a terrible mother? Did I raise a horrible child?" Yes. "I have wondered whether he might have put the cat in there intentionally for attention."

"No!" I cry in delight. "That can't be!" Finally Otto is getting his rightful share of blame. If only I could tell Tess about the poisoned cookies, the decapitated bird in the bathtub, or the theft of my husband's lock of hair. If only I could call his grandmother in California to compare notes on his wickedness. I want every one of Otto's sins paraded out in the open, including the worst one, the evilest of them all, calling me up pretending to be my dead Julia. But I must let Tess figure out the monstrosity of her son on her own.

"Look," I say in the voice of wisdom. "If that's the case, if he did kill those birds, maybe it's a sign that he's deeply unhappy here. Yes, I thought the Royal Karnak would be a good home for him, but now I think he might need his father. You said that Alain"—I glance at her uncertainly, to bury the fact that his name springs from my lips so easily—"had a bad temper and could be a little . . . strict. Maybe Otto needs the strictness of his father right now? Maybe some harsh discipline is precisely what's missing in his life?"

It's my best offer of a last-minute reprieve. But Tess scrunches her face at my description of Alain. Then she shakes her head, her turquoise earrings slapping against her jaw. "Wait, no. Alain isn't like that. He's exactly the opposite. He's so gentle, so thoughtful. I've hardly ever heard Alain raise his voice. He's unbelievably patient with Otto. These past few years, once we were all together again, Alain's been the best husband and father we could ask for."

I glare at Tess through the beam of sunlight that separates us. She's a liar. I remember her words distinctly. I've whispered them like a prayer to myself. *There are moments I've felt scared for my own safety around him, and then he'd be perfectly loving and sweet the next moment.* "Tess, at the tombs, you told me you felt frightened around him. That one moment he'd be violent, and then he'd turn around and be loving. Please tell me you aren't in denial about your husband's abuse?"

She lets out an affronted laugh. "Maggie, you misunderstood. I wasn't talking about Alain." She leans toward me, her green eyes flinching as they enter the shaft of light. She drops her voice. "I was talking about Otto. That's why we had to leave Paris. He started up again, acting out, turning violent. I really think it's due to being trapped in that apartment with no end to the pandemic in sight. I mean, to put a box around a child, his whole generation forced to bunker down and prepare for a disease that might wipe out everyone they know . . . It got bad. Really bad. And there was no one to help us; no psychiatrist would see him during lockdown. We were all just stuck in three small rooms in a city under militaristic stay-at-home orders, spiraling out of our minds. And then, well, god, can I be totally honest with you?" Her eyes scan my face, but she doesn't wait for my consent. "About a month ago, Otto started coming into our room at night while Alain and I were sleeping—" She has trouble breathing and leans back in the chair. "He would stand on Alain's side of the bed and just watch him. Staring at him until Alain woke up and asked what was wrong, and Otto would say 'Nothing' and stumble back to bed. But he wouldn't stop doing it, even when I asked him not to. Standing there, watching his father for minutes or hours." The ceiling becomes the focus of Tess's attention. "Then one night, Alain woke up and saw Otto standing there and decided he couldn't take it anymore. He jumped out of bed and picked up his son to carry him back to his room and, well"—she chokes—"I'm sure he wasn't going to use it."

"Use what? What did he have?"

"A child's saw. It fell out of his hand when Alain picked him up. I mean, it wasn't a *real* saw. It could cut, it had metal teeth, but it was tiny, for a kid, with a plastic handle. It came in the tool set we bought for him to help his daddy around the house. I mean, he was just holding it for protection. That's what he told me later when I talked to him about it. He wanted to protect us. He couldn't have hurt Alain with it?" She delivers that last remark in the tone of a question. "But the incident spooked Alain. He started to wonder if Otto had been holding the saw every night that he stood staring at him while he was asleep. I tried to reassure him, *Calm down, kids are weird.* But Alain began acting uneasy around him, even though he's truly a sweet kid and was only trying to protect his family in the middle of an unprecedented global emergency! There are no rules we've been given on how you're supposed to act during a plague!" A tear runs down her cheek, chased by a second and a third. Her voice starts to break. "That's why Alain has been so reluctant to join us here. And I have a feeling he heard about the bird incident, because he hasn't responded to any of my texts for the past day. Complete silence, which isn't like him. Even his assistant won't answer me." No, dear, I want to tell her, that's not the reason. It's because he thinks you're fucking Zachary. Tess tilts her head back, as if she no longer has the strength to hold it up, and for nearly a minute I watch the thin cylinder of her neck gulp air. Then, she lowers her head, and her eyes meet mine. "No, you're right. The birds in the garden had to have been an accident. He loved them. They were the first thing that made him happy in such a long time aside from video games. He wouldn't kill them. He's not a monster."

"What about school?" I counter. "Wasn't he kicked out of one even before the pandemic started?"

Tess grunts in irritation. "I suppose Zachary told you that. I shouldn't drink with those guys. Yes, he was expelled from school for bullying another student. But that was a misunderstanding. Otto says that she was bullying him, and he was simply defending himself."

"*She?*" I wheeze. "It was a little girl he bullied."

Tess shakes her head. "That doesn't mean the same thing it did when you or even I was young. Girls are tough now, often tougher than boys. She had a crush on Otto, and he wasn't interested, and you know how girls can get. She became aggressive. He showed me bruises on his arms. The whole situation got out of hand. She had an asthma attack on the playground, and the teachers accused Otto of hiding her inhaler. It was ridiculous, and the girl was perfectly fine. But the school refused to listen because we're Americans and the French always defend their own. So it became Otto's fault. To be perfectly honest, I blame them for . . ."

I stare at the idiot across from me. It's always the parent who can't see the true nature of their children, blind to the obvious, refusing to connect the dots. But it's the fact that it was a little girl who he nearly bullied to death that hits me the hardest. And now he's conjured the voice of my little girl. I can no longer count on gentle, thoughtful Alain to rush down and rid me of this beast.

"A little girl," I repeat.

"I'm telling you this in confidence," Tess says. "Please don't mention it to anyone."

"Tess," I say firmly, as if to wake her from a daydream, "why don't you send him back to your mother in California. Just for a little while. Get some space for yourself. I can tell you're worn thin. Because if he did kill those birds . . ."

Her face pales. "I'll never leave my son again. And even if I wanted to, I can't send him back to California."

"Yes, I know there are travel restrictions right now, but surely there's a—"

"My mom won't see him. I told you, she's a religious fanatic. She doesn't want to set eyes on her grandson again. She thinks . . ." Tess won't say it, but I know the words that finish her sentence because I've thought it too: *She thinks he's evil.*

"But they're best friends," I remind her.

"We don't send the postcards he writes her. We don't mail the gifts. Otto doesn't remember a thing about his time in San Francisco. He loves the idea of his grandmother, and I really wish she loved the idea of him."

"Oh, Tess," I sigh. *I'll have to kill him, I hope you realize that.*

Tess smiles optimistically. "I want you to know, despite that tantrum in the cave, Otto promises that from here out he'll be on his best behavior. I sat him down yesterday and made him swear, no more acting out, no more causing trouble. A fresh start! He understands. He promised!" She's grinning, faithful to her own delusions. "And Maggie, I wouldn't be shocked if Otto surprises you with an apology. He really is fond of you. All yesterday he was tapping away on his phone, and he finally lifts his head and asks, 'Do you think the nice old lady in room 309 is the Maggie Burkhardt from Tampa or the one from Milwaukee?'" She giggles. "He wants to know all about you! I swear, he's going to end up working for the CIA."

I have been moving my hand back and forth between our chairs, and Tess finally takes notice. She watches as my fingers pass in and out of the sunlight. Back and forth, my hand goes, in and out of the bright shine, through the sun's warm waves.

"The light takes on the color of the Sahara," I tell her. "Isn't it beautiful?" Stupid woman. If only Tess looked carefully at my hand in the light, she'd see the septic-green blots blooming right below my knuckle. Then she might have realized the monster she's just mistaken for a friend.

23.

"*Psst!*"
    The gigolo doesn't hear me. He's leaving the men's changing room right off the fitness center. It's the closest bathroom to the pool, reeking of ammonia, and its batwing doors judder in his wake. A soft pack of cigarettes is tucked into the waistband of his maroon Speedos, and he pauses to take one out, along with a yellow Bic lighter.

"*Psst.*"

He spins around, searching, his brown eyes picking through the foliage of bushes and wildflowers. Thick veins run from his neck down into the circuitry of his lean shoulders. He flexes his chest muscles, his maroon nipples going oblong, his bony throat swallowing as he notices me in the shadows—maybe he spots my glinting eyes, or the shine of my teeth, or the metal of my umbrella handle. "*Psst.*" I step out into the open so that he can recognize the harmless old woman beckoning him.

The gigolo squints and brings his cigarette to his lips to take a deep drag, his cheeks hollowing from the inhale. The fingernails on his right hand have already yellowed from his habit. He looks more bemused than curious at my presence. I supposed he's accustomed to propositions from old ladies, which is presumably how he affords his poolside days at the Royal Karnak. I expect that, like the hotel, he too has been hurt financially by the loss of tourism and might be hungry for cash. *Can I help you?* he asked me at the pool the other day. *It depends on what you want.* Today I know exactly what I want.

"A minute of your time," I say in a friendly whisper. I gesture toward the dirt road behind the fitness center. I don't want anyone who happens to be passing through the garden to catch us in conversation. He decides to humor me, walking along the brick path as I stomp through the flower bed to reach the mud-baked driveway, as far away from the hotel as possible. One of Seif's wheelbarrows, filled with mossy bricks and hanks of ripped weeds, blocks the gigolo's way. He dances around it, showing off his athleticism by hopping on the stone ledge and tightrope walking across it with his bare feet as it follows the road. The cigarette dangles from his mouth, his eyelids low to shield the smoke. When he jumps down, he prefers to stand out in the sun, as if even this momentary detour affords him the opportunity to tan. I stare into his eyes. Those young, brown pleasure-seeking orbs stare back in invitation.

The gigolo is a beautiful man, and for a split second my mind drifts from the proposition I have in mind for him. I imagine leading him up to 309 and stripping him out of his Speedos. How exhilarating an hour with his young body would be, his thin hips between my legs, his hairy thighs clenching, his head hanging down between his shoulders to watch the ecstatic expression on my face. I nearly break into a sob over that lost rapture. I'm doomed never again to take up space in someone's arms.

"Are you interested in making some money?" I ask.

Tess signed Otto's death warrant the moment she told me that he was researching me on the internet. I don't want to think about the crumbs of biographical data he's already compiled from his marathon searches. Is that how he learned my daughter's name? What else will he dredge up to torture me with? A decade ago I, like so many of my generation, was peer-pressured into creating a Facebook profile in the promise of staying "connected." Peter had the foresight to refuse, but I covertly made a page for him too, filling his updates with photos of me and Julia along with snapshots of the backyard rosebushes that he monastically tended. Later, after their deaths, try as I might, I couldn't figure out how to delete our profiles from that wretched human inventory. Our accounts just kept popping back up like ghosts from a grave. I worry Otto has found those profiles and is mining them for fresh ammunition. What else could he dig up? Articles in the *Milwaukee*

Sentinel or the online neighborhood bulletin, the *Klode Park Crusader*? Peter's obituary? A Swiss police blotter, or a Reddit subgroup dedicated to guest horror stories submitted by hotel staff in the Alps? I have no idea what lethal riptides flow underneath the glittering surface of the internet. But Otto probably does. He's hunting for my weak spots, just as he did with his grandmother and the schoolgirl he bullied.

"Money?" the gigolo repeats, letting the smoke roll out of his mouth like a lethargic dragon.

"Yes, money," I say confidently. "A lot of it." The gigolo laughs, and so do I, as if money were the funniest subject in the world.

He thinks for a minute, his fingers absentmindedly readjusting the Speedo fabric that covers his testicles. "What kind of money?" His voice is high-pitched, but it doesn't waver. I yank the tote bag from my arm and hold it open as if it were a feedbag. He cranes his neck and stares down at the stack of Egyptian pounds.

The gigolo whistles. He lifts his head in fresh curiosity, his eyes softening as he takes me in. He puffs another drag, but kindly blows the smoke out the side of his mouth so that it doesn't waft in my face.

"You want me to do something for the money?" he asks lightly, like I'm challenging him to perform a small childish dare. *Climb that tree! Run around the pool naked.* My dare is far more serious.

I look at him, nearly begging him for help with my eyes. I wish I could explain to him that I can't get rid of the boy on my own, that I'm too old, too weak, too bound by the confines of this gated property, and that the last time I attempted to kill him, all I got in return was a black eye. I wish I could explain that Otto stood with a weapon in his hand at his own father's bedside, and that his grandmother refuses in fear of the devil to see him. I wish I could tell him what it was like to lose everyone I love and have that loss exploited by an evil child. I need an accomplice, someone strong and nimble who can help get rid of Otto once and for all, and I have the money to afford that sort of friend. But how do I propose such a thing?

"I'm afraid what I need isn't very nice. It's risky."

He gazes at me in confusion, but after he picks a piece of tobacco off his tongue, another spell of giggles erupts from him. "I like risky," he says. I know he does. Both Ahmed and Yasmine have told me as much. Still, I hesitate, fearful of his reaction, my mouth so dry that my tongue sticks to my teeth.

"You might not be the right person for this job. But maybe you know someone who is? A friend in Luxor who needs money badly, someone who could handle a job that is very risky and disturbing? I could pay you for the introduction."

He pinches the butt of his cigarette, then rolls it back and forth between his forefinger and thumb. He doesn't look the least bit alarmed by my insinuations. I pause, waiting in a silence of hissing sprinklers and echoing traffic for some indication that we're on the same page.

"I know lots of people," he brags with a shrug. "What is this job? Tell me what you need."

Still, my lips falter. No one wants to kill a child. I won't ask him outright. I'll make subtle inroads to that destination. I can always chalk it up to a misunderstanding if he recoils. A language barrier. A beloved old American woman asking to murder a random child?

"The boy," I say cautiously and hold out my hand, measuring roughly Otto's height. "You've seen the little boy running around."

"Little boy?"

I nod and circle my eyes with my finger to indicate glasses.

"Ah, yes, the little boy," he says. "The one who liked the birds."

"Yes!" I exclaim, "the one who killed the birds! Precisely." I shake the money bag again, and the gigolo's eyes instantly shift to it. "That little boy," I continue. "I need you, or your friend—whoever, I won't ask their name—I need them to . . ." Here I must be delicate. But how do you delicately ask a stranger to erase a child? I drop my voice into a whisper. "For *all* this money, I need the boy taken out into the desert. *Far out.*"

"Far out?" His forehead creases. He doesn't understand. How do you describe a destination that doesn't exist on any map?

"*Very* far out. So far out that he can never find his way back."

"No way back," he repeats.

"Yes! As far as possible." I can't hold back now. He's hooked, and I start reeling. "I need your friend to get rid of him."

"Forever?" he asks dumbly. But he's not dumb. He's catching on to the assignment at hand.

"That's right!" I rasp. "For all this money and much, much more, your friend needs to"—this last word I can only speak in the breathiest whisper—"dispose of him."

He flicks his cigarette into the flower garden. "You mean . . ."

Is the gesture for killing universal? I drag my forefinger across my throat.

"The boy with the glasses?"

I jiggle the tote bag. The gigolo goes quiet, staring distantly at the wheelbarrow's lopsided tire. I can't tell if he comprehends the full brunt of what I'm asking, so I pull the knife from my kaftan pocket to demonstrate. "You see," I say, and let the sunlight catch the blade, showing off its razor-sharp edge.

His eyes fly back to me, scanning my face for some particle of humor. That's when I know I've made a terrible mistake. "You want me to kill a little boy? For money?"

I close the tote bag and return it to my shoulder, as if concealing the money deletes the request. Before I can return the knife to my pocket, the gigolo grabs my wrist, squeezing it with all his might, the muscles of his face tightening with the effort of hurting me.

"Are you crazy? Are you sick? You are very sick woman, asking me to murder a child." My arm is shaking in his grip as my brain sputters for a method of walking back my words. But for once my mind is failing me. I can't think how to fix the *non*misunderstanding. I'm too consumed by how reckless I've been. All these years so careful and deliberate, only to turn so appallingly sloppy over an eight-year-old boy.

"You!" the gigolo cries. "We go now to the hotel, and you tell Ahmed what you ask me." He gives my wrist a violent jerk, and the knife flies from my fingers up the driveway.

"I'm sorry," I stutter. "I didn't mean *murder*. I meant to take him into the desert, for him to see how vast it is, only to scare him, a funny joke . . ." But the gigolo doesn't buy the explanation. "You can have the money! Take it! You don't need to do anything."

"I don't want your money," he hisses. "You need jail." He lets go of my arm and stomps across the dirt to fetch the butcher knife.

"Please!" But he isn't listening, and there's no time to convince him to hear me out. The gigolo is threatening to destroy the only home I have. This sanctuary of love and safety is disappearing right in front of me. I grab a chunk of brick from the wheelbarrow, its cool, wet underside slippery with moss. I coerce my feet to hurry into the sunlight, heading toward the gigolo, who is bent down, picking up the knife.

"Yes, I agree, we must talk to Ahmed immediately, because you have misunderstood." I utter this with warm conviction as I advance to allay his suspicions. "I want to see Ahmed this very instant!"

I lift the heavy brick, and as he turns his head, I slam it down on the back of his skull. He falls to one knee, and I'm forced to strike him again, even harder this time, until the brick slips from my grasp and rolls onto the dirt. The gigolo collapses, dropping onto the ground. His head is bent awkwardly, and a bubble of blood forms in one nostril. I fall to my knees, leaning over him, half terrified that I've killed him and half terrified that I haven't. A beautiful man in the prime of his youth—nineteen? twenty?—his skin still so hot to the touch. "Hey," I whisper. And, because I don't know his name, "Hey you. Can you hear me?"

He can't.

24.

I want to rest for an hour against the rock wall. I want to sit in one of the plastic chairs stacked in the driveway and bury my head between my knees. I desperately want to run to my room, shut the door, draw the curtains, and lie in bed until night falls. My hip throbs. The arthritis and rheumatism in my fingers, on most days only a nagging ache, have chosen this moment to flare with fury. My ankles do not feel capable of dragging a young man's body one more inch, let alone twenty feet. But I must get the gigolo out of the open. I'm lifting him by the armpits, his heels trailing in the dirt, my sandals fumbling backward along the rutted driveway, my ears on high alert. It's agony. My bent back is dripping with sweat, and I'd rather turn myself in to the police than keep my fingers taloned around his shoulder bones.

Seif's voice shatters the peace. He barks a command at an underling somewhere in the garden, and I drop to my knees, the gigolo's torso falling across my lap as if he's a dying soldier who I'm sending off to heaven. I hold my breath and listen as the head gardener's boots stomp off toward the pool. Quickly, fighting a muscle spasm in my back, I continue my work. I refuse to fixate on my panic and exhaustion and aching bones until I've dragged the gigolo behind a pile of mulch bags, stacked chairs, and wheelbarrows. Only one hiding spot has come to mind. There is no other.

I peel back the striped fabric over the car and search for the magnetic box by the front tire. My fingers finally locate it, stuck to the inner fender, and inside I find the key. I tell myself—in gasps, because even the voice inside my head is fatigued—that I will find another hiding place in the saner, calmer, less sunlit future. The company car is only temporary. I keep wrenching the fabric cover off the Peugeot until I can unlock the back door. Grappling with the gigolo's body, shrieking in my throat but muffling the scream with the clamp of my teeth, I slowly manage to heave him onto the hot leather back seat, pulling him in until his feet lift from the ground and only his broken toenails and scratched soles stick out the side. It's dark in the car, the back windows are tinted, and it carries a stale, dank reek that I didn't notice the night Ahmed drove me to his house for dinner. The staleness reassures me that the car is barely used, and I recall the dust and dry leaves exploding off the cover when Ahmed removed it.

I scramble off the gigolo's body, nearly toppling onto the ground in the attempt to wiggle out of the car. As I jam his feet farther inside, I spot his pack of cigarettes and yellow lighter lying near the mulch bags. I toss them in the back seat, slam the door, and lock it with the key. Wiping the key with my kaftan, I return it inside the magnetic box to its hiding spot. Finally, I smooth the cover over the vehicle, taking great care the same way Yasmine does my bedspread every afternoon, not a wrinkle out of place.

An unnerving serenity passes over me as I walk across the driveway to gather the knife, my umbrella, and the bag of Egyptian pounds. Relief from physical exertion is so easily confused with a sense of accomplishment. What have I accomplished, other than murdering an innocent man? I crave the oblivion of cold air-conditioning and a dark room. The scent of lavender wafts along the brick path through the garden, a delicious comfort I don't deserve, and a maid smiles as she passes, carrying a pile of fresh towels. Behind me, I can hear splashing in the pool and a girl calling to her father to join her in the deep end. There is a dead man thirty feet from that girl, his body just beginning its long, arduous process of decomposition.

My fingerprints on the car's door handle, my DNA on the brick that rolled into the dirt. As I reach the door to the lobby, my fingers slip from the handle because they're covered in the gigolo's suntan oil. Under no circumstances will I picture his face, only a few minutes ago squinting at me with the throb of life still in it. The woman who used to be Maggie needs to go up to her room, lie down, and start her day all over again. Leg stretches and tornado arms and Peter in the shower.

My body is shivering as I enter the lobby, and with each step I feel vomit crawling up my throat, scalding my windpipe but refusing to breach my mouth. Even in my current state, I can sense something is amiss at the reception desk. Ahmed is searching through his accounting books, his hair too freshly combed and gelled for the lateness of the day. I sleepwalk toward him, my feet shuffling over the balding carpet, my fingers rigid from dragging the body, my lower back muscles crying, *Oh, you'll pay dearly for that exertion tomorrow.* As I reach the front desk, I see the door behind Ahmed hanging open. It leads to a manager's office that's usually never used. Inside I catch a glimpse of a woman in her late forties, stout and efficient, with platinum hair pulled back in a ponytail, standing over a laptop at the desk. With horror, I imagine her watching surveillance footage of the driveway behind the fitness center. I picture the angle of the camera, a downward shot of me bludgeoning the gigolo to death. But as I stare more intently, the screen's glow reveals a grid of spreadsheets, nothing more.

"I didn't think it would happen so soon," Ahmed is saying to me, and I force my eyes to sweep over his face.

"Me neither," I admit.

"We'll have to be on our best behavior from here out. They will be looking for the smallest mistakes."

"Yes, they will."

The woman in the office lifts her head and glances out at us. I step to the side so that Ahmed blocks her direct view of me, not that she would recognize me, not with my dyed hair and flowy kaftans and my bruised and wrinkled face. I've changed so much, but she hasn't changed in the slightest. I recognize her instantly, Liesbeth de Clerq of Richesse Resorts, the oversight manager dispatched during a crisis to steer a wayward hotel back into the corporate fold. The last time I saw her was in a chalet in the Alps after the violent murder of a hotel guest.

"Maggie, what's that in your hand?" Ahmed asks. I glance down. I'm holding the butcher knife, along with my umbrella.

"Oh. This. I found it on a table in the garden."

Ahmed smiles appreciatively, the way he once smiled when we were close friends. "Thank you for retrieving it. But maybe it is better not to carry a knife around the lobby while the boss from HQ is here."

"Yes. I'll return it to the kitchen." I put the knife in my kaftan pocket. "I'd better let you get back to work."

Ahmed nods, and I slowly turn away, not wanting to attract the curiosity of Liesbeth. I'm just an old lady living out her final years in a crumbling hotel on the Nile. I could be any old woman. It is imperative that I avoid Liesbeth de Clerq at all costs. As I reach my hand for the staircase railing, the last thing I want shouted across the lobby comes out of a child's throat.

"Hi, Mrs. Burkhardt."

I see swinging feet, fluorescent-orange sneakers with lime-green socks and hairless little-boy legs. I step back and stare into the unlit corner under the stairs where my nemesis sits on his iron throne chair, his hands curled over the ends of the armrests like a crowned prince. He's wearing a KN95 mask over his mouth, and his muffled breathing, escaping through the top, is fogging up his glasses. The mask makes it impossible to read the expression on his face, but I sense that underneath it lurks a smile of hatred.

"Hello, Otto," I answer cordially. "You don't need to wear a mask inside the hotel." A demon temporarily takes possession of me. I want to plunge the knife into the boy's chest, not once but forty times. I want to break his legs at the knees and bite into his calves, swallowing down ripped child flesh. I want to smash his glasses into his eye sockets, grinding the shards into his discolored irises with my thumbs. I want to pull his tongue out for mimicking the voice of my Julia.

"I'm waiting for Zachary," he tells me. "We're going to surprise Ben at the museum today, and we need to wear our masks to visit. They have treasures thousands of years old."

"That's so sweet of you," I reply. "Ben will love a surprise visit from you. Who wouldn't?" *What are you plotting? What traps await me today?* I move away from him, back to the staircase.

"Oh, Mrs. Burkhardt?" Again, he loudly broadcasts my name, as clear as a bell through the mask, and I pray Liesbeth isn't listening.

I pause. "Yes, Otto?"

"Where were you before you came here?" He asks this question in a tone of innocence, "You told us you've been living at this hotel for a few months. But where were you before? I mean, where did you go after you left Klode Park?"

Although he's mispronounced it, he's already learned of my old neighborhood in Milwaukee. Has he seen the house, Peter's rose garden, the pool? Before I can stop myself, I shoot toward him, entering the unlit corner where I hover over him. I think of the brick I slammed into the gigolo's skull—which is the boy's fault, an act I was forced to undertake because of him—and I jam the rolled-up end of my umbrella between his legs, right into the triangle of his crotch, where his tiny testicles bunch. He squeals at the unexpected jab. His glasses stop fogging, and his eyes peer up at me through the condensation. I'm about to punch the umbrella into his scrotum as hard as I can. I want to damage his testicles before they're capable of producing sperm. But I hear Liesbeth's voice calling to Ahmed in the office.

Instead, I bend toward Otto and whisper lovingly into his ear. "Where have I been all these years? I've been inside your head, touching things."

25.

Eighteen hotels in five years. I was a different woman back then, or at least unrecognizable as the one you see today: gray hair tied in a bun that sat high on my head; long, high-waisted tweed skirts; a cream silk blouse buttoned to the neck and wrists; a bra, pearl earrings, a blue sapphire ring, low-heeled leather shoes, pantyhose, and plenty of makeup. The ulcerous European light did not flatter my complexion, and I spent an hour putting on my face at the bathroom mirror each morning (eighteen different mirrors, but it's always the same mirror, just as on holiday it is always the same sea, only different points of entry). There you have her, Maggie Burkhardt in her carapace of prudence and control, lost somewhere between tragedies—the annihilation of her family and the unprecedented world-scrambler of the pandemic. Her art, as I've told you, is rescuing the trapped.

It all started with the innocent desire to help a girl. In an alpine hotel in Klosters, under the stony shadow of the great Graubünden peaks, I watched day by day as a twelve-year-old girl endured the punishing mood swings of her boorish stepbrother. They'd been newly thrown together because of their parents' second marriage. More than double her age, a college dropout who'd backpacked through Indonesia for the past three years, a walking hangover who consumed his first drink at breakfast, he would make snide jokes about her undeveloped body, mock her ruthlessly for the smallest misstep, and by cocktail hour smother her in kisses and ass-pinches as she froze, terrified, pressed against his chest. Her eyes always seemed to find me in these moments, pleading for help. The father was not on the scene, and the mother, a career diplomat, was too glued to her laptop to notice. But I saw the life slowly draining out of this girl, and I decided I had a moral obligation to act. I needed to make the mother realize the reptile she'd adopted for a stepson. Without any proof, I was forced to invent some. (It only took stealing the period-stained underwear of a thirteen-year-old Norwegian girl staying at the hotel and planting them in the young man's hiking bag, which I left hanging open on the mother's door.) The very next day he was sent off to his father with a dire warning never to find himself alone with his stepsister again. The whole thing was so astoundingly easy, an entire life set right by a tiny intervention. So many years of future suffering prevented by simply licking my fingertips and reaching out to pinch the flame. I had found my calling. The more I helped, the more the world around me brightened, and the more my blotches receded and became an affliction of the past.

In a ski chalet in Gstaad, Switzerland, a German couple with three kids teetered on the brink of divorce. They had planned the getaway as a last-ditch effort to save their marriage, yet it was plain as day that they had inflicted too much damage to trust each other again. Quietly, imperceptibly, I massaged the world around them until they reached the rightful conclusion. They departed separately a few days later to seek divorce lawyers. In Bad Gastein, Austria, in an overheated Victorian thermal spa whose springtime rooftops were still dandruffed with snow, I saved a lesbian couple from their rash plan to adopt a child. In a former monastery in the foothills of the Dolomites, its grounds zippered in grapevines, I prevented a rich widow from forgiving her unctuous son. In Chamonix I stopped a marriage proposal and saved two men, both inveterate cheaters, from years of passionless heartbreak. On the off-season Lido in Venice, I convinced a self-hating financier to abandon her husband and four-year-old daughter and embrace a new life in Argentina. In Verbier I prevented a renewal of vows. In Zermatt I sent a daughter packing. On the lakes of Trento I thwarted the disastrous reunion of two estranged sisters. My portfolio of good deeds goes on.

I always knew there were risks—and I don't mean only in terms of my personal safety. I understood that such radical life changes don't come without costs—friendships wrecked, emotional support lines fractured, future children no longer conceived, homes with heavy mortgages sold at a loss. But those are the sacrifices we make to be free. For the most part, despite an occasional overattentive maid or a wheelchair-bound valetudinarian parked in the lobby while his family threaded down the slopes, no one had any inkling of my handiwork. That is, until I tried to help save two newlyweds last December at a resort at Sils Maria. The couple was completely mismatched, shockingly wrong for each other, anyone could see it. Two tall, attractive Hungarians in their early thirties, they had just gotten married and escaped the Covid-ridden districts of Budapest for a few weeks of skiing in the Upper Engadin Alps. He was bookish and quiet and stalked the edges of the hotel's communal rooms with a meek, frightened expression; she was loud and quick-witted, laughed constantly, and walked around as if a pop song were playing in her head. He went to bed early and waited for her with the light on, while she drank Scotch in the bar with the older couples and shot pool while talking to anyone who would listen (anyone but her husband, Bajnok). It was a doomed situation—a few months of lust, the forced coinhabitance of an apartment during the pandemic, and the foolish idea that marriage would solve their lingering doubts about each other. They made a terrible union, the husband hopelessly in love, the wife growing more bored with him by the minute. I felt the tremendous urge to help them realize their mistake. If I worked quickly enough, Hanna and Bajnok could probably get an annulment. I was in a double time crunch because the wife's sister was scheduled to join them for the last week of their vacation. A meddlesome third party only adds complications: they pay too much attention and disrupt reliable routines; worse, they offer themselves as counselors and negotiators when a more decisive break is needed. I had to act fast.

Bajnok was my primary concern, sweet man. I dropped a few well-placed clues, more than hinting at infidelity, which he took longer than I'd hoped to recognize. But finally, forcefully, like being stabbed in the stomach, he understood.

"Hanna is cheating on me," he wailed during one of our private conversations. "Maggie, how can that be? I can't believe it. I *won't* believe it. And yet I have proof." He was inconsolable, his eyes glazed with tears.

At that point I had become his trusted confidante, and I played my part to perfection. "Oh, my dear, I hoped that you wouldn't discover it. I'm afraid all of us at the hotel know. I think we simply assumed it was a passing phase. Of course you're absolutely right, sleeping with the bellboys, especially on a honeymoon, isn't a very . . . I'm sorry I didn't tell you. I didn't want to break your heart."

His sobbing neared hyperventilation. "Only two weeks ago we were married! Only yesterday Hanna talked about having children! How could she betray me? *How?* I could kill her!"

I knew Bajnok lacked confidence. He wasn't a strong soul; he didn't possess the innate self-assurance needed to leave his wife. He was still so morbidly in love with her, I feared that he would decide to forgive her. That would only make him more miserable than he'd been before I got involved on his behalf. I needed to bolster his determination, to gild the lily, so to speak, to push him over the edge before the wife's meddlesome sister turned up. "Yes, of course you should want to kill her. I'd have murdered my husband if he took up with all the cleaning ladies behind my back, rest his soul. You need to end it. Once and for all. Before you have a child together and she's still cheating on you right and left. Trust an old woman. It won't get better. End it, Bajnok. This is your last chance."

Hanna was found by housekeeping the next morning, strangled in bed, the covers pulled over her head. The search for the perpetrator didn't take long: Bajnok had hanged himself in the staff stairwell.

How could I have known he'd go so far? Or had I known, flirted with the idea of finality, seen death as the only assurance that someone as meek as Bajnok would not remain locked in unhappiness forever? Needless to say, I was racked with guilt, unable to eat or sleep. The hotel was in a collective state of shock and panic, and it didn't help that Hanna's sister, Madlen, materialized that same afternoon, expecting to find her sister alive and in love.

The hotel's parent company, Richesse Resorts, sent one of their top managerial heads, Liesbeth de Clerq, to quell the storm. Bajnok had left a note, a long, incoherent ramble of accusations about his wife's infidelity. In it he made two references to me, the first time thanking me for my friendship and willingness to speak the painful truth, and the second time alluding to my eyewitness account of Hanna's adulteries with hotel staff. Naturally, I denied any knowledge of what he was referring to. I had barely spoken to the newlyweds, had only vaguely learned their names, and frankly they seemed quite happy, very much in love. Baja-nik? That was his name, right? Poor, poor man.

The police seemed to buy my ignorance. Then two porters came forward, claiming that they'd seen me entering the newlyweds' suite on multiple occasions, and speaking intimately with Bajnok on the evening of the tragedy. The grieving sister heard their testimony and between that and the suicide note, became convinced I was to blame. "What did you say to him that brought him to strangle my sister?" she screamed at me in the lobby, while Liesbeth tried to calm her. "You bitch! You sick, twisted *kurva*! I knew him. He wouldn't have hurt her if you hadn't spread your lies!"

Madlen went to the canton's chief of police, demanding an investigation, refusing to let the case rest as a run-of-the-mill honeymoon murder-suicide. Finally Liesbeth requested a meeting with me and the cantonal police chief, promising to sort out the "unfortunate misunderstanding."

I checked out in the middle of the night. I felt certain there was no solid evidence against me, and with the pandemic death toll spiking over the winter solstice, the police were overtaxed enough without adding libelous accusations against a wealthy American senior citizen to their workload. After all, I'm not the one who strangled Hanna. But it was better to be gone than sorry.

I paid my bill, called an Uber, and fled south, searching for a country on another continent whose borders were still open to Americans. Egypt was the nearest port that didn't require a mandatory quarantine. Yes, it perturbed me that Richesse Resorts had colonized all the grand hotels along the Nile, but what choice did I have? I was innocent. I hadn't been accused of a crime, and the company's Brussels head-quarters lay on the other side of a vast desert and a sea. The colossal, overwhelming chaos of Covid made smaller, less urgent chaoses nearly impossible to keep track of. Especially a chaos the size of an old woman.

. . .

Bajnok. A gentle, sensitive man, attuned to other people's emotions like a piano teacher to the notes on a scale. He took long sighs between his sentences, his mouth often pensively covered with his fingers; his shirtsleeves never reached the end of his arms, leaving his long, delicate wrists exposed. I still feel guilty, still hate myself for failing him, even if my intentions were good. I had grown sloppy in Sils Maria because of my success rate. I promised myself when I fled Europe that I was of-ficially retired, no longer implicating myself in strangers' doomed lives. But in trying to help Shelley, I've been sloppy all over again.

As evening begins to darken my room, purpling the walls, I lie mo-tionless in bed. For a moment I see Bajnok swaying above me, the red curtain sash around his neck, his head slung forward, his long, delicate feet skimming my stomach. His face doesn't look peaceful, nor is he any happier now. I turn onto my side to stare out the window at the garden's treetops. There lies another death for which I am to blame. I squeeze my eyes shut at the thought of the gigolo, packed in the back seat of a car hidden under a shroud of striped fabric. Under my eyelids, I see the faces dearest to me in all the world—Peter and Julia, also dead, beyond help. All I am is a graveyard.

Night is falling, and yet I haven't heard the bell calling every-one down for sunset. Tonight will be another victory for the boy, one more day of his domination of the Royal Karnak. I half expect another phone call from him, impersonating Julia. The silence con-tinues, almost itching my ears with its emptiness, and the sun is now fully setting. Why no bell?

My curiosity gets the better of me. I climb from bed and enter the bathroom, brushing my dyed hair over my forehead in front of the mirror. Unrecognizable. I use concealer on the green dots on my hand and the purple blot above my collarbone. No other marks are evident, and I don't dare check the state of my skin underneath my clothes. After swallowing down a second risperidone, I open the door and sneak along the hall, my hip jackhammering with pain. I grab the railing as I descend, orbiting around the chandelier chain. Has the gigolo's body already been discovered? Is that the reason Otto hasn't rung the bell? Is this my last descent at the Royal Karnak before my arrest? They wouldn't hang an old woman, would they, for murder?

As I worst-case predicted, uniformed officers throng the lobby's reception desk. Six of them. And yet they look more like military than police, in slender green fatigues and black caps emblazoned with the insignia of an eagle. Their pistols hang in leather holsters at their hips. My heart is pounding as I reach the lobby—I've never seen soldiers inside the hotel before. Yasmine and two maids stare with terrified expressions from the side hall. It can't be a coincidence that these soldiers have shown up on the very day of the murder, yet there is no sign of a medical examiner or detectives with evidence boxes and latex gloves. The part-time manager of the fitness center is talking to the soldiers in Arabic, his ragged voice pleading. Ahmed stands next to him, and when he spots me, he uses me as an excuse to leave the tense conversation. He shakes his head as he hurries over, acknowledging the strangeness of the situation.

"Don't worry," he assures me, "there is no emergency. The officers are only searching for someone who's missing. I am sure it is all a misunderstanding." *An unfortunate misunderstanding.* That's the term Liesbeth de Clerq used in Sils Maria, and I notice her standing at the back-office door, her finger looping around her neck chain as she watches the officers conduct their interrogation.

"Who are they searching for?" I can hear the needling fear in my voice. The gigolo has only been dead for half a day. How are members of the Egyptian military already on the hunt for him? I figured it would take a week before anyone noticed the delinquent's disappearance.

"Rafik." Ahmed stares at me as if the name is supposed to conjure a familiar face. I play dumb with my eyebrows. "The young man who enjoys the pool on many afternoons." *Many?* Try all. Ahmed doesn't seem to recall my asking about the gigolo, or his response to me: *That one. He is not important to you. Pay him no mind, Maggie.* "He was here today, but he seems to have vanished."

"Vanished? Maybe he just went home."

Ahmed shakes his head. "He meets his father every evening at five for tea. He did not show up today, and his father grew concerned. It is strange, Maggie. The manager of the fitness center, he finds Rafik's street clothes, phone, and money in his locker, meaning he did not get dressed after his day at the pool. He is only wearing his swimsuit." The tight maroon Speedos, browned by the mud as I dragged his body along the drive. "Many missed calls from his father on his phone. So where did he go? He could not have just walked off, wearing a small swimsuit, into busy Luxor. He didn't even have his shoes."

"Maybe he's with a girl?" I propose. "A woman in the hotel? Or perhaps a different distraction? Friends in a car?"

Ahmed winks and quiets his voice. "That is a possibility. Rafik is a nice young man, but he does have a mischievous streak. When he was younger, he got into a little trouble, selling some stolen goods. But he has straightened out. It would be unlike him to miss tea with his father, even for a beautiful woman." Ahmed laughs. When the officers hear him, they glare in warning. He clears his throat. "I am sure that he will be found soon, and all will be well."

"The father called the military when his son didn't show up for tea?"

Ahmed sucks on his teeth, as if sucking on an ugly fact. "His father *is* the military. Rafik's father is the top general of the southern division. A very important man in Luxor. That is why Rafik is welcome to use our facilities. I'm afraid his father is very upset by his disappearance. His officers won't be allowed to return to their camp until they find him."

My brain drops, plummeting so far into my body that I keep waiting for it to crash-land at my feet. I asked the son of an army general to murder a little boy. The gigolo was not a poolside hustler but a pampered prince living out his days of leisure. No wonder Ahmed warned me not to pay him any mind. No wonder Yasmine feared crossing his entitled path. He has far more power and connections in Egypt than I do, and now his father's troops won't stop until they locate him. I need to sit down. Or lie down, even right here on this carpet. But I catch Liesbeth glancing over at Ahmed, and I don't so much as slump my shoulders for fear of attracting her attention.

"No worrying!" Ahmed exclaims, as if trying to convince himself. "You could be right about a rendezvous with a guest in her room. Where else could a handsome young man in a small swimsuit go in a gated hotel? I only pray he didn't fall somewhere and hit his head."

26.

It's after eleven at night. The hawkers on the corniche have long dis-banded, but men's cries outside infiltrate my room. "Rafik, Rafik," the officers shout, and the beams of their flashlights penetrate the win-dow, briefly flaring across the walls. Unable to sleep, I crawl from bed and watch them in their search, as if the gated back garden were an im-penetrable forest and Rafik were lost somewhere in its depths, unable to find his way out. Two hours ago, the soldiers searched every hotel room, tapping on each door, apologizing, explaining that a man's son was missing—they failed to mention that Rafik is an adult—and asking to check the closets and bathroom. I assumed they'd make the briefest scan of the quarters of a feeble old woman, but they were thorough in room 309, yanking the closet hangers aside, getting to their knees and checking under the bed. *You have nothing to hide*, I kept reminding my-self. *Everything you've done is beyond these walls.* I forgot about the butcher knife I'd stashed in the nightstand drawer. When a young soldier by the bed inexplicably reached for the drawer handle, I cried out, "Please don't touch that!" He glanced at me suspiciously, and I quickly appealed to his commander at the door. "My lotions and medications are in there," I quavered, nearly in tears. "I have a terrible skin condition!" It was the tears that saved me, or the anguished voice that reminded him of his grandmother, and the commander signaled to the soldiers to continue their sweep of the rooms. Rafik's father must be an extremely important man for Richesse Resorts to allow such an intrusion into the privacy of paying guests. If I weren't so consumed with my own paranoia, I would worry how this latest imbroglio is going to impact

Ahmed's career. Liesbeth de Clerq can't be pleased. But right now it's my future, not Ahmed's, that terrifies me.

At the window, I feel the warm night air rinse my face and smell the aroma of the flowering orange trees in the garden. The officers' boots patter along the brick paths in the dark. At any moment, they might find the body. I didn't bury him in a hole. He lies in the back seat of a Peugeot, less than two hundred feet from my window. There's no way I can move him farther away at my age, let alone during an active search, and sooner or later, he will be found. "Rafiiik!" they call. "Rafiiik, Rafiiiik!" Maybe they'll eventually give up, assume he went off with a woman, that perhaps he felt trapped by his domineering father and broke free to start a brand-new life.

I pray for rain to drown their voices, to wash away any clues I left on the driveway—the drag marks that his feet made, bloodstains on the brick. But prayers are rarely answered in the desert. Rain only falls in Luxor once a year.

27.

The sun looms directly overhead. My umbrella casts a tight black orb on the brick around my feet. As I cross the garden, two Saudi girls run past, dripping from the pool, their black, wetsuit-like burkinis covering their legs and arms. I follow their watery footprints in the opposite direction along the walkway, through patches of jacaranda and spiky callistemon. A soldier is stationed by the vacant aviary, eyeballing the guests. Another soldier is patrolling the far edges of the garden, nearing the fitness center, curious about the small crawl space underneath the changing rooms. He disappears around the back, perhaps wandering down the dirt drive, and my heart clenches, fearing he might head the wrong way and take an interest in a vehicle sheathed in fabric. My hands are shaking as they tighten around my umbrella handle. Trying to stick to my routine, I climb the steps to the pool and am relieved to find Ben there, hunkered under a table umbrella, cross-legged and using the laminated menu as a fan. I lift my arm in a wave. *Act normal. Pretend it's just another day. Smile. Like the fake smiles I gave in the hospital when Peter was dying, sunny and optimistic, as if my entire world wasn't crumbling right before my eyes.*

"Hello, dear!" I say as Ben groans "Mags!" A pile of books, T-shirts, sun-lotion bottles, loose American quarters, and a plastic toy sword clutter the tabletop. As my eye skips across the turquoise-blue rectangle, I notice Otto in the water, splashing around the balding head of Zachary.

"Yep, he's still playing dad," Ben reports as I drop into the chair next to him and place my umbrella on the table. I glance at the surrogate father and son. Zachary is splashing back in retaliation. The mere sight of Otto laughing, not a care in the world, makes me fantasize about accidents in the desert, a boy crawling through the sand in search of a tiny drop of water, licking dry stone, vultures swooping and pecking chunks of meat from his back. He should be the one lying in the back seat of the Peugeot, not our beautiful gigolo. In response to Ben, I offer a wise, sympathetic sigh.

"Well, the boy does seem to make your husband happy. I guess that's all that matters."

Ben rolls his eyes, and then a sneeze overtakes him. Spring has brought exotic allergies to this flowering oasis. He wipes his nose before broaching the day's most pressing topic. "Did they search your room last night?" he asks. I nod. "They stayed in ours for nearly ten minutes, looking at everything!"

"You do have the largest suite," I remind him.

"One of the soldiers even quizzed me on my work here, as if I might be trying to lure Egypt's handsomest young men into a life of poorly paid academia. Call me old-fashioned, but I don't find it reassuring when a military dictatorship pokes around my hotel room." He shakes his head. "Where the hell could that guy be?" We both make a show of looking around the pool area, as if Rafik might suddenly pop up from under one of the teak loungers. I notice the officer with the more thorough search instincts moving through the shadows of the trees on the other side of the pool.

"It's possible he met a friend and went off," I say, and mime gripping motorcycle handlebars. "As it turns out, our gigolo is a child of privilege. We really got him wrong."

"You mean, *you and Zachary* got him wrong," Ben clarifies, somewhat erroneously. "I was open to all possibilities. Naturally, Zachary was thrilled to find out his crush is also obscenely wealthy."

"But his privileged family explains his disappearance. You know rich kids. They're notoriously irresponsible. He's probably off running amok with friends. Maybe he's high on drugs in the desert right now. Who knows?"

"That's exactly what I told Zee!" Ben exclaims. "An irresponsible teenager. What's all the fuss? He'll turn up. You know, the soldiers gave Carissa a particularly intense interrogation last night." I lift an eyebrow to encourage him to continue. "I guess they looked at all of us and singled her out as the only guest he might have been screwing. Naturally, Zachary was offended that *he* wasn't grilled as a potential love interest."

"Well"—I can't resist the old habit of stirring suspicion—"you *are* gone all day, Ben. Who knows what your husband gets up to?"

Ben doesn't take the bait. "Carissa was so outraged by their sexual insinuations that she lodged a complaint with the manager. Not Ahmed, the more senior one from Europe. She's leaving tomorrow."

"Who's leaving tomorrow?" I urgently ask. "Liesbeth, the senior manager?"

"No, Carissa. She's going back to Athens once and for all. Bought tickets and everything. I guess it took military intervention to finally convince her to leave. We never really got to know her, did we? I enjoyed her piano playing. She was part of the family. The oddball second cousin."

I'm not interested in sentimentalizing Carissa right now. I return to the subject of Rafik. "You know, I heard our gigolo has a criminal record. He was caught selling stolen goods a few years back." This bit of gossip from Ahmed is like food to a starving traveler. Ben leans toward me with renewed interest.

"You don't say. Like a fence? So he does have a criminal history! See, we were right! And there's a healthy black market in Luxor for stolen antiquities. That's probably where half the museum's collection has gone. Our sweet, handsome gigolo, selling ancient treasures?"

"Who knows if it's true," I add airily to distance myself from the rumor.

"But don't you see, Maggie? That explains his disappearance. Kidnapped by Luxor's crime syndicate for owing money. Or maybe he was held for ransom as the son of a powerful man. Or both?" I can't gauge whether Ben's theories are beyond the realm of possibility. The fun of our poolside chats lies precisely in how much we blur the boundary between reason and fantasy. Nevertheless, these absurd speculations give me hope that Rafik's murder could be blamed on elements other than the elderly guest in room 309. Maybe his death could be a revenge killing at the hands of religious zealots because of his godless military father. But I can't keep up this line of wishful thinking. My smile turns agonized, and I stare at Ben with pleading eyes. He is still young and ambulatory, he could help me move the body. Together, in the dead of night, we could take the gigolo into the desert, where no one would ever find him.

"What?" Ben asks, reading my face.

"Nothing."

I spot the soldier circling back toward the dirt drive, wandering near the wheelbarrows and stacked plastic chairs. A tortured whine escapes my lips. Ben hands me the menu, mistaking my keening for hunger.

"Hummus plate?" he suggests.

The boy climbs out of the pool. Over his bony shoulder, his play-mate is still bobbing in the deep end. Zachary waves to me, and I wave back, but my eyes are focused on the boy, who shivers in the bright sunlight, leaking chlorine from his board shorts, his skinny legs shuffling through the fluorescent fabric. He hurries toward the table to claim his plastic sword. He stiffens when he notices me in the um-brella's shade—the last time I saw him, I jammed my umbrella into his crotch—but makes an effort to appear unfazed.

"Hello, Mrs. Burkhardt!" he says gingerly, grabbing his green T-shirt from the table and using it as a towel to wipe his face. On the front of the shirt is a graphic of a cartoon turtle on a skateboard sticking his tongue out.

"Hello, Otto. Enjoying the pool?"

He nods furiously, emphasizing his happiness. His young skin is so drum-tight over his body, I can make out the delicate architecture of his ribs, the tendons of his neck, and the thin white surgery scar on his stomach. He would be so easy to dissect. You could almost use your fingernails to cut him open. He finishes wiping his face and tosses the T-shirt back on the table.

"Why don't you come for a swim?" he asks me, and I match his smile and raise the bet with the baring of my teeth.

"I'm afraid at my age I can't be out in the sun."

He laughs at this response, shuffling back on his heels, the way teen boys do when they flirt with girls, the off-balance sensation of a dance.

"Lots of old people like the sun," he replies, pointing to a shriveled European couple across the pool.

"Does your grandma like the sun, your best friend in California?" I ask. His smile tightens. "Why don't you call her up and ask her? Call her right now. Surprise her. Grandmas love to hear from their grand-children. No grandma wouldn't speak to their grandchild by phone, not if they're best friends."

"Grandma doesn't like to use the phone," he replies dismissively, refusing to be thrown by my remark. "Is that why you're always walk-ing around with your purple umbrella? You're scared of the sun?"

"That's right," I say agreeably.

"What would happen if someone took your umbrella, and you were forced to—"

"Do you want some food, Otto?" Ben gruffly interrupts as a mora-torium on nuisances. Instead of answering, Otto spins around with the sword in his grip and hurtles, weapon held high, toward Zachary in the turquoise water. Ben turns to me with rolled-back eyes.

"That kid never stops talking," he groans. "On and on, the *con-stant* questions, and yet he doesn't pause to hear their answers. And his hands are always touching things, testing every surface, even in an exhibition hall where there are signs every five feet informing you in English that touching is strictly forbidden." I presume Ben is referring to Otto's surprise visit to the museum yesterday. "What could I do, hide in the back until they left? Zachary was so excited. *Look, I brought a little boy!* I was forced to give the kid a short tour of the collection. By *short*, I mean I spared ten minutes, but even then, it was questions, questions, questions. I thought he'd be interested in the relics of Tut. But our Otto only had eyes for the gold figurines. 'Like the one on the mantel in your hotel room,' he yelled when he saw the others in the collection. I could have slugged him. And don't think I didn't watch his pockets!" Ben draws a breath. "The problem with Otto is that disliking him makes me feel like the world's worst person. Isn't this pandemic supposed to have taught us to appreciate the young? They've given up their childhoods so that their elders don't drop dead from the spread.

I mean, finally. About time children are last in line for something on this planet."

I feel a vibration against my upper thigh. It comes from the cell phone tucked in my kaftan pocket. I so rarely receive texts that the sensation is as alien as an electric shock. The last text I received was from Otto's father in Paris. I pull out the phone and find, with alarm, that the sender is my sister, Claire. I haven't spoken to her in five years. In the first months after Peter's death, we tried to feign a sisterly phone relationship, but the daily nagging interruption of each other's lives didn't yield the intended results. She made a few paltry attempts to check in on me at the start of the pandemic, but I ignored her like I did the rest, and eventually my phone went as still and silent as a stone.

I don't want to read her message, and yet my eyes have already violated that decision, zipping through the first lines of the text.

> *Dear Maggie, I hope you're well. It's been so long since I've heard from you. When the pandemic began, I tried calling and I sent you several messages to your phone as well as on Facebook to ensure that you were taking precautions. But maybe you don't check Facebook anymore? I still do, and I feel I should tell you that I received a rather strange message this morning. A boy, it seems, from Paris, maybe an American? His profile is confusing, but he says he met you on a recent trip to Egypt?*

My eyes lift up and flash to the pool, where Otto has mounted Zachary's shoulders, wielding his sword like a conqueror. I return to the screen.

> *He asked me a bunch of questions that I wasn't sure how to answer. Questions about Julia. I don't know what information he was looking for, or why he would ask me. But I suppose he saw that we are related on Facebook. I thought you should know. I do worry about you and think of you often. No one in Milwaukee has any idea where you've gone. Egypt? Is that where you are? A hotel in Luxor? If you ever want to talk, I still have my old landline number, although Daryl and I have put the house up for . . .*

"Maggie? Maggie?" Ben's chair screeches back, and his hands are on my shoulders, shaking me. My head has fallen forward, and I can't find the strength to lift it. I also can't seem to work my tongue. "Maggie, I'm getting a doctor. Hold on." Just as Ben withdraws his hands, a flicker of strength runs through me.

"No, don't worry, I'm fine," I tell him, resurfacing, gripping the table as I right myself in the chair. I wonder if I need to up my dosage of risperidone to three pills instead of two. "Sorry, I just had a little faint. It's common with my blood-pressure medication. I've had these spells for years." It's a lie, and Ben stares at me doubtfully.

"Are you sure?" He digs through the clutter on the table for a bottle of water. Unscrewing it, he hands it to me.

"I'm fine. I promise," I say lightly, gulping the water down. "Thank you." But hatred is shooting through me, infecting every cell. Otto has reached into my past, prying out as much information about my dead daughter as he can, opening her coffin and touching her bones. In the pool, saddled on Zachary's shoulders, he brandishes his sword at imaginary enemies, beaming triumphantly, a child king. "Hi, Mommy!"

Tess heads toward us from the changing rooms. She's wearing her giant sunglasses, a red bikini top, and a pair of jean shorts. Mercifully, behind her, the snooping soldier has reemerged, walking in the leisurely manner of a man who has not discovered a dead body. As Tess crosses the edge of the pool, she puts on a brave face and waves to her son. "Hi, honey!" But when she turns to us, it's clear that she's been crying. She sits down at the table and pulls off her sunglasses to reveal swollen eyes. Then she engages me in a prolonged stare, as if I can be relied on to ask the obvious question that will allow her to pour out her heart. Only a fool confuses curiosity for compassion.

"Heavens," I say on cue, "what's the matter?"

"I wish I knew!" she replies, crossing her arms over her chest. "It's Alain. I thought because of all the silence from him, he might be on his way down here to surprise us. It turns out, he's changed his mind altogether." Her lip quivers. "He decided he isn't coming to visit us at all. Like I've done something wrong, like I deserve to be punished.

He says I've destroyed his trust and I should stay where I am and enjoy myself." The photo I sent him has produced the opposite effect. Alain was still my long shot hope of outside intervention to clear the Seebers from the Royal Karnak.

"I'm sure he's just in a bad mood," I say. "Don't give up on him. Are you certain you shouldn't pack up this afternoon and head home to try to patch things up?"

I reach my arm across the table toward her in a beseeching manner, my palm open as if to share her pain. But when I pull my arm back, I am holding Otto's balled green turtle T-shirt in my hand. I slip it onto my lap.

"It would be cruel to Otto to take him back," Tess says. "He can't go through another lockdown. He's having such a nice time here."

I turn my attention to Ben. "Dear, do you have any aspirin in your room? I have a splitting headache. The doctor says an aspirin helps with the fainting spells." Ben starts to get to his feet. "No, no. I'll fetch it. It's time I go inside anyway. It's too hot for me."

"The bottle is on the bathroom sink, next to Zachary's hoard of vitamin supplements." He pulls his keycard from his wallet and slides it across the table. "Leave the card at the front desk. I'll pick it up when I get back from work."

"You're a lifesaver."

I say my goodbyes, feigning exhaustion, and hurry through the garden to the hotel. I hold Otto's damp T-shirt balled against my chest. Perhaps there is more than one way to make a boy vanish. As I climb the stairs, I think of my sister's message and realize that she didn't say whether she answered Otto's question about Julia. Her end is a tragic story, too horrible for a child's ears. It's a shame that a story can't kill a person upon delivery, entering the ear like a bullet and exploding on impact inside the brain. Stories can destroy a listener, can break a person into a million pieces. But they can't kill. I know because I once heard a story that should have killed me.

Egypt? Is that where you are? A hotel in Luxor? Otto has divulged my whereabouts. Now my past knows where to find me.

28.

I don't head to the Sultan's Suite directly. First, I make a pit stop in my room to collect the figurine that I bought for Ben at the market. As I carry it down the hallway, its gold paint flecks off on my fingers. The figurine was meant as a gag replacement when Ben returned his relic to the museum's collection. Now it's just a replacement.

If I'm honest, what frightens me most about my plan is the smell. Two days in 110-degree heat in a locked car. What does that do to a body, even one as beautiful as Rafik's?

I hurry down the hall, careful about the tripwire of an orange vacuum cord, saying hello to a maid restocking minibars. There's no need for me to be furtive. I have permission to enter another guest's room. A quick swipe of Ben's keycard, and I'm in.

Hurricane vases filled with fresh-cut yellow roses. A marble bar top with the powdery green remnant of protein shakes spilling across it. White oak flooring, newly laid in straight lines, unlike the chipped parquet that checkerboards all other guest rooms. The curtains are different too, not pilled satin but raw linen glowing in the sunlight. A wide U of an overstuffed white-leather sofa faces a massive flat-screen. It's as if the suite has been teleported from a boutique hotel on South Beach, and I wonder whether it's the trial run for Richesse Resorts' impending renovation. No wonder Liesbeth wants all the old employees fired. Richesse Resorts can perform its insidious makeover without the inconvenience of nostalgic staff. The old and stubborn only get in the way.

As I move around the sofa, I notice a pile of toys heaped on the floor: a plastic shield to match the sword that Otto was wielding at the pool; a stuffed-animal lion; a red-eyed, battery-operated sphinx. They're bribes of affection in Zachary's trial run as father. Fortunately, the toys confirm that Otto has access to this room. On the mantel I find Ben's tiny gold Set figurine, propped up by a pink hotel matchbook. I grab it, replacing it with the souvenir facsimile. It's nowhere close to a perfect match. Even the most casual assessment would confirm the preposterous substitution, which is exactly the reaction I'm hoping to elicit. Only a child would be dumb enough to presume an archaeologist would fail to notice the swap. Ben's figurine is heavier and more substantial. Even mid-theft, I can't resist admiring the beauty of this object, buried from the world for forty-four centuries, lost under deep leagues of sand for thousands of years. Its jackal head is covered in rosettes of purple stones, like the floral swim caps my mother wore in pools when I was a child. The jeweled orbs of its eyes are the blue of Mediterranean water. I recall Ben telling me once that blue was the symbol of eternity for the Thebans. All the Renoirs on the planet couldn't compare to this little artifact, which I drop into my kaftan pocket. The figurine still has one more journey through the underworld to take, but I won't be able to make that trip until nightfall.

Before I leave, I dip into the bathroom. Amid the vats of creatine, hair-rejuvenation pills, and vitamin supplements, I find the aspirin. I pop two in my mouth and leave the lid askew to corroborate my alibi. In the mirror I steal a glance at the purple mark on my neck. I've been avoiding my body, shutting my eyes when I shower, staring at the wall as I change. But now I see that a second blotch, the size of a nickel, has emerged above the first on my neck. It's not huge, but larger than the first, a sign of what's to come if I don't take better care of myself—get a good night's sleep, keep out of the sun, and, most importantly, dispose of Otto.

I take the stairs down to the lobby, where I hear muffled arguing behind the closed door of the back office. The Coptic bellboy is covering the reception desk. "Sul-tan's Suite," I tell him, and slide Ben's key-card across the desk. "Return to owner. Okay?" I could tell this kind young man anything—that I murdered the gigolo, that I engineered the deaths of a couple in the Alps, that I desperately want to end the life of a little boy whose room I'm currently subsidizing—and he would smile and nod and say thank you. "Sultan's Suite!" I repeat, guiding him with my pointer finger as he places the card in the appropriate cubbyhole behind the desk.

The arguing in the office intensifies, and I make out the husky voice of Liesbeth de Clerq, followed by the calmer, dignified responses of Ahmed. If only I could burst into the office to defend him.

I decide to wait for Ahmed to finish with his meeting; he'll need a friend after such an abrasive confrontation. At first I sit on one of the front sofas, but my eyes fall on the shadowy corner with Otto's iron chair, and I can't resist the temptation to sit in his favorite seat. From that throne, I stare out at the dusty lobby; like the merchandise in an antique store, its decorative coherence lies solely in the shared sense of having outlived a far more glorious era. I try to see it with Otto's eight-year-old eyes. I try to imagine how the blood feels in his fawnlike arms and legs, how much oxygen he takes in with his clean lungs, how his budding hormones spring his steps. But it's as impossible for me to re-call the sensation of being young as it would be for him to imagine the slow-motion plane crash of old age.

Finally Ahmed appears, shutting the office door behind him. He emerges from behind the reception desk and marches past without no-ticing me in the corner. "Ahmed," I cry as I jump from the seat. His own name spooks him, and he gasps as he spins around, horror filling his eyes when he takes me in.

"Maggie! I'm sorry," he says, as if he should apologize for being frightened of me. Sometimes I'm frightened of me too. Maybe we can reboot our friendship on that shared sentiment.

I step closer, shrinking the distance between us. "I heard the yell-ing," I whisper. "It's Liesbeth, isn't it? She's not very nice. Is she giving you a hard time?"

"It's fine," he says reassuringly. "We have differences of opinion, but we will work through it to find the best solution for the hotel."

This diplomatic answer is not what I want to hear. I want Ahmed to confide in me like he used to, telling me his petty aggravations.

"Is she upset about the recent rash of complaints?" Ahmed doesn't answer. "First the Bradleys, then I hear Carissa is furious about the grilling she received from the officers. That woman! First she breaks up Geoff and Shelley's marriage. Now she might have carried on a torrid affair with the gigolo."

"The who?" he balks. I've overstepped. I smile as I touch his arm with affection, sliding my fingers up toward his shoulder. But Ahmed jerks his arm away.

"Ahmed, what's wrong?" I whimper, tears crowding my eyes. "Why are you acting so distant with me? Have I done something to offend you? Is it because I invited you to sleep in my room that night? I only meant . . ."

Ahmed bites his lower lip, and he breathes ponderously through his nose. He seems to be struggling for the right words in English. "No, Maggie, that is not it, and you have not offended me. No, it is only . . ." He retreats from the truth. "I must remain professional, especially now that Richesse Resorts is here, I must treat each guest . . ."

"We used to be friends! And rely on each other. And talk to each other honestly!"

He inches forward, his eyes narrowing. "That night you came for dinner, sitting with my family, you spoke of your daughter."

"Yes, I remember talking about her. Was I not supposed to—"

"You told them she died as a little girl. But, Maggie, you told me she passed away only a few years ago. You said that to me when you first arrived." He shakes his head. "I don't know why you'd lie, either to me or to my family. It is your business, what happened to your daughter. But I feel . . . well, it makes it hard to trust you."

I can't bear to hear his doubts about my integrity. "She died!" I cry. "My daughter is dead, and I was confused. I get flustered. I don't remember everything clearly all the time! That's what the pills are for, the ones you always remind me to take. They help me keep everything straight! But, every so often, time swings in and out of focus, the past so close and the present so far away!" I'm not merely playing the dementia card. It is true, I forget sometimes what year Julia died or how exactly it happened. But I was wrong at the Ramadan dinner. Peter passed away first, and then Julia a month later.

Ahmed gives a compassionate frown, and as if to prove there are no hard feelings, he deigns to pat my arm. "I am sorry that I have been distant," he says with sincerity. "It has been very hard on me, having this manager from Belgium looking over my shoulder, threatening my job and livelihood. Please do not be offended."

"I understand." I nod vigorously. "And if there's anything I can do . . ."

While I'm nodding, he shakes his head, as if we can't even sync up on the most basic responses. "Do not worry. *Inshallah*, all will work out for the best. It is just . . . I hope the hotel will return to normal. Something is very *wrong* here of late."

It takes all my effort not to reply, *That's my doing, Ahmed. This is my home. I moved in, and I redecorated.*

29.

Otto has a history of violence. Terrorizing his grandmother. Bullying a schoolgirl. Haunting his father's bedside with a saw clamped in his hand. Slaughtering the pet birds that he was pretending to nurture. Killing a cat, then a dog—a classic escalation. It was only a matter of time before he committed a murder. At least, that's the conclusion I hope the police will draw.

In my room, I wrap the gold Set relic in the boy's green T-shirt emblazoned with its skateboarding turtle and knot the ends. Otto has already shown a strong desire to possess the figurine. Rafik has a criminal past that involves selling stolen goods. He and the boy could have met at the pool and hatched a plan. I might even hand over the note Otto wrote me on hotel stationery, demanding I buy him a game console. I practice my doddering-grandmother act: *I just assumed he was being silly, you know, a typical greedy boy, I didn't hear about him threatening to kill his father until later. Not until after he gave me this black eye during one of his wild tantrums. Goodness, I almost bought him the XTMegaBox that he was determined to have at any cost. Do you think if I'd bought it for him, Rafik would still be alive? How could I have known?*

All I need to do is leave the T-shirt-wrapped Set figurine in the car with Rafik's body when the coast is clear. I'm terrified of what I'll find in the car—worse, possibly, than the odor. Rafik sprawled on the sticky leather seat, his skin fusing with the upholstery, flies finding their way through the tiny gaps, crawling into his nose and mouth, his hands already stiff with rigor mortis. I would prefer to make the attempt in the middle of the night, but I can't remember if the Peugeot's interior lights turn on when a door opens, and I can't risk that lone beacon in the darkness, especially if the soldiers are on guard. I slip the butcher knife into my pocket for protection and tighten my sandal straps.

At six o'clock, Otto rings the bell for sunset. He walks the halls, first the second and then the third, tolling as he plays the vendor of time—"Fresh, hot sunset, get your fresh, hot sunset before it's gone." Doors open, guests stream toward the staircase. I slip out into the hall, pretending to join them, smiling wildly. "I'm going to take the elevator as a favor to my knees!" I press the call button. Instead of the first floor, I descend to the basement. From there, through carpeted corridors, past the business center and the maintenance rooms, I use the employee entrance that brings me out into the garden.

Unwittingly, Otto has done me the favor of gathering all eyewitnesses to the front of the hotel. I hurry through the back garden, scurrying along the brick path. Gnats cluster above hose puddles. Long shadows bend over stone. Flowers droop mournfully from the loss of the sun. I keep my eye out for soldiers, for gardeners, for anyone who might notice me, but there isn't a soul in sight. I head toward the fitness center, my hand already gripping the wrapped figurine in my pocket. I slip past the changing rooms, veer around a cypress tree, and just as I turn down the last stretch of shaded brick, I nearly collide into a stranger standing alone in the bluing dusk. No, not a stranger at all. Liesbeth de Clerq, in a gray skirt and blazer. She holds a lit cigarette between her fingers. A few strands of platinum hair have fallen loose from her ponytail, and there are pouches of exhaustion under her eyes. She stiffens at the sight of me, like a grazing animal rearing up in defense. I draw back from her with a cascade of *Ohs*. Liesbeth must be sneaking a smoke out of sight during the terrace sunset. She's not the kind of employee to flaunt a bad habit in front of guests.

"I'm sorry," I gasp, trying to disguise my voice, flattening the Wisconsin vowels. "I wanted to book a massage for tomorrow. Is this the entrance to the fitness center?"

She fixes the collar of her blazer while casting a smile of managerial efficiency, tender but inflexible, accustomed to handling frivolous requests with solemn dedication. She displays no sign of recognizing me. "No, ma'am, the fitness center's entrance is on the other side, if you follow the brick path to the front. Although you can also book an appointment from your room." I'm relieved by "ma'am." Let's start over, Liesbeth, let's keep it professional this time, neither of us interested in getting bogged down in past mistakes. It doesn't seem to have occurred to Liesbeth to examine the list of current Royal Karnak occupants. Why should she? For once, it's the staff and not the guests who are the problem. I begin to turn back, when Liesbeth stops me.

"Are you enjoying your stay, Ms. . . . ," she prompts. Her foot is squashing her half-smoked cigarette in slow half circles while her tired blue eyes remain fixed on me.

"Margaret," I reply, avoiding Maggie while remaining true to my passport. "Yes, I've loved my stay at the Royal Karnak Palace. Really such a unique hotel. And a terrific staff, particularly Ahmed." I want to sing Ahmed's praises, but I fear uttering too many sentences, in the chance I'm tuning her memory back three months to a previous crisis. Casually, I try to brush some of my hair over my face.

"You're an American?"

I nod. If she asks, I won't say Milwaukee. Sioux Falls comes to mind. Montpelier. Dover. Random cities that even I can't picture.

"And how long have you been a guest here?"

"A few weeks. It's been *very* nice." I'm cheating on the math, and yet still I worry I'm catching the faintest glint of recollection in her eyes.

"Margaret, have you ever stayed at any of our other Richesse Resorts properties?"

"Oh, now let me think. I'm not sure. You have so many, don't you? It's possible, many years ago. Perhaps in Spain?"

"We don't have a location in Spain. Most of our signature properties are in Italy, Switzerland, and France. You weren't visiting any of those destinations recently? I'm usually very good with faces."

I shake my head, withdrawing my voice from the evidence table. How could she forget a murder-suicide in one of her signature properties? I fear it's coming back to her, the old me. My hand lingers in my pocket. I've let go of the figurine, but my fingers curl around the knife handle. No one's around, just the whistling traffic beyond the hotel gates and the occasional echo of touts on their last call for carriage rides. Our white skin is glowing as night begins its claim on the garden. I could jam the blade into her neck before she has time to scream and drag her body to the car to load on top of Rafik. I would love to do it, just to be rid of her. For both me and Ahmed to be left in peace. But there would be too much blood, and I don't have the strength to carry her all the way down the dirt drive. My fingers, though, won't let go of the knife.

"Oh well," Liesbeth says with a laugh. "It will come to me sooner or later." She pulls another cigarette from her pack, in an overt display of informality that makes me nervous. "Some advice. Try the Nile Escape."

"Nile Escape?"

"It's a ninety-minute Balinese deep-tissue massage with a milk and honey facial. Does wonders for the skin. Beyond relaxing!"

30.

I wait until daybreak to try my luck again.

Several times last night I climbed out of bed and considered putting on my shoes to sneak through the garden to the car. But, leaning out the window, I thought I heard footsteps, possibly belonging to the soldiers. Sleepless as the minute hand drew its ceaseless circles, I stared up at the cross on the ceiling. *Why keep fighting?* That's what I asked myself in the dark. *The Royal Karnak was never your home. You don't have a home. Pack your bags and leave this second. Get rid of all this trouble by getting rid of you. Let that brat and his mom have full run of the place before you get caught or your affliction worsens. Take the first morning flight out to . . .* That's when the wheel in my brain jammed. A flight to where? What country would admit me, when most borders are closed in lockdown? At this point, I wouldn't even be permitted back into Europe. *Go where? Where is safe?*

I rolled over, struggled to find sleep, tried to relax the muscles in my eyelids while visualizing a calm, silver radiance flowing through my veins. Eventually I pictured the pool cleaner, my twilight counterpart, rising from his bed on the outskirts of Luxor, dressing in his uniform, collecting his gear, and making the long slog over to the Royal Karnak in the dishrag grays of predawn. He unlocks the gate and silently gets to work, expertly picking at the weft of his net like a tennis player before casting his first stroke into the water. His net catches leaves and bark peelings, fireflies and bees. He discards the litter in the garbage bag knotted at his belt. His stroke is as calm and steady as an oarsman. His net glides through the pool and dredges up ancient coins and girl's white underwear and chunks of red meat. Peter is shouting in agony through the speakers that hang in the trees, violent with rage, the world around us suddenly whistling like a jet engine, a father jumping into a Wisconsin lake with his frightened daughter . . .

I wake a few minutes after ten, panting, kicking at the sheets, the mattress wet with sweat or a worse leakage, my nightgown ridden up to my stomach. Bluish-yellow blotches streak my thighs, one nearly black as it disappears below the elastic of my underwear. I don't have time to agonize over this latest eruption on my body, even though I fear it almost more than what awaits me inside the Peugeot. I'm late for my task, horribly late, the garden already crawling with workers and guests. But I must try. Rafik's murder would have been committed for nothing if I don't connect Otto to it. I decide I won't place the bundle in the gigolo's hand; I'll merely lob it into the back seat and shut the door. As I swallow my pills, slip on a kaftan, and load my pocket with the wrapped artifact, the logic of the plan begins to fray. I don't allow myself to second-guess it. *Be an ant, carry this piece of leaf across the dirt and into the hole. No thinking required.* I strap my sandals on my feet and fly out the door.

In the hallway, porters are steering wobbly luggage carts toward vacant rooms for the latest check-ins. They've commandeered the elevator, leaving me to take the stairs. I don't look at the reception desk. I want no joking banter with Ahmed. I race outside through the lead doors and realize with a jolt that I've forgotten my umbrella. The unshaded stretch of brick is glazed in sunlight, and out of habit I halt mere inches from it as if it were a cliff's edge. But it's too late to take precautions, the affliction has already begun to spread, and I push on, dashing through the daylight into the garden. Two gardeners are fixing up the bird aviary, scraping off the old paint and stapling fresh netting to the sides. They nod in greeting. The younger gardener has eyes the luminous blue-green of sea glass.

Hurrying along the path, feeling glimmers of leathery sunlight on my face, I am relieved that I don't hear any splashing from the pool. But as I round the back of the fitness center, I'm stopped by the sight of Seif at the far end of the driveway. He's standing only a few feet from the covered car. He's wearing his work jumpsuit, his back hairs sprouting up at the collar, the prayer knot on his forehead as thick as a bottle cap. Like a madman hearing voices, he seems to be following an invisible entity through the air. He shuffles past the wheelbarrows and then moves in a figure eight around the stacks of chairs and garbage bins. I grab the figurine wrapped in Otto's T-shirt, as if I might be able to sneak past him during his delirium. But when he turns in profile, I realize that he's guided not by hallucinations but by a stench, his neck thrust out and his nostrils flared. There is only one way his search will end. Seif staggers toward the shrouded Peugeot, his hand lingering on the hood as he again arcs his nose. I stuff the figurine back in my pocket and retreat, fearing I'll hear his scream at any moment. I run back across the rectangle of bright sun. I don't want to hear Seif's cry. Somehow it feels safer to learn of the discovery secondhand.

Rushing into the hotel, I hear a man shouting in the lobby. How could Seif have beaten me into the hotel? But it's English being yelled, a voice so angry and deep I don't recognize it as belonging to Ben until I see him standing by the sofas, his finger wiggling down at Otto.

"Where is it? I know you took it!"

"I didn't take anything." The boy's face is red with blamelessness, and he glances up at the staircase as if for rescue, prompting me to look there too. Zachary is rounding the steps, worry etched on his face. "Ben," he wheezes. "Stop it." Tess is following behind him, anxiously rubbing her hands, as if she suspects there might be some truth in Ben's accusation. Ben realizes his time is limited before the cavalry comes to the boy's aid.

"Where the fuck is it?" he shouts. "It's a priceless artifact. Worth more than anything you've ever touched in your puny, little life! Jesus fucking Christ, it's not a toy. You need to give it back to me this instant! NOW!" Ben is not attuned to parental modes of persuasion, but his rage, nearing desperation, is convincing. Otto backs up, the backs of his knees pressing against the sofa, his head mutely shaking out noes. "Quit lying, you little shit."

"Ben, stop it. Otto said he didn't take it." Zachary speeds down the last flight of steps, only to adjust his gait as he reaches the lobby, moving with slow, deliberate steps as if trying to lull a wild animal into a false sense of security—*see, no one's upset, look how leisurely I'm walking, let's all relax.* "Are you sure you checked under the couch? It probably rolled under there."

"It didn't roll under the—" Ben takes an exasperated breath. "He swapped it with this action figure." He brandishes the cheap souvenir. "Thinking, presumably, *what?* I wouldn't notice? Zee, I need to return that artifact to the museum. Don't you understand? I should never have—" Ben's voice cracks in anguish, the full horror of his carelessness made abundantly clear. Even during a global pandemic that threatens to wipe out the human race, it is not okay to take the world's treasures home with you.

Ben latches onto the boy's shoulder. "Give it back!" he screams as he jiggles him. Otto's eyes are no longer so mismatched. Magnified by his glasses, they are little colored islands floating in broad lakes of white. "Right now, before I rip your head—"

Zachary grabs Ben by the arm to pull him away from the boy, and Ben, overcome with rage, reacts with a blinding swing, making direct contact with Zachary's eye. In return, Ben is struck with an elbow to the ribs, and the two men wrestle to the ground. Tess tries to reach her son, but she's temporarily blocked by the husbandly melee of punches. There is nothing for us to do but stare down at them in shock. Despite myself, I'm admittedly impressed. Otto has accomplished what I couldn't conceive—he's managed to wreck the unwreckable couple. I wait until the boy glances over at me to give him a smile.

"Oh, Otto, did you take it?" I ask. "It's okay to admit that you did. But it was very valuable."

He glares at me, the fright in his eyes morphing into hatred. We could have been such good friends.

"Of course he took it," Ben rasps, his lip bleeding as he lies inertly on the carpet. He and his husband have stopped fighting and are lying side by side, trying to catch their breaths. "He's been playing in our room!"

Tess reaches her son, kneeling down and pressing her hand flat on his chest. "Honey, be honest. It's okay. We just need to know if you took it without realizing that it's an important relic."

The important relic is currently wedged in my kaftan pocket. I grip the back of an armchair in the role of fraught onlooker, serious about teaching our youngest generation the meaning of respecting private property. "Otto, please," I beg him, "be a good boy. Tell us where it is?"

He sputters with laughter as he shakes his head, his lips snarled. "You probably took it!" he wails at me. "She's a monster! An evil old lady! She took it, not me!"

"Otto, stop!" Tess shrieks, as if her last motherly straw has snapped. She grabs him roughly by the shirt collar, the blue veins of her fingers showing off her tiny diamond-chip wedding ring. "What's wrong with you? Why are you acting like this? Why would you steal something from these nice men?"

He tries to pull away, and she slaps him in the face.

I want to savor this moment forever. What the angels must have felt watching the devil fall. Total bliss. But the paradise ends too soon, when Yasmine and a young maid run screaming into the lobby.

31.

We were told to stay in our rooms. Ben chose the absolute wrong moment to demand a thorough search of the hotel for his missing antiquity. The staff ignored him—just another crazy tourist bleeding from the mouth and flapping his arms with a ludicrous request—while they rushed through the lobby, some coming, some going, some crying and screaming and praying to God, one or two cooler heads phoning the police.

As I retreat up the steps, I feel a twinge of disappointment in not connecting Otto to the murder. I think of his teary eyes on me as he went mute and accepted his punishment, his mom yelling at him to stop misbehaving as she struck him. It was a vindication, a moment to preserve in amber. And yet I haven't won. Otto is still here, a guest of the hotel, humbled but not defeated, a child-size monster sleeping in a king-size bed.

The invasion of the garden occurs within the hour. First there is a flurry of high-ranking officers—black caps, short-sleeve camo shirts, blousy green pants, and polished dress shoes—and then young soldiers, heavily armed, as if Rafik's death is a national emergency. I spend the afternoon at the window, unable to calm the fears rushing through me. I'm muttering that I'm innocent, an elderly woman on vacation, and if anyone killed the gigolo, it had to have been the boy with the violent past. I happen to have the proof in my kaftan pocket, a figurine of the god Set tied in a T-shirt that I found . . . where? . . . No, that doesn't work. Start over. *I am an innocent elderly woman on vacation . . .*

In the middle of the afternoon, a heavyset man with a bristly gray beard enters the garden. He wears a blue dress shirt, disheveled, mis-buttoned, and an entourage of lieutenants surrounds him. I assume this is Rafik's father. *I know what it's like to lose a child*, I want to yell down from my window in consolation. *Sir, I know only too well what you're going through. The pain never leaves you. You'll wake up thirty years from now and want to gouge your heart out. The death of a child is a vacuum bomb. It destroys you over and over and over every minute of the day.* The general marches toward the scene of the crime, disappearing below the tree cover. I watch as two soldiers escort an inconsolable, frightened Seif, head bent as if he's been beaten, along the path to some undisclosed location. Seif found the body. Does that make him a prime suspect? Did he do it? I wonder if he might have. There is no sign of Ahmed from my third-floor lookout. I consider calling reception to check on his well-being. I want to be there for him as a friend and confidant. Ahmed, who do you think did it? There's a rumor that Seif is the killer, but I don't believe it. What did Seif have to do with Otto? *Ahh . . .* because of the birds? You think Seif and Otto killed Rafik together? I hadn't thought of that. Maybe it was over the Egyptian artifact that I just found in Tess's purse? *No, no, that doesn't work.*

I force myself to leave the window, but the room's blank walls are no comfort. They offer only the space and time and close confines to obsess about ancillary horrors. This morning new blotches appeared on my thighs, and I wonder how badly they've spread. I can almost feel them underneath the kaftan fanning up my pubic bone, joining forces at my stomach, feathering up my ribs. I wiggle up the kaftan's skirt to my knees but stop myself. Don't look. If you don't see, you don't know, and if you don't know, the worst hasn't happened yet.

A little after four, when the day's heat begins to weaken, I emerge from my room, taking tentative steps down the hall. There are still officers swarming the garden, but most of the activity has moved beyond the trees, in the service area behind the fitness center. I picture the general demanding that his squad round up suspects in the Luxor criminal world, if they haven't already decided to arrest Seif for the murder. Perhaps during his interrogation, Seif will bring up the slaughter of the birds, and the arrows will point naturally toward Otto? From the top of the staircase, I spot Zachary standing below me on the second-floor landing, staring down at the lobby. The police can't expect us to remain locked in our rooms indefinitely, can they?

I sheepishly wave down to him, respectful of his privacy after his fight with his husband. Zachary rolls his eyes and signals for me to join him. As I descend, I notice the bruise swelling on his left eye, worse than mine, with red streaks running across his purple eyelid.

"We match," I whisper.

Zachary smiles, which aggravates the bruise, and the smile immediately turns into a wince. He speaks robotically, trying not to use the muscles in his face. "Who knew Ben had such a solid right hook?" I can smell alcohol on his breath; likely he's been making use of his suite's minibar to ease the pain.

"Where is Ben?" I ask. "Has he found the figurine?"

Zachary shakes his head. "He's up in the room, cooling off, I hope. Although he threatened—he's such a drama queen—that he's going to draft his resignation letter. *Dear Harvard . . .*" Zachary tosses up his hands. "He feels like he betrayed the trust of the museum as well as his profession. And maybe he did. But we've all gone a bit crazy this past year. Aren't we allowed to be a little insane after everything that's happened? And it's not like the museum is going to notice the absence of a knickknack that's been sitting in the back of a filing cabinet for four thousand years." He sighs. "Oh, well, Mags. I'm afraid we might not be long for Luxor."

"I'm sure it will turn up," I say, and then add with meaningless conviction, "It's got to be somewhere!"

"I don't believe for a second that Otto stole it." But right after Zachary makes that declaration, he lets himself believe it. "He couldn't have. Or could he? Am I that blind and desperate for a child's affection? Honestly, I think that fight with Ben in the lobby was less about a misplaced artifact and more about how much he and I have drifted apart these past few years. Like I can't want kids because ten years ago I made a vow to Ben that we'd be childless assholes for eternity. Like I'm not allowed to change." He leans on the railing, his body sinking between his shoulder blades. "I really thought we were happy. But one day you wake up and realize you've been running on the fumes of what your relationship used to be."

I place my hand on his back. "Don't let some selfish boy test the profound bond that you two share." Testing bonds is my job. I decide those life-changing moments, not Otto.

"I don't know," he says wearily. "But what does it matter? That poor young man by the pool is dead." Zachary, who was the one to coin Rafik's nickname, no longer feels the compulsion to use it.

"You don't think Otto could have been responsible for that too, do you?"

He glances at me with a rumpled forehead. "Huh?"

"Nothing," I reply, withdrawing the possibility. "I heard they took Seif into custody."

"Really?"

"Yeah, apparently Seif hated the gigolo. Who knows if there's any truth to it? Hotel gossip."

"That's weird," Zachary replies, "because the police are downstairs arresting Ahmed."

My breath stalls in my throat. It won't move up or down my windpipe, an obstruction made entirely of air that's now choking me. Ahmed, who brought me to his house to meet his wife and children, who every morning steps out from the reception desk to examine his watch and hector me about sleeping late, who looks after me and makes certain I order my medication. *No, no, no.* I'm actually repeating that word aloud, whimpering "*No!*" into Zachary's beaten face.

"Apparently he's the only one who used the company car and knew where the key was hidden," Zachary says. "The doors were locked when they found the body. I mean, what does that prove? But Egypt is just like our United States, Mags. It doesn't matter whether they've caught the right person. It only matters that they have someone in custody to blame." He snaps his fingers. "But maybe Ahmed hated the young man as much as Seif did. Do you think that's possible?"

I'm not listening. I'm already rounding the staircase, hurrying down the steps. I need to clear up this terrible misunderstanding, to explain that Ahmed had no part in the murder, that it was all the evil little boy, he's the one who beat the gigolo with the brick and dragged the body into the back of the car, before tossing in his cigarettes. I nearly trip down the last flight as I spot police officers gathered at the office door behind the reception desk. I see Ahmed inside, in handcuffs, and they're leading him out to take him to the precinct. I stop, my hand gripping the banister, Zachary nearly crashing into me as he skids to a halt on the step behind me. Ahmed sees me. He's crying, with heavy perspiration shining on his cheeks.

"Maggie," he calls pleadingly, like a man about to be ripped away from his life forever. "Maggie, please tell them! Tell them I drove you! That's why I used the car. Tell them, please!"

I'm about to lift my voice in confirmation when Liesbeth appears at the office door, staring over at me with renewed interest, as if she's on the verge of placing me at another hotel murder three thousand miles away. My tongue refuses to move, and Ahmed is swallowed by the sunlight as he's led out the door.

32.

I'm shivering on a white-leather sofa, wrapped in a blanket that the boys have thrown over my shoulders. Out the windows of the Sultan's Suite, the last flares of sun invade the room, bruising the walls purple and red. Zachary stands at the bar, filling a glass with vodka. Ben paces from coffee table to sofa to window, his incessant worry taking the shape of an isosceles triangle as he tongues his bloody lip from the fistfight. The three of us, waylaid with too many injuries, are stuck in our own distinct states of dread: me on the arrest of Ahmed, Ben on his professional future, and Zachary on his disintegrating marriage. If only we could band together and agree that these three problems all stem from the same foul source. A little boy named Otto, agent of havoc, destroyer of peace.

"Do you want something to drink?" Zachary asks twice, before I realize he's talking to me.

"What?"

"A drink. Alcohol. Do you want something to calm your nerves?"

"No," I snort. "I have a headache. I'm sick to my stomach. I'm dizzy, and my hands feel numb." But the primary symptom is guilt, an agonizing culpability for the charge of murder lodged against my dearest friend, whom I did nothing to protect. I glance at these two lost, ineffectual men, my only remaining allies, desperate to conscript them into collective action. "Boys, we must do something to help Ahmed. Can't one of you tell the police that everyone in the hotel knew where the car key was hidden? That the magnetic box was an open secret?" Zachary is paying closer attention than Ben, so I speak directly to him. "You could say that you borrowed the car, Zachary. Or even better, that Otto told you about the key, that he was always playing inside the Peugeot! That he bragged about hiding things in its back seat!"

He slurps his vodka, and I'm worried he's going to ask how I know the make of the car. But that's not the part that unnerves him. "Why on earth would I tell the police that?"

"To help—"

"Maggie, I'm not going to implicate a little boy just so—"

Ben spins around. "No, of course you won't, Zee. You're always protecting that brat. Your own husband, *the man you married*, the one you've chosen to spend your life with, finds his entire career in jeopardy, everything he's worked for, because of that boy who you've known for about ten minutes, and all you do is protect him!"

Zachary's face reddens. "So I'm the bad guy? You threaten to rip a child's head off in the hotel lobby, and I'm being the unreasonable one!"

"He stole a museum artifact! Do you understand the gravity of that offense? Do you? He didn't steal Maggie's umbrella or your cell phone. It's a sacred cultural treasure." He straps his hand over his forehead, the veracity of his words shocking him all over again. "Jesus, Zee, I know he stole it, and so do you!"

"You mean, the sacred cultural treasure that you voluntarily removed from the museum? No one forced you to keep it on the mantel."

"I'm going to forgive you for saying that because you're drunk."

"Boys!" I cry. "Right now the most important thing is to get Ahmed out of custody!" But they aren't listening, Ben pacing, Zachary slurping, each rambling on with a marriage's worth of slights, a chorus of pent-up resentments filling the room as the sun dies out the window. I fling off the blanket, climb from the sofa, and beeline to the bathroom. "I need an aspirin."

Switching on the light, I watch my hand tremble as it hovers over Zachary's pharmaceutical stockpile. I'm so shaken by the day's events that, reaching for the aspirin bottle, I knock over a plastic canister of vitamins. A cascade of bullet-shaped pellets spills to the floor. Bracing myself against the counter, I slowly crouch down to collect them, light-blue capsules scattered on the marble, pills the exact shape and color of my most recent risperidone refill. Picking three up from the ground, I study them closely—blue and squishy, a perfect match to the medication in my room that's been prescribed to keep me sane and hallucination-free. The wonder drug that, for the past five years, has succeeded in keeping my monstrous affliction at bay. I try to recall when my last refill was delivered from the pharmacy. The bag was dropped off the evening that I went to Ahmed's house for dinner. The pills sat unattended behind the desk all night, until Ahmed handed them to me the next morning.

I stagger out of the bathroom. The boys are still quarreling, but I shout over them, holding up the capsules in my palm. "What are these?"

Zachary saunters over with his drink in his hand. "Ahh, those are my amino-acid supplements." He picks one up and pinches it. "It helps muscles recuperate after workouts. Or so my trainer in Boston always proselytized."

"Amino acid," I repeat dizzily, the ringing in my ears growing intense. "And you let Otto play in this room. Unsupervised."

Zachary purses his lips. "Mags, what's wrong with—"

"What's wrong?" I cry. It's as if *what's wrong* is calling to me from my room on the opposite side of the hotel. *What's wrong* needs to see me instantly so it can confront me about how gullible I've been. I push past Zachary and veer around Ben, seeing myself out without so much as a goodbye. I march down the hallway, refusing to turn around when Zachary peeks his head out, calling after me, "Is everything okay?" I don't respond because nothing in my world is okay. Passing the staircase's gleaming chandelier chain, I envision Otto riding it like a tire swing, laughing as he rocks from one side of the shaft to the other, the Royal Karnak his playpen now.

Safe in my room, I rush to the bathroom and open the prescription bottle of risperidone. Spilling the magic pills onto the counter, I compare them to the amino-acid supplements from Zachary's stockpile.

A perfect match. Right down to the minuscule trademark script running along their slender blue bellies. I glance dumbfoundedly at the woman in the mirror, the one with purple blotches running up her neck, needing her to comprehend the extent of the deception. "Do you see?" I shout at her. "Do you get what the boy has done to you?" I've been swallowing vitamin supplements for the past three days to fight the monsters in my head.

33.

The landline on the nightstand rings and rings, and then it stops for a half hour and rings again. I won't answer it. I can't listen to the boy pretend to be Julia. No exercise this morning, no shower, no point in tossing back the pills at the sink. After I strip out of my nightgown and before grabbing a kaftan, I allow myself the tiniest peek at my naked body in the mirror. Half a dozen oval blue-black bruises swim like a school of minnows up my back toward my shoulder blades. I don't dare turn around to examine my breasts or stomach. The condition is back in full force, almost reaching a stage unseen since Klode Park. Otto has nearly succeeded in erasing me. Soon I won't be able to leave my room.

But not yet. It's after eleven by the time I exit my room for the day. My errand is too important for any further delay. I've taken along my umbrella and tote bag of cash for safe measure. Before I shut the door, I considered grabbing the butcher knife in the nightstand, but I'm not a murder suspect—at least, not yet—and it seems unwise in the current climate to be caught carrying around a deadly weapon.

As I pad down the hall, the realization hits me: I haven't thought of Peter for even one second this morning. Did I think of him yesterday morning? Or the day before? That's another thing the boy has taken from me, the very worst of all his thefts. He's stolen the past as I re-member it. The exquisite, jewel-bright moments of the day when Peter comes alive again, if only for a few seconds, vivid and tender-eyed, unobstructed by memory blanks. For that theft alone, Otto deserves his death.

The elevator seems the safer option. Safe from being looked at too closely, safe from any ambushes that Otto might have in store. As the elevator groans to the lobby, I'm already regretting the decision not to bring the knife with me for protection. I practice using my umbrella as a shield, as a bayonet, as a club. Julia, at age fourteen, begged me to let her take karate lessons. *Please, mom, pleaazzzzzzz.* "What for?" was my response. "What could you possibly be frightened of in Klode Park? Do you plan to karate-chop Vanessa, the neighborhood's first woman mail carrier? Flip-kick Ryan Keiser, the deaf boy who rakes our yard?" Looking back, I should have been the one to sign up for karate lessons. For *any* defense classes. How could I have been so blind not to foresee that Peter would die before me, and I'd be left to fend for myself? How did the basic facts of existence escape me all those nights when Peter and I snuggled up on the couch to watch nature documentaries, where inevitably the old lions were devoured by young hyenas? That's the natural order. Nothing in the wild dies peacefully of old age.

I expected the hotel to be plunged in mourning for its lost leader. But despite Ahmed's arrest, the lobby is busier than ever. A swarm of new guests, fresh from the airport, throngs reception, waiting to be checked in, their impatient grumbles and moans audible over the chorus of the hawkers on the corniche. Liesbeth stands behind the desk, drowning in the protocol of guest registrations, trying to familiarize herself with the Royal Karnak's outdated system. Next to her, the Coptic bellboy points the temperature gun at each foreign forehead, grinning too exuberantly as he aims the laser between their eyes and pulls the trigger. Liesbeth pleads for patience. "Patience, please, one at a time. You will all get your rooms, not to worry! I know it's hot, but our chef is bringing out some—where's Hamza?—cold refreshments. Can someone please check on Hamza?"

Oh, Ahmed, if only you could be here to witness this managerial meltdown. Liesbeth was so certain she could sail along without you as captain, unaware of the rapids you fought daily to keep our ship from smashing into the rocks. I'm careful as I watch her—the small, blond head, so delicate and crushable, even a boot heel would do it. The note that Ahmed and I put at the reception desk warning of the heat has

been discarded. In its place hangs a computer printout: POOL CLOSED
UNTIL NOON TODAY. FITNESS CENTER CLOSED UNTIL FURTHER NOTICE.
Liesbeth must have drafted this bland, impersonal announcement. My
heart aches for my dear friend. Have they locked Ahmed in a cell until
he confesses? Have they threatened to hurt his sons if he doesn't admit to the murder? Will they let him speak with a lawyer? I want to
beeline to the front of the reception line and demand an update from
Liesbeth. Surely she must know the latest on Ahmed's plight, tracking
his doom through the Richesse Resorts' public-relations machine. But
I can't risk sparking her curiosity in me. Instead I shuffle toward the
front door, grateful when I catch sight of Yasmine dry-ragging the
windows.

She jumps at the sound of my voice in her ear. "How's Ahmed?" I
whisper. "What have they done with him?"

I can tell, as she turns around, that she's on the verge of weeping,
her brown eyes welling, her lips fighting the rebellion of a quiver. She
shakes her head before nodding toward the reception desk. "Maggie,"
she murmurs. "We are forbidden to speak on the matter. Forbidden."

"We'll find a way to save him," I promise, wishing I could give
her a hug. "We'll find a way to blame the boy." She blinks at me as
I continue to the door, open my umbrella, and enter the furnace of
the day.

• • •

The errand is a disaster. The morning's heat brought a scarcity of taxis,
and I was forced to accept the offer of a carriage ride to the pharmacy.
Its giant wood wheels juddered over every pothole, and the gray mare
pulling us suffered relentless diarrhea, its smell wafting back as I sat on
the torn vinyl seat. My biggest mistake was looking back. As we began
clopping off up the corniche, I swiveled around to catch a parting view
of the hotel. Amid the near-obliterating shine of the sun on white marble, I spotted Otto on the front terrace, his arm held high, waving an
exaggerated goodbye to me.

I could just make out his voice squealing above the traffic. "You're getting smaller and smaller," he shouted. "There's so little of you left, I can barely see you. Only a sliver. Going, going, going . . ." We rode out of earshot before I could hear the final word. *Gone*.

One unfortunate consequence of the construction of the Aswan High Dam in the 1960s was the eradication of giant Nile crocodiles downriver. It's a shame that Luxor's riverfront hasn't been repopulated with its native carnivores. How convenient it would be to have those champion apex bone grinders twenty feet from the boy's playground. All I'd have to do is drag his little body across the road.

As the carriage pulled up in front of the pharmacy, I handed the driver thirty pounds.

"The price, madam," he said, "is one hundred."

"We agreed on thirty at the hotel."

The driver feigned outrage: not only was he being cheated out of his wage, but his honor was being called into question. The adulation that he initially expressed for foreigners when I climbed into his carriage—"I love Americans! The greatest country! We welcome you!"—quickly turned into disgust. "On the lives of my children, we said hundred! Thirty is not enough to feed my horse. Do you want us to starve, madam, is that why you have come to my country, to bleed us, to—" I added seventy pounds to the total and hurried into the cool dark of the drugstore.

"Yes, more! I need more!" I appealed, my hands held together in pleading prayer. "Urgently. Risperidone. Please, urgently more!" The pharmacist reminded me that he'd refilled that prescription not four days ago. "I lost it! It was stolen from me, if you want to know the truth. It's gone, all gone, and I need it for the preservation of my mind, you see, I can't *not* take it. My doctor in the United States, Dr. Reiselman, requires it for me!"

The bona fides of being a card-carrying member of the American health-care system didn't spur the pharmacist into a flurry of action. He simply watched me from the other side of the counter, as if noting the erratic symptoms he'd failed to detect on my previous visits. He then reminded me of the difficulty of locating that medication during the current crisis; moreover, he was not in the habit of refilling strong antipsychotics multiple times a week, even for Americans.

"It's a matter of life and death!" I cried and opened the tote bag of cash. "I'll pay double. Triple if you insist on holding the medication hostage! Just so you're aware, there's been a murder at my hotel. And the manager who did it is my best friend!"

"I think, Mrs. Burkhardt," the pharmacist said calmly, as if demonstrating how much sanity he had to spend, "that if you kindly obtain a new prescription from one of our local doctors, I'll be more than happy to continue serving you."

A taxi returns me to the hotel in defeat. It's nearly two thirty by the time I climb the horseshoe steps. The lobby is quiet. For a second, I half expect Ahmed to be standing at the reception with a smile on his face: *I'm back, Maggie! It was all a misunderstanding. Seif was the real killer after all!* As I glance into the dusty gloom, I spot two shiny lenses staring out at me from the dark corner under the staircase. Marching toward them with my umbrella gripped like a billy club, I find only the glinting corners of the iron chair as it catches the window light. Where is the boy? Upstairs, waiting for my return? Instead I head to the pool, safer in numbers.

There's no sign of Seif in the garden. I wonder whether he's still in custody, locked in the same cell as Ahmed at the police station. And yet I don't catch a glimpse of any of the other gardeners either. The brick paths are littered with brown pine needles and shriveled hibiscus flowers, Seif's fastidious tending already giving way to disorder. The fitness center and the dirt drive are roped off with green police tape, but the pool is a throb of activity, the hotel's newest arrivals seeking refuge on the teak loungers. Two sullen Italian teenagers play blackjack on the lounge chair that the gigolo once occupied. My eyes scan for faces I recognize. Thankfully, I spot Ben and Zachary on the opposite side of the pool, both seated in the shade of a table umbrella.

"Boys!" I shout, trying to induce the playful spirit of the old days. Their faces look somber and drained. Only Zachary makes the slightest effort to welcome me, removing his feet from one of the chairs in invitation. His hand is clenching an empty cocktail glass, the ice cubes stained peach from whatever alcoholic concoction he's been ordering. A full pizza sits on the table between them, the toppings picked off, leaving the cheese and marinara looking like the skin of a burn victim. "Help yourself," Ben says without enthusiasm. I can tell they've been discussing important matters—in other words, fighting in modulated voices. Ben's bloody lip has scabbed, and Zachary's bruised eye has faded yellow. These are my people.

"At least you aren't punching each other," I remark as I shut my umbrella and set it on my lap. Ben squints at me, and I attempt a smile. "You're taking a late lunch from work today, Ben?"

"I didn't go to work," he says stoically. "Not today, and maybe not ever."

Zachary rolls his eyes and tries to harvest a last sip of alcohol from the melted ice in the glass.

"You aren't the only one playing truant," I reply. "Where are all the gardeners?"

Zachary sets his glass down and eyes me bleakly. "Apparently, they're all at the police station having their testimony taken. You know, did any of them witness suspicious activity in the vicinity of the car. Did they catch Ahmed sneaking around the garden in the dead of night? Or better yet, did they happen to notice the hotel manager dragging a dead body through the flower beds?"

I shut my eyes, trying to recall whether any of the gardeners spotted me wandering suspiciously around the garden. A vision of a young worker with sea-glass eyes cleaning out the aviary comes to mind, followed by the sound of the brick hitting a skull, over and over, as if I struck him a hundred times. My hands grip the edge of the table, like it's spinning in space and I might go flying off if I don't hold on. Have the police already forced a confession out of Ahmed? Or is he right now describing the old woman in room 309 who he drove to and from his house, the one who helped him tuck the car in at night and watched him hide the key?

"Ohhhhh . . ." The moan leaks out of me. When I open my eyes, the boys are staring at me worriedly. "Those *poor* gardeners," I invent.

"You know, Maggie," Ben says more caustically than I've ever heard him pronounce my name, "you have an unhealthy obsession with the hotel staff. I doubt they've ever once bothered to wring their hands over you."

"Hey!" Zachary snaps. "Don't turn on Mags just because you're in a crash-and-burn mood."

Ben winces, chastened, and reaches over to pat my hand. "I'm sorry. Zee's right. I am in a terrible mood, and it has nothing to do with you. It's that eight-year-old psychopath running around—"

"We already discussed this," Zachary grouses, but Ben knows I'm on his side when it comes to Otto, and he leans toward me to fix my attention.

"That brat was in the bushes a half hour ago, staring at me, *just watching*—"

"You don't know he was watching you specifically," Zachary cuts in.

"Yes, I do! From right over there." He points to the pocket of foliage where the bludgeoned orange cat had lain. "Hiding in the leaves, just staring, waiting for his chance at me."

"Naturally, Ben ran toward him shouting and waving his arms like any sane adult would," Zachary adds.

"All I could think of was getting my Set figurine back!" I, too, think of the Set figurine, the jeweled little god, wrapped in Otto's green T-shirt and hidden in my room. "A guilty person doesn't run off when you approach them. And get this, Mags, as he sprinted away, he looked back at me and laughed."

"He wasn't laughing," Zachary retorts.

"He's been laughing at us all along," Ben says, doubling down. "Probably laughing at Ahmed as he was arrested. Probably laughing at the dead body in the garden." Ben glares across the table at his husband. "He's laughing at you too, Zee. At your groveling devotion. At your hopeful eyes. You're a perfect game for children."

Going, going, going . . . I picture Otto waving goodbye to me from the terrace this morning, and as I replay the scene in my head, he's laughing as he screams those words. My eyes track the pool for Otto, checking to see if he's hiding in the shadows, waiting and watching, his laugh stirring the tree branches, wilting the rosebushes, crawling in our ears to lay its eggs. I'd rather wake up in the middle of the night to a stranger's voice in my bedroom than hear Otto's laughter in daylight at my back.

Ben and Zachary start bickering again, leaving me far behind. I can only sit there mutely, clutching the table for support. Their voices are like two hammers trying to hit the same nail, but my attention is caught by a commotion on the brick path leading to the hotel. First I spot Liesbeth advancing at a rapid clip, her eyes skimming the tables by the pool. She jogs back into the hotel, only to reappear with a trio of baggy-suited Egyptian men. Their faces are pale and expressionless, impossible to decipher beyond the locked jaws of serious intent. When Liesbeth points directly at our table, I know that they've finally come for me. Did Ahmed break down in his cell and finger me as the only other possible suspect? Or was it Otto, one step ahead, warning me just this morning from the terrace that my time here was limited? Of course, how stupid I've been, the boy's been plotting to frame me for the murder just as I've been trying to do the same to him. How could I have failed to foresee this trap? The three men in suits begin making their way around the pool. I lurch to my feet, the chair toppling over behind me, my fingers too numb to gather my umbrella. When Ben asks where I'm going, I mumble, "Far away forever." Staggering into the sunlight, I can barely see, my arms making broad swimmer's strokes through the warm air. Perhaps my limbs are simply enjoying their last moments of freedom. My feet are slow and clumsy, and I expect the men to overtake me at any moment, arresting me for murder, leading me in handcuffs to their patrol car while Otto watches, laughing from the terrace. But as I veer off the concrete into bushy shade, the acokanthera plant's lacy white flowers falling like confetti around me, I realize no one's behind me.

Turning, I look back in confusion. At the table, Ben is now standing, and the three baggy-suited men are gathered around him. I can't see Ben's face, but Zachary is making exaggerated gestures, his face a stew of fear and rage. What has Otto done? Finally, Ben flails his arms in defeat, and the men lead him away. Zachary scampers behind, announcing to anyone who will listen that he was once an important lawyer in America.

Then I spot the boy. Not twenty feet away, crouched in a different patch of bushes. Otto amid the leaves, hiding, waiting, watching, laughing.

34.

Zachary doesn't return until late in the evening. It's nearly ten by the time he climbs the staircase, pausing at each half landing to gather his strength. I've been waiting for him, standing guard in the third-floor hallway, attracting odd stares from guests as they return to their rooms after dinner. "Can I help you?" I snap when their eyes linger on me for too long. "Am I bothering you by standing here? Is my mere existence making you uncomfortable?" I'm relieved when I spot Zachary's balding blond head as it slowly circles up the three flights. First Ahmed. Then Ben. If I lose Zachary, I'll be left all alone.

On the final turn, Zachary's balance falters, and he stumbles backward before catching himself. I get the impression he's stopped off for a few drinks on his way home. I don't want to startle him, so I move out in the open, standing at the top of the stairs.

"I've been worried!" I exclaim when he's within arm's reach. I manage to scare him anyway, his face shooting up, his mouth gasping for breath.

"God," he wheezes, using his wrist to wipe spittle from his lips. He stops two steps short of the top, as if unwilling to commit to the final landing. He casts his eyes up at me, but they seem to pause on my neck. It's hard to tell in the stairwell's gloom, but I instinctively cover the blotches with my palm.

"What are you looking at?" I demand, both mortified and perversely hopeful that Zachary might acknowledge my affliction. Finally, someone else sees the damage as acutely as I do. "It was Otto. He made these spots appear on my neck!"

"What?" he balks. "Maggie, I'm tired. I don't know what you're—"

I let go of the accusation and quickly reroute the conversation. "*Well?* Are you going to tell me what happened to Ben? I've been waiting for you all night."

The question sobers him, and he trudges up the final steps. "Mags," is all he says in reply. He flexes his jaw muscles, staring forlornly at the carpet.

"Does it have to do with the gigolo?" I prompt. I might be in the clear for the murder, but it occurs to me that I could soon be forced to make a horrible choice. Ahmed or Ben, which do I prefer to lose?

Zachary shakes his head. "No, no, it's nothing to do with that. Ben's not in jail. More like an uncomfortably cramped office. They brought him in to *talk*." His fingers make air quotes around the last word. "Like he had a choice in the matter. I'll need to call the embassy tomorrow, as well as the department chair at his university. It's a mess. It's probably the end of his career."

"I don't understand. If he wasn't arrested for the murder of—"

"Stop with the murder!" Zachary hisses, his drunken exhaustion lighting a fuse. "It was the Antiquities Ministry, not the police. 'Supreme Council of Antiquities,' they call themselves, like it's a religious sect. They're accusing Ben of looting artifacts. When those soldiers searched our room for the missing young man, one of them reported seeing that stupid relic on our mantel. Apparently, everyone's an informer in this town. I guess you get points for ratting people out. But for Christ's sake, Ben's an accredited Egyptologist. Isn't he expected to keep a few ancient tchotchkes lying around? Anyway, that's not what landed him in hot water. This morning they received an anonymous call from someone at the hotel, claiming that Ben was trying to sell artifacts to wealthy guests. Seeing as Ben has unrestricted access to the museum collection, that allegation sent the Supreme Council into a paranoid frenzy. So now Ben's sitting in a hot, windowless office, using his arm as a pillow. They're trying to scare him into confessing, hoping to hold him there until he breaks."

"A guest at the hotel called in a tip?" When I repeat the sentence, it's no longer a question. "A guest at the hotel called in a tip! Can you guess who that someone might be?" Finally there's a crack of hope in the darkness. For once, Otto has overplayed his hand. Up until now he's been so skillful covering up his deceits, but his childish inexperience has finally caught up with him. I have to contain the note of celebration in my voice. "Any ideas, Zee? I wonder if it could be the guest Ben screamed at yesterday about his missing artifact. Or perhaps it was the guest who was watching Ben from the bushes this afternoon, just waiting for something bad to happen to him?"

"Maggie, please." Zachary's shoulders droop, and he casts his eyes down the hall to his door. "You don't need to convince me. Ben said the same thing."

"I'm sure that boy has Ben's figurine stuffed in his suitcase. It's his room they should be searching! It's him they should arrest!"

"My god, Maggie. He's just a kid."

"A kid." Tears sting my eyes. "I didn't want to tell you, but he has a history of violence."

"He bullied a classmate in school. Big deal."

"It's so much more than that," I wheeze, and I'm suddenly so overwhelmed with emotion that I can't get my tongue to function properly. "He would stand by his father's bed. His grandmother in church. My Julia."

But Zachary isn't interested in a victim's list. "I'm going to take care of it," he says decisively. "I'll speak with Otto. He and I have a special bond. I'll get him to admit that he made up the accusation. Then they'll have to let Ben go. Don't worry, we've—" He stops mid-sentence, his attention drawn to the bottom of the staircase. My eyes peer over the banister, following the links of the chandelier chain. Far below, I spot the dim shape of Otto walking up the steps, his glasses shining like silver coins in the murky darkness.

"Jesus, shouldn't he be in bed?" I rasp. But Zachary raises a hand to shush me.

"I'm going to have a word with him." He turns and begins his descent, running his hand along the banister.

"Zachary," I plead, but when he glances back, nothing further

224 • *Christopher Bollen*

leaves my mouth. I watch Zachary go, his steps surer, as he shakes off his intoxication and summons the role of surrogate father.

"Hey buddy," I hear him say as he disappears onto the second-floor landing. I want to listen in on their conversation, particularly the point at which Otto whimperingly admits his maliciousness. But I can't risk creeping down the steps for fear of him spotting me. Instead, I squat down on the landing, gripping the railing bars to ease the weight on my hip. Holding my breath, I concentrate on the voices one flight below. I hear only murmurs, Zachary's gentle baritone interrupted by Otto's whisper-whine. After a minute, my hip begins to spasm, and I lift myself up. It dawns on me that I'm wasting an invaluable opportunity. While Otto is safely occupied, I have free rein in the hotel and the chance to plant the Set figurine somewhere that will indisputably implicate him. The boy might not take the fall for Rafik's murder, but at least he can be convicted of theft. I limp-jog toward my room, my mind ransacking the hotel's geography for the perfect hiding place. The aviary? The iron chair? Should I leave it in the bushes by the pool where he last stood?

I'm halfway down the hall when the cry reaches me. It isn't so much a scream as a whinnying moan, followed a split second later by a series of thuds. I spin around, my hip pinwheeling with pain, and run back toward the staircase. Peering over the banister, I can only make out a solitary arm stretched out on the stairs two flights below. The rest of Zachary isn't visible. Clutching the railing, I hurry down, orbiting the chandelier chain, my heart and eyes on high alert, scared of every shadow for fear that it hides a boy. After darting across the second-floor landing, I finally locate my friend. He's sprawled out on the lower flight of stairs, belly up, feet aimed toward me, his arms out wide. One of his legs is bent in a painful dislocation, like a paper clip twisted far out of alignment, and I know in my heart that he's dead. I race down to him and kneel by his head. Touching his chest, I feel the sweaty warmth of a live body.

"Zachary," I whisper. "Can you hear me?"

His eyelids flutter, revealing veiny white orbs rotating underneath.

I grab his hand and squeeze it, encouraging him back to the world of the living. "Zachary, I'm right here. I'm with you."

The irises roll down and lock into place, the pupils widening, his hand squeezing back, and he mutters something too faint to understand. I lean over him so that all he can take in is my face.

"Zachary, it's me. It's Maggie." More whimpering from him. I gently shake his shoulders, requiring his full attention. I need him to confirm the evil I'm up against. "Did Otto do this? Did he push you down the stairs?" I watch Zachary's lips struggle to respond, the air that pours from them reeking of alcohol but lacking speech. I grip his chin so that he can't turn away. "Tell me," I beg. "Before you lose consciousness, say it! Say that Otto tried to kill you!"

Sweat drips from his forehead. His blue eyes are frantic as they stare into mine. The air in his throat finally finds a key. "My leg!" he shrieks. "My leg is on fire! Hospital! Ambulance! For fuck's sake, Maggie, get help!"

Out of the corner of my eye, I detect movement in the lobby below. When I gaze over the railing, I find my nemesis standing at the bottom of the stairs. Otto, the killer, stares up at me, our eyes meeting, and a shiver runs through me, as cold as the deepest depths of any lake. It is only us now. But in another second, that supposition is proven wrong. Before I can cry out for help, Otto is joined on the stairs by Liesbeth de Clerq, and the two begin their ascent to finish the job. I don't have time to rescue Zachary from my enemies. I drop his head and climb the stairs, hands and feet grappling in a desperate bid to get back to my room, an old woman running for her life through the halls.

35.

I buried Peter in Forest Home Cemetery, a few miles south of Klode Park. His gravestone is red granite, flush against the ground, surrounded by grass so green and shorn in the spring that it could double as a golf course (in late summer it's a scorched yellow, and in winter bouquets of red roses pierce the blanket of snow). All these years later, I can't shake the question of what Peter looks like in his coffin. I don't mean his appearance the moment they closed the lid; I was there for that final sealing. I mean right now. Six years he's been lying underground, on white satin in a simple oak casket, wearing a suit we bought on sale at Gimbels that proved too small for him in life. After his death, when I was forced to endure the minor hell of funeral preparations, I picked a wood coffin not because it was cheaper but because it seemed more humble, and that was the kind of man Peter was. But I never thought to ask the funeral director about durability, whether the wood was impervious to insects, air, water, or small burrowing mammals. I can't stop wondering—does my Peter still look like the man I knew for nearly sixty years? If I dug down and opened the lid, would I recognize the body lying there as my husband? Or has the flesh already pulled from the bone, the chest collapsing like a fire-charred log, his silvery white hair sprinkling the shoulders of his suit coat like cheap Christmas tinsel? If I opened his lid, would I find the color of his eyes faded? Is any of my Peter left under that slab of red granite stenciled with his name? *Loving husband and father.* Or was it *Loving father and husband*?

I bought the grave right beside him as my future resting place. I asked Julia at the time if she'd like the plot next to mine, my treat, but she shook her head. "*God no.*" (I tried not to take that reaction personally.) Now I wish I'd bucked Burkhardt family tradition and chosen cremation. If you're already ash, no one can touch you. Your bones can't be dredged from the dirt, exhibited, picked apart.

The Royal Karnak sits on a riverbank, facing one of the most astonishing graveyards ever conceived. For millennia those pharaohs slept in peace under a thick quilt of sand and limestone, only for future invaders to disturb them with their shovels and pickaxes. All those treasures kept safe for centuries, only to end up tossed around in the clumsiest hands. Gnarled pharaonic bodies wheeled out and paraded around like a circus show. I feel the strange compulsion to swallow the gold Set figurine or stick it up my vagina, protecting it inside my vessel of flesh, where not even the Minister of Antiquities could find it.

Who will be left to see me one last time in my coffin? The answer is no one, which is just as well. I stand at the bathroom mirror, undo the sash of the hotel robe, and let the waffled cotton fall open. The affliction has progressed too far to be contained. No wonder drug would temper it now. Right above the patch of gray pubic hair and the sag of skin across my pubic bone, the blotches have multiplied, engulfing my stomach, ribs, and breasts. As black as tree rot, yellow-edged, plum-veined, and if I stand completely still, I can almost observe their borders expanding, the decay devouring the pink. I should try to get out before they cover every inch of me.

What time is it? Day or night? My suitcases are splayed on the bed. I stop packing to say a prayer for Ahmed, that he isn't being tortured in a military prison, and another for Ben and Zachary, that they aren't in too much pain. I've turned on the hot water in the shower to steam my wrinkled silk blouses, the costume of a previous life. Sensible leather shoes. A wool skirt. Shirts buttoned at the wrist and the neck. You'd wilt wearing such an outfit in the desert.

I can't use the Set figurine, but the figurine can use me to keep it safe for at least another few decades—or however long the Royal Karnak is spared the wrecking ball of extensive renovation. I turn off the shower and push aside the curtain of blouses. Squatting in the tub, I remove the drain's metal covering. The hole is just big enough to fit the miniature god, like a long throat descending deep into the earth. It will be safe here. The very fact that it's fallen into my hands after all these millennia only proves how endangered it is. I let go of the treasure, and the drain accepts it without a sound. Gone, like an eye that takes in the most beautiful wonder and remains open, hungry for more.

I hear feet moving in the hallway, approaching or departing. I stare out the peephole, but there is only the blurry fish-eye view of the door across the hall. Of course a child standing at my door would be too small to spot, and I'm convinced Otto is on the other side.

"Otto," I whisper. Then louder, "Otto? What do you want? Get away from my room! I'll kill you if you get near me! Do you hear? I'm going to kill you." I remember his mismatched eyes staring up at me in the stairwell after Zachary's fall. He thought he'd won because he'd succeeded in stripping me of every friend I had. I press my ear against the wood to catch any threats he might be uttering. I hear only the light whooshing of air, like the sea caught inside a shell.

Ringing invades the room. It's my cell phone, and I follow the sound around the bed to where the device has fallen behind the night-stand. I crouch down and struggle to pry it free. No sooner do I get my hand around it when it stops ringing, replaced by the insistent wailing of the landline. I'm scared to answer it. According to the screen, the call is from reception, and in a surge of hope I wonder if Ahmed has returned. *I am back, Maggie! There will be no more trouble from the police! They don't care about the murder anymore. Can I sleep in your room tonight?* Grabbing the handset, I place it tentatively to my ear.

"Hello?"

A series of clicks, like a cigarette lighter that won't catch, followed by a brief high-frequency whine. Then a voice, far away, yet horribly close: "Mom?" I don't respond, because what can you say when a tidal wave slams into you in the middle of a desert? "Mom, it's me, Julia. What's going on?" The voice is screechy and familiar. "What are you doing? What have you done?" The voice pauses, then delivers its vile threat. "Mom, I'm coming to get you!"

I know the boy's trick: he patched the call through reception to ensure I'd answer. I refuse to be terrified by his threats, refuse to let him win. I slam down the phone and rush to the door. Tearing it open, I fly down the hall, taking the stairs so rapidly I almost trip. I'm breathless, my chest heaving by the time I reach the Royal Suite. I pound my fist against the door.

"Open up! I want to see Otto!" I realize I should have brought the butcher knife with me for protection. "Get him out here *right now*!"

After a minute, Tess's groggy voice reverberates through the door. "Maggie?" it asks cautiously. "Is that you?"

"He knows what he's done!" I cry. "How could he? She was my daughter!"

"Maggie, Otto's in bed."

"Like hell he is. Open up!" I pound more ferociously, right in the spot where I imagine Tess's face to be. "I want to see him in the flesh." I want to dangle him over the stairwell railing. I want to hold his head underwater in the pool. I want to smear my skin against his body until he contracts the same insidious affliction. I want to take him up to the rooftop and watch him splatter on the horseshoe steps. "Open this door, Tess! Stop hiding him! Your mother was right! He's evil, and you're only making things worse!"

"Go to bed," she hisses. "You need to sleep. You're acting crazy."

"I'm crazy? Your son murdered Rafik and almost managed to do the same with Zachary! Have you seen the bruises all over me? Those are thanks to your son!" I try the knob, but it's locked. When my knocking produces no further response, I return to the stairs and continue down to the lobby. In my fantasy, Ahmed is waiting for me at the reception desk. *My job is to help you*, he assures me. The lobby is deserted, the dim lamps radiating dust. At reception, I rap my knuckles on the marble, calling out, "Hello, hello." To my regret, it is Liesbeth who opens the office door, the pouches under her eyes nearly black from fatigue, her tight smile conveying a strangled hostility at the late hour.

"Hello, Liesbeth," I say firmly. "I know you're new at this hotel. If Ahmed were here, he would explain. You see, I've been paying for the mother and son to stay in the Royal Suite on the second floor. Well,

Otto has been harassing me, and I refuse to put up with it any longer. I want you to kick them out of the hotel tonight. Right this minute, in fact! I won't wait until tomorrow. They've been terrorizing me for a week, and I don't know that you're aware, but the boy stole a priceless artifact that belongs to the museum."

Her eyes slowly sliver, taking me in. "I don't understand," she says politely. "Perhaps you're overexcited from the events of the past few days . . ."

"No, I'm not excited. Look it up! I'm paying for their room, and I want them out!" I wait for her to jump into action, but she doesn't move a muscle. "Do something!" I shout. "I had a daughter. That boy is pretending to be her!"

"The boy? Pretending to be your daughter?"

"A dead daughter!" I cry. "Call him down here if you don't believe me! Or are you in league with him? Is that it, Liesbeth, you two have made a pact? Let's get him down here right now and bring it all out in the open!" I grab the silver bell from the desk and begin to ring it above my head, like a teacher calling the children in from recess. "Otto! Get down here! Sunset! Tell this woman how you've been tormenting me!"

"Please," Liesbeth entreats, grabbing my wrist and lowering it to the desk. My fingers remain clenched on the bell handle, refusing to let go. "You're tired, Mrs. . . ."

"Burkhardt!" I snap. But I catch my mistake as I watch the bullet of my last name enter her forehead. Her eyes widen, and she stares into my face.

"You," she stutters. "You were the woman in Sils . . ."

The bell comes alive, its tongue lolling around in its mouth as I swing it back and send it crashing into Liesbeth's temple. One strike, and then my arm swings in the opposite direction before swiveling back again, slamming the bell against the other side of her head. I have no control over its movement, this is what the bell does, this is how it makes room for the next day. Liesbeth lets out a shriek and sinks behind the desk, covering her head, and the bell slips from my fingers to follow her over the edge, dropping with a clang onto the floor.

I run. I lift my kaftan to anticipate the climb, leaping up the steps two at a time, faster than I ran in my youth, so grateful that my ankles don't ache. Tess said I was acting crazy. How can a person live for eighty-one years on this deranged planet and not be crazy? Why must I feign total sanity for the comfort of those who've been here such a short time? I reach the second floor, and then the third, and soon I see the door to my home, where I used to hang a wreath every winter, and two crisscrossing American flags in July, and we never locked the door, that's how safe life was. The kids in the neighborhood came and went, and I never thought to ask what they were doing inside my home.

36.

I lie on the bed, dressed in the old manner: a tweed skirt, a high-collared silk blouse tucked in at the waist, my dyed black hair tied in a bun. I'm buttoned at the neck and the wrist. I could only find one of my pearl earrings, and slipped it into my left earlobe so I wouldn't have to remove it in the event of an urgent phone call. This is how I want to be buried, hands on my heart, eyes open, staring up, so I can look at them when they come to rob me.

I pushed the bureau against the door, and then the desk against the bureau. Crime has gotten so bad in Klode Park. It's insulting really, when you think of how hard we all worked to make it a safe neighborhood. But the new people come in and smash things. That's the way life goes. Last night, they tried to get in. I heard them picking the lock and repeatedly slamming the door against the bureau, trying to barge their way inside. They must have read my name on the mailbox, because they kept using it. *Mrs. Burkhardt, please. Maggie, we want to make sure you're okay. Would you mind moving the furniture aside and opening the door? No one wants to hurt you.* Right. Don't they know I worked as a loan officer in a bank? We did annual training drills to prepare for robberies. Why didn't I insist on installing a security system in our home? Peter said he didn't like cameras, didn't want Julia growing up in a prison. I relented as I always did. We didn't even have a neighborhood watch. No one was watching. Why would you ever think to watch?

The phones keep ringing—first my cell until it dies, and then the landline on the nightstand. I don't pick up. I take one of the light-blue capsules for my sanity, rub the five pink hairs that I've preserved of my husband against my lips, go back to sleep. When I awake it is evening, and I hear an electric drill boring a hole through the front door. They're so shameless, they'll do anything to get in. I scream through the bureau, telling them I'll jump out the window unless they stop. The drill falls silent. I'm not hungry. It's marvelous. I need nothing now except to be left in peace. Why did I waste all that time doing leg lifts and tornado arms? I'm so happy in this burial chamber. But as a precaution, I drop my sapphire ring down the hole in the tub for safekeeping.

The next afternoon I have a vision at the window. Under the scorching sun, on the garden brick, I see my Julia walking with Tess. Julia's much older than she was when she died, her brown hair dusted gray at the top, her thighs and shoulders plump, her sides bowing outward instead of in. Tess is pointing out various sights to her, and she nods amiably. In this hallucination, they both look up at my window, and I quickly step backward into the darkness, holding my breath. After a minute, I return to the glass. The only one standing in the sun is the boy. He's staring up at me with his thick glasses. Otto is not a hallucination. He knows he'll be able to get inside my grave eventually; he just needs to wait me out.

The phone rings, and I answer it. "Mom, it's Julia. It's your daughter. Mom. Why won't you open the door?" I slip over to the window, and Otto is no longer standing below it in the sun.

"You little fuck," I whisper before hanging up. "I want you dead."

The phone rings again, but I don't answer. A few minutes later the front door is tried, Otto's voice again, mimicking her: "Mom, open up. I'm here. Why are you doing this? Don't you want to see me?"

I take the butcher knife from the nightstand drawer. There are no pockets in the tweed skirt like there were in the kaftans, but in the bathroom mirror I practice holding it against my side until the gleam of the blade takes on the camouflage of brown wool. It only needs to be hidden long enough to get close to him. *Don't you want to see me?* Yes, I do.

37.

Three weeks after Peter's funeral, Julia stopped by the house. I made tea and arranged a plate of cookies. We sat in the living room, staring through the casement windows out to our front lawn dotted with daffodils (no one would believe they grew wild in our yard, but they did). Julia was crying—well, we both were, our loss could still be counted in hours and days, not yet bundled into months or seasons. For me, it never stopped being days. Even though Peter had been in the hospital for an extended period before he died, his presence could be seen all over the house—there were traces of him everywhere. His loafers in the hall. His newspapers piled next to the fireplace. His ear and eye medications on the rack under the kitchen television.

We hugged, or rather Julia let me hug her, squirming and fidgeting, not allowing me to fix my hands all the way around her. She smelled unshowered, which surprised me. Julia worked as a social worker, and she believed that good hygiene encouraged the same self-respecting habits in others. We sat in the armchairs, the yellow upholstery swirling with tiger lilies, and the most tremendous light, a pure Wisconsin white, shone through the windows onto us. "Dad always liked to sit here in the afternoons," I reminded her. I poured her some tea, and let her sob, and told her that maybe in the summer we could start going through the stuff in the attic, not throwing things out, just rearranging them into neater piles. Then, inexplicably, in the chair next to me, both our feet warmed by the same sun, my daughter, in her last act of her life, began to fill the air with lies about Peter, about what he'd done to her when she was a girl.

"The deer always eat the daffodils," I told her. "We're lucky if we get a week with them before they're all gone. But the prairie violets and the anemone will sprout next, and that's always a treat for the eye. After that, we don't have to wait long until we get the best stuff, the poppies and the lady's slippers."

"Mom, did you hear me?" Julia rasped. She was already dying; most of her was invisible by that point. "I want you to know what happened. What he did to me. Did you have any idea? If you did, please just admit it."

"Your father loved the summer months because of the roses, but because you insisted on spending so much time at the lake, he couldn't tend them as he wanted. You always had to get your way."

"Don't you remember those long swims he took me on up there? And you just watched us go, waving from the dock. My god, Mom, were you really that blind? I would come back crying and lock myself in my room. Don't you remember all the bruises I had as a little girl? They were all over my body from the way he held me down. Tell me you at least remember the bruises."

When people are dying, the wiring in their brain gets distorted, and they're liable to say all kinds of nonsense. You can't blame them for it.

"How could you have seen those marks on me, and not for a second wondered what was going on?"

"What was the name of that gardener we hired to look after the roses one summer? The one with the gambling problem?" I asked. "You know, I think I might have a photo of Dad with his rosebushes upstairs."

I went up to look for the picture. I was rummaging around in the study and didn't hear Julia shout up a goodbye. Through the upstairs window, I watched her car pull away. It must have been only seconds later, right after she disappeared down the block, that she died. I never saw her again.

A light pattering sound fills my room. At first I mistake it for rain. I gaze out the window, but there is only bright desert sunlight. No, the pattering is coming from the door, someone drumming their fingers insistently on the wood, the tempo of a drizzle turning into a downpour. I know it's Otto standing on the other side before he even speaks. I'm frightened he's going to mimic Julia again and make more terrible accusations against me. I wait, wishing I could shove the butcher knife through my own ears.

"Mrs. Burkhardt?" he asks. As if there's anyone else in this tomb but me.

38.

She said the bruises on her wrists came from volleyball drills, and I offered to write a note excusing her from gym class. She wore oversize, long-sleeved shirts and baggy pants to school—nothing flashy or attention-grabbing, nothing that would make her stick out. Even still, she blamed a cluster of brown neck bruises on a bullying clique of eighth-grade girls. I threatened to march into the principal's office the next day, but Julia sobbed, begging me not to, *Don't you dare, if you love me, you won't,* and Peter promised to talk to her about strategies for keeping out of the older girls' crosshairs. She developed severe acne long before puberty, and her skin regularly broke out in hives. I treated her to a day at the makeup counter and introduced her to concealers and the essentials of a healthy skin-care regimen. She didn't get her period until she was fifteen (I, too, was a late bloomer), but early on, she possessed a moody teenager's obsession for privacy, refusing to let me accompany her into changing rooms and screaming if I happened to put away towels while she was in the shower.

Peter rubbed my shoulders and told me that all girls go through an anti-mom phase. "My mother and sister fought like demons," he swore. "For a year it was the Battle of Antietam every afternoon, and then one day, peace reigned."

The summer months at the lake cabin were the toughest. Julia was out so often, I couldn't keep track of her whereabouts. The shy, quiet, homebound girl prone to panic attacks in Klode Park became, for those ten weeks, feral and unreliable, hanging out with a motley band of lakeshore friends, rarely informing us whether she'd be back at meal-times in an attempt to dodge her coddling parents. Peter pushed the father-daughter swims as a family ritual. I endorsed them in the spirit of a new Burkhardt tradition, reckoning that even if she wrinkled her nose at me, at least she maintained close ties with one parent. I was the enforcer, waking her up at 7:00 a.m., waving her bathing suit in front of her like a matador's cape, goading her out the door and down to the lake. She had bruises. On her inner thighs from biking around all day on a borrowed boy's ten-speed. On her shoulder from falling off a rope swing. Purple, blue, the sickliest greens. It was summer, and she was a kid, and Peter said you couldn't bubble-wrap youth. He was right, of course. *You're right, dear. You're always right.* I walked them down to the dock every morning and watched them jump in, and I waved until I lost sight of them in the sun glare, and I was proud of my two favorite darlings, and I didn't worry about her during those morning hours, not once, because she was with her father, and that meant she was safe.

39.

He stops drumming his fingers on the door, and I wait for his voice to speak more than my name. The distance between us is a vast universe. The distance between us is ten feet separated by an inch of wood.

"Don't go yet," Otto says sweetly, like a boy asking for a ride home in the rain. "Stay with us just a little longer. There's one more surprise for you. It's better than any sunset. But you have to come downstairs."

One rule of life is that it's easier to lodge than dislodge. I have difficulty pushing the desk aside and need to set the butcher knife down to drag the bureau from the door. There's no sign of Otto in the hallway. I slip down the corridor as quietly as I can. I may need the element of surprise to overtake him. Thankfully I'm not dressed as the person they knew, not Maggie of Luxor, but the old brokenhearted widow haunting Europe's highest mountain peaks. I hear the pulse of activity in the guest rooms I pass—a reality show playing on a television, an argument between a jet-lagged couple, the gurgle of a sink drain. It is the quiet hour at the Royal Karnak, a drowsy coolness penetrating the halls during the deadly heat of the afternoon. I circle down the staircase, the knife pressed flat against my side, nodding to a Spanish family that's climbing the steps after a morning of sightseeing.

The Coptic bellhop is stationed at reception. "Where's Otto?" I ask. He peers over at me and freezes, his smile turning to wax on his face. I hear the din of conversations coming from the ballroom down the hall. Could there be a new medical convention? Perhaps they'd let me sit in and listen to the latest advancements on the regeneration of organs or the recalcification of bones. Doctors can do amazing things these days, except stop death. Only they did stop a boy from dying in infancy eight years ago, and think of all the pain they could have prevented had they simply let him go. Sunlight is streaming through the ballroom, flooding the herringbone floor and making oatmeal of the Persian rug. A few chairs have been arranged in a semicircle, the two Louis XIVs mixing with metal foldouts, like an AA meeting on acid. Are they waiting for me to speak on my condition? Doctors, it's the opposite of what you think: disappearing weighs you down. Vanishing from the world makes you heavier, not lighter. I'm disappointed there isn't a larger audience, even in these Covid times.

I step through the doorway, searching the backlit faces for the boy. The first person I recognize is Ben, more by the shape of his body than by his shadowed face. Next to him is Zachary, sitting in a metal chair with crutches and a thick white cast covering his leg. Zachary extends his hand toward me, but I can't take it because I'd lose the knife in my grip. "Maggie," he whispers.

"Hello," I reply, wishing I didn't sound so sad. "Have you been to Klode Park before? I'd be happy to show you around."

As my eyes adjust, I notice Liesbeth de Clerq standing behind him, her bruised eyes locked on me. I want to scream at her—*You have no right to barge in and renovate. Newness is an infection, spreading across the globe, erasing all of us with it.* But then I spot Tess next to her, smiling feebly, her brow pinched. It was kind of her to attend.

Before I can search the shadowed corners of the ballroom for Otto, a voice calls out behind me. "Mom." My heart nearly stops. I'm too frightened to turn around.

"Mom, it's me," the voice persists. "I'm here." It's chilling how much Otto sounds like my Julia—so much more so than he did in his phone calls. I'd rather go on facing the wrong direction, believing it *could be* Julia, miraculously back from the dead, than turn around and find an eight-year-old boy smiling at me. "I flew over as soon as I learned where you were," the voice continues. Then a pause, so deep the whole world could be swallowed up in it. "Mom, *please?*"

I take a breath and turn, my eyes struggling to acclimate to the room's heavy darkness. At first, I only make out a looming shape. Then, by some miracle, there she is, not ten feet from me, the same specter I saw strolling through the garden with Tess from my window. Below her lank, graying hair, her forehead is scored with lines, and her cheeks and jaw have widened. I haven't seen her since her last visit to the house in Klode Park right before her death. That was six years ago. Like me, she's become an old woman.

Her eyes shine with tears, and tentatively she reaches out her hand. "I had no idea where you were. All this time, without any word from you. I called and texted when the pandemic started. Why didn't you answer? Jesus, Mom, I've been worried sick. I wasn't sure you were even alive."

"*Oh*," is all I manage to reply. My whole body is trembling, even the muscles of my throat, which can't seem to swallow down air. I watch Julia stare at me in equal wonder, trying to account for this strange old lady in disguise who once looked like her mother. I have so much I want to tell her. I have only one thing to ask her: How is it possible to come back from the dead?

She reaches both arms out, inviting me to embrace her. I feel the strength of the sunlight on my back, as if it's pressing me forward. I'm scared she'll vanish if I take a single step toward her. He impersonated her voice. Why not the rest of her? I won't survive another trick.

"I don't understand . . . ," I say cautiously. "How did you find me?"

Julia laughs, just like she always did, an unpleasant snigger to hide an ugly fact. "The boy. He's the reason I'm here."

I feel the blood draining from my chest, the spit drying in my mouth. "*The boy?* Otto brought you back?"

She nods eagerly, her arms still held open to me. "Yes," she cries. "I wouldn't be here without Otto. He tracked me down and brought me back to you. I don't know how we can ever repay him. We owe him so much gratitude."

"I see. Yes. Gratitude." I try to find the smallest glitch, but Otto's impersonation of my daughter is seamless. The round face, the dimpled chin, the extra-wide groove between the nose and lips. He's outdone himself.

"Everything's going to be all right now," the impostor says as she jiggles her outstretched arms like bait. "Mom, I'm here to take you home."

It's a beautiful mirage. Who could blame me for wanting to believe in it? But I don't waste any more time. I cross the ten feet of ballroom that separates us, slip between her embracing arms, and drive the knife into her chest. Screams erupt behind me, and I understand their confusion, because I, too, was tricked.

"It's okay!" I cry, tears in my eyes, as I thrust the knife as deeply as I can. "Don't worry! My daughter's dead. It's Otto! It's the boy!"

For an instant, there is a terrific calm. Then the knife slips from my grip and the body falls and it becomes impossible to ignore a set of eyes in the doorway. Staring. Mismatched.

A boy runs with the sunlight through the halls.

ACKNOWLEDGMENTS

———

There is a majestic hotel on the banks of the Nile that provided a good deal of inspiration for this novel. In fact, the idea of the story came to me in a flash while sitting in the hotel's back garden in the late pandemic days of April 2021. That said, the Royal Karnak Palace Hotel and the people associated with it exist wholly within the author's imagination.

Special thanks to my friend, agent, and fellow plotter, Bill Clegg, as well as the support team at the Clegg Agency, including Marion Duvert, Simon Troop, MC Connors, and Rebecca Pittel; thanks to my brilliant editor Millicent Bennett, who believed in the book from the start and saw a method in so much madness. Thank you to my family at Harper for your help and faith, especially Jonathan Burnham, Liz Velez, Milan Bozic, Maya Baran, Katie O'Callaghan, and Miranda Ottewell. Thank you Shelley Wanger for the kind help. Also thank you to Michael Cendejas on the West Coast.

This novel started as a short story and grew and grew until it took over my life and sanity. For those sharing my life and sanity, thank you for your patience and kindness. Those include Thierry Conrad Reutenauer, Wade Guyton, Thomas Alexander, Alexander Hertling, Zadie Smith, Sloane Crosley, T. Cole Rachel, Patrik Ervell, Jack Pierson, T. J. Wilcox, James Haslam, Joseph Logan, Adam Kimmel, Olympia Scarry, Jeremy Tamanini, Connor Monahan, Scott Rothkopf, Danko and Ana Steiner, Luchino, Lauren Tabach Bank, Kelly Brant, Zoe Wolff, and my mom and sister in Cincinnati.

About the Author

CHRISTOPHER BOLLEN is the author of the critically acclaimed novels *The Lost Americans*, *A Beautiful Crime*, *The Destroyers*, *Orient*, and *Lightning People*. He is a frequent contributor to various publications, including *Vanity Fair*, the *New York Times*, and *Interview*. He lives in New York City.